Casting Spells

Titles by Barbara Bretton

CASTING SPELLS
JUST DESSERTS
JUST LIKE HEAVEN
SOMEONE LIKE YOU
CHANCES ARE
GIRLS OF SUMMER
SHORE LIGHTS
A SOFT PLACE TO FALL
AT LAST
THE DAY WE MET
ONCE AROUND
SLEEPING ALONE
MAYBE THIS TIME
ONE AND ONLY

Anthologies

THE CHRISTMAS CAT
(with Julie Beard, Jo Beverly, and Lynn Kurland)

Casting Spells

BARBARA BRETTON

**Doubleday Large Print
Home Library Edition**

B
BERKLEY BOOKS, NEW YORK

This Large Print Edition, prepared especially for Doubleday Large Print Home Library, contains the complete, unabridged text of the original Publisher's Edition.

THE BERKLEY PUBLISHING GROUP
Published by the Penguin Group
Penguin Group (USA) Inc.
375 Hudson Street, New York, New York 10014, USA
Penguin Group (Canada), 90 Eglinton Avenue East, Suite 700, Toronto, Ontario M4P 2Y3, Canada (a division of Pearson Penguin Canada Inc.)
Penguin Books Ltd., 80 Strand, London WC2R 0RL, England
Penguin Group Ireland, 25 St. Stephen's Green, Dublin 2, Ireland (a division of Penguin Books Ltd.)
Penguin Group (Australia), 250 Camberwell Road, Camberwell, Victoria 3124, Australia (a division of Pearson Australia Group Pty. Ltd.)
Penguin Books India Pvt. Ltd., 11 Community Centre, Panchsheel Park, New Delhi—110 017, India
Penguin Group (NZ), 67 Apollo Drive, Rosedale, North Shore 0632, New Zealand (a division of Pearson New Zealand Ltd.)
Penguin Books (South Africa) (Pty.) Ltd., 24 Sturdee Avenue, Rosebank, Johannesburg 2196, South Africa

Penguin Books Ltd., Registered Offices: 80 Strand, London WC2R 0RL, England

This book is an original publication of The Berkley Publishing Group.

ISBN 978-1-60751-258-5

PRINTED IN THE UNITED STATES OF AMERICA

**For my husband, for everything
XXXX and counting**

ACKNOWLEDGMENTS

Many thanks to knitters/designers extraordinaire Wendy D. Johnson and Dawn Brocco for their friendship, their talent, their blogs, and their generosity.

A virtual basket of quiviut to each and every writer and reader who has made Romancing the Yarn such a terrific experience. Special thanks to Fran, Cindi, Jamie, Janet, Elizabeth, Laura, Georg, Kenyetta, Nicole, Ellen, Cathy B, Carol, Nephele, and Linda D.

Love to Nancy Herkness, who is simply the best of the best in all ways possible: a superlative friend and knitter.

And a special 4 dpn salute to Dallas Schulze, the finest needlewoman on the planet! You almost make me want to try spinning again. I don't know what I'd do without your friendship.

1

CHLOE
SUGAR MAPLE, VERMONT

Do you ever wonder why things happen the way they do? All of those seemingly random decisions we make throughout our lives that turn out to be not so random after all. Maybe if I had closed the shop twenty minutes earlier that night or gone for a quick walk around Snow Lake, she might still be alive today.

But I didn't and that choice changed our lives forever.

At the moment when it all began, I was

down on my knees, muttering ancient curses under my breath as I tugged, pulled, and tried to convince five feet of knitted lace that it would be much happier stretched out to six plus.

If there were any magic spells out there to help a girl block a shawl, I hadn't found them, and believe me, I'd looked. Blocking, like life, was equal parts intuition, brute strength, and dumb luck.

(Just in case you were wondering, I usually don't mention the dumb luck part when I give a workshop.)

That Monday night I was two hours into Blocking 101, teaching my favorite techniques to three yarn-crawling sisters from Pennsylvania, a teacher from New Jersey, and a retired rocket scientist from Florida. We had been expecting a busload of fiber fanatics from northern Maine, but a wicked early winter blizzard had stopped them somewhere west of Bangor. Two of my best friends from town, admitted knit shop groupies and world-class gossips, rounded out the class.

By the way, I'm Chloe Hobbs, owner of Sticks & Strings, voted the number one knit shop in New England two years running. I don't know exactly who did the voting, but I owe each of those wonderful knitters some quiviut and a margarita. Blog posts about the magical store in northern Vermont where your yarn never tangles, your sleeves always come out the same length, and you always, *always* get gauge were popping up on a daily basis, raising both my profile and my bottom line.

Sometimes I worried that this sudden, unexpected burst of fame and fortune had extended the tourist season beyond the town's comfort zone. Hiding in plain sight was harder than it sounded, but for now our secret was still safe.

A blocking board was spread open on the floor. A dark blue Spatterware bowl of T-pins rested next to it. My trusty spray bottle of warm water had been refilled twice. I probably looked like a train wreck as I crawled my way around the perimeter, pinning each scallop and point into position, but those were the breaks.

Since blocking lace was pretty much my only cardio these days, when the wolf whistle sailed overhead, I didn't bother to look up.

"Wow!" Janice Meany, owner of Cut &

Curl across the street, murmured. "Those can't be real."

If I'd had any doubt about the wolf whistles, Janice's statement erased it. Last I heard, not too many women were ordering 34As from their neighborhood cosmetic surgeon.

"Implants," Lynette Pendragon declared in a voice that could be heard in the upper balcony of her family's Sugar Maple Arts Playhouse. "Or a really good wizard."

It was times like this when I wished I had inherited a tiny bit of magick from my mother. Just enough to render my indiscreet friend speechless for a second or two. Everyone in Sugar Maple knows we don't talk about wizards in front of civilians unless the conversation includes Munchkins and Oz.

Fortunately our guests had other things on their minds.

"I'm glad my Howie isn't here," one of the Pennsylvania sisters breathed. "She looks like Sharon Stone. Howie has a thing for Sharon Stone."

"Sharon Stone fifteen years ago on a good day," the New Jersey schoolteacher added. "A *very* good day."

What can I say? I'm only human. (And a nosy one at that.) I dumped the lace and glanced toward the front window.

Winter comes early to our part of Vermont. By the time the last of the leaf-peepers have headed down to the lesser glories of New York and Connecticut, we're digging out our snowshoes and making sure our woodpiles are well stocked. In mid-December it's dark and seriously cold by four thirty, and only the most intrepid window-shopping tourist would even consider strolling down Main Street without at least five layers of clothing.

The woman peering in at us was blond, tall, and around my age, but that was where the resemblance ended. I'm the kind of woman who could disappear into a crowd even if her hair was on fire. Our window shopper couldn't disappear if she tried. Her movie-star-perfect face was pressed up against the frosty glass and we had a full-frontal glimpse of bare arms, bare shoulders, and cleavage that would send Pamela Anderson running back to her surgeon.

"Am I nuts or is she naked?" I asked no one in particular.

"I think she's strapless," Janice said, but she didn't sound convinced.

"It can't be more than ten degrees out there," one of the Pennsylvanians said, exchanging looks with her sisters. "She must be crazy."

"Or drunk," Lynette offered.

"I'll bet she was mugged," the rocket scientist volunteered. "I saw a weird-looking guy lurking down the block when I parked my car."

I was tempted to tell her that the weird-looking guy was a half-asleep vampire named Buster on an ice cream run for his pregnant wife, but I figured that might not be good for business.

The possibly naked woman at the window tapped twice, mimed a shiver, then pointed toward the locked door, where the CLOSED sign was prominently displayed.

"Are you going to make her stand out there all night?" Janice asked. "Maybe she needs help."

She definitely isn't here for a new set of double points, I thought as I flipped the lock. Not that I profile my customers or anything, but I'd bet my favorite rosewoods that she had never cast on a stitch in her life and intended to keep it that way.

My second thought as she swirled past me into the shop was, *Wow, she really is naked.* It took a full second for me to realize that was an illusion created by a truly gifted dressmaker with access to spectacular yard goods.

My third thought—well, I didn't actually have a third thought. I was still working on the second one when she smiled at me and somewhere out there a dentist counted his T-bills.

"I'm Chloe," I said as I looked into her sea green eyes. Eyes like that usually came with magical powers (and more than a little bit of family history), but she had the vibe of the pure human about her. "I own the shop."

"Suzanne Marsden." She extended a perfectly manicured hand and I thought I caught a shiver of Scotch on her breath. "I think you might have saved my life."

"Literally or figuratively?" I asked.

I've dealt with lots of life-or-death emergencies at Sticks & Strings, but most of them included dropped stitches and too many margaritas at our Wednesday Night Knit-Ins.

She laughed as Janice and Lynette exchanged meaningful looks I tried very hard to ignore.

"I can't believe they wouldn't seat me early at the Inn. I thought I could flirt with the bartender until my boyfriend arrived but no such luck."

It was probably the first time anyone had ever refused her anything, and she looked puzzled and annoyed in an amused kind of way.

"The Weavers can be a tad rigid," I said, studiously avoiding eye contact with my townie friends, who knew exactly why the Weavers acted the way they did. "I promise you the food's worth the aggravation."

"I left my coat in the car so I could make a big sweeping Hollywood entrance, and now I not only can't get into the damn restaurant, I locked myself out of my car and would probably have frozen to death out there if you hadn't taken pity on me and opened your door."

"Honey, you're in Vermont," Janice said. "You can't go around like that up here. You'll freeze your nipples off."

"She said she has a coat," I reminded Janice a tad sharply. As a general rule I find it best not to discuss politics, religion, or my customer's nipples in the shop. "It's locked in her car."

"With my cell and my skis and my ice skates," Suzanne said with a theatrical eye roll. "All I need is to use your phone so I can call Triple A."

"Oh, don't bother with them," Lynette said with a wave of her hand. "They'll take all night to get up here. My daughter Vonnie can have it open in a heartbeat."

Suzanne's perfectly groomed right eyebrow rose slightly. "If it's not too much trouble, that would be great."

Clearly she thought Vonnie was majoring in grand theft auto at Sugar Maple High, but that was a whole lot better than telling her that the teenager could make garage doors roll open three towns away just by thinking about them.

There were some things tourists were better off not knowing.

I shot Lynette a look. "So you're going to go call Vonnie now, right?"

We both knew she had already put out the call to her daughter, but we're all about keeping up appearances here in Sugar Maple.

"I'm on it," Lynette said and went off in search of her cell phone.

I turned back to our visitor, who was up to her elbows in a basket of angora roving waiting to be spun into yarn, while Penelope, the ancient store cat who shared the basket, ignored her.

"This is glorious. I've thought about learning to knit but—" She shrugged. "You know how it is."

Well, not really. I've been knitting since I was old enough to hold a pair of needles.

"I'll be spinning that next week," I told her while we waited for Lynette to return, "then knitting it up into a shawl."

She wandered to the stack of shawls on the shelf and fingered a kid silk Orenburg I had on display. "Don't tell me you made this?"

"Chloe knitted everything in the shop," Janice volunteered.

"Impossible!" Suzanne Marsden looked over at me. "Did you really? I love handmade garments and this is heirloom quality."

She might have been lying through her porcelain veneers but it was all the encouragement I needed. I whipped out the Orenburg and was treated to the kind of adulation usually reserved for rock stars.

"Amazing," Suzanne breathed as I laid the shawl across her slender shoulders. "You couldn't possibly have made this without divine intervention."

I started to spout my usual it's-all-just-knit-and-purl shop owner spiel when to my surprise the truth popped out instead. "It almost put me into intensive care," I admitted to the background laughter of my friends, "but I made it to the other side."

And then I showed her the trick that either sent prospective knitters running back to their crochet hooks or won them over forever. I slipped my mother's wedding band off my right forefinger and passed the shawl through the small circle of Welsh gold.

"How much?" Suzanne asked.

"It's not for sale," Lynette answered before I had the chance to open my mouth. "Chloe never sells her Orenburgs."

"In my experience there are exceptions to every absolute." Suzanne favored me with a smile that was a half-degree away from flirtatious. "Name your price."

"Dangerous words to use in front of a shop owner," I said lightly, "but Lynette is right. The shawls on that shelf are for display only."

Suzanne met my eyes, and I saw something behind the smile that took me by surprise.

Pretty people aren't supposed to be sad. Isn't that the story you were told when you were a little girl? Pretty people are supposed to get a free ride through this life and possibly the next one too.

That was the thing about running a shop. Every now and then a customer managed to push the right buttons and my business sense, shaky at the best of times, went up in smoke.

I swiped her platinum AmEx through the machine and slid the receipt across the counter for her signature.

"Would you like me to wrap it for you?" I asked while Lynette and Janice kept the other customers amused.

"No, thanks," she said, pirouetting in front of the cheval mirror in the corner. "I'll wear it."

Lynette popped back in. "Vonnie texted me," she said to Suzanne. "Your car's unlocked and the Inn is open for business."

Suzanne flashed us a conspiratorial grin. "My boyfriend always keeps me waiting. It wouldn't hurt him to do a little waiting himself."

But she didn't keep him waiting long. She signed her receipt, made a few polite noises, then hurried back out into the darkness.

"I'd give anything to see the boyfriend," one of the Pennsylvania sisters said after the door clicked shut behind Suzanne Marsden. "I'll bet we're talking major hottie."

"Johnny Depp hot or George Clooney hot?" the schoolteacher from New Jersey asked, and everyone laughed.

The rocket scientist gave out a cross between a snicker and a snort. "That woman has future trophy wife written all over her. Odds are he's old, wrinkled, and rich."

"Maybe she loves him," I said then immediately wished I'd kept my big mouth shut.

Janice and Lynette exchanged glances and I didn't need extrasensory powers to know exactly what they were thinking. I shot them my best "don't you dare" warning look.

One thing I didn't need was another lecture on love from Sugar Maple's two most dangerous matchmakers.

Blocking lace seemed a little anticlimactic to me after Suzanne's minidrama. I was seriously tempted to excuse myself for a minute then race up the street so I could peek through the front window of the Inn and eyeball the guy she was meeting, but that wasn't how Sticks & Strings had maintained its ranking as the number one knit shop in New England two years running.

So I stayed put, but that didn't mean I was happy about it.

It was a little before ten by the time everyone exchanged names and phone numbers and e-mail addresses. I handed out goodie bags of knitting gadgets and yarn samples and smiled at the oohs and ahhs of appreciation. Welcome to the dark side, ladies. Before long they would need an extra room to house their stash.

I let out a loud sigh of relief as I sank into one of the overstuffed chairs near the Ashford wheels. "I actually broke into a sweat blocking that shawl." I flapped the hem of my T-shirt for emphasis.

Janice rolled her eyes. "You're not going

to get any sympathy from me. Try giving a full body wax to an overweight eighty-five-year-old man with more wrinkles than a shar-pei. Now *that's* a workout."

Too much information. What went on behind the closed doors of Cut & Curl was none of my business.

"Seriously. I thought that shawl was going to get the better of me."

"Our visitor is the one who got the better of you," Lynette said. "You barely recouped the cost of the yarn."

Lynette was always trying to give me business advice, and I was always doing my best to ignore her. "I thought we had a great group tonight. Definitely better than the carload of mystery writers who drove in for the finishing workshop last month. Now that was a big mistake."

Leave it to mystery writers to wonder why the Inn flashed a NO OCCUPANCY sign but didn't have any visitors.

"I'm talking about the shawl. She practically stole it from you." Lynette could be like a dog with a stack of short ribs.

"Don't exaggerate."

"You must have spent twice that on yarn."

"I didn't spend anything. That was hand-spun from my mother's stash." When my mother died, one of the things she left me was a basket of roving that remained full to overflowing no matter how many hours I spent at my wheel, and another was a love of all things fiber.

"Good gods," Lynette shrieked. "It's worse than I thought."

"I'm not crazy," I said, slightly annoyed. "Lilith checks the roving twice a year to make sure it's free from any traveling spells."

Lynette was mollified, but just barely.

"You really should drive down to Brattle-boro and take a class in small business management," she went on. "Cyrus said it's the best money we ever spent."

Lynette and Cyrus were owners/opera-tors of the Sugar Maple Arts Playhouse at the corner of Carrier Court and Willard Grove. Cyrus was one of the SMAP's fa-vorite performers, which, considering the fact that he was a shapeshifter, made cast-ing a snap. Lynette and their daughters Vonnie and Iphigenia were also shapeshift-ers and had been known to round out Cyrus's repertory company on more than one occasion. Their sons, the unfortunately named Gilbert and Sullivan, were occasionally pressed into service too, but Gil and Sully were quickly reaching the age where it would take cash to turn them into orphaned pirates.

"So you'll think about it?" Lynette pressed. "If you sign up before the end of the year, Cyrus gets a fifty-dollar rebate."

"I'll think about it," I said, "but it's pretty hard to get away these days."

"You don't want to get away," Janice said as she rinsed out the teapot.

"That's right," Lynette observed as she swept crumbs off the worktable and tossed them into the trash. "You're all about the work these days."

"It would do you good to take a little trip." Janice reached for the coffeepot. "I can't remember the last time you went away for a night or two."

"I can," Lynette said as she fluffed up the pillows on the leather sofa near the fireplace. "It was when she was seeing that lawyer from New Hampshire."

Janice frowned. "That has to be—what? Four, five years ago?"

"Almost six," I said, "and I don't want to talk about it."

"You can't possibly still blame us for that."

"Putting a spell on our car wasn't very funny. We could have frozen to death up there in the woods."

"We moved the relationship along," Lynette broke in. "You should be grateful."

"Lynnie's right," Janice said. "We saved you from making a terrible mistake."

"Howard was handsome, smart, and independently wealthy. Where's the mistake in that?"

"He was human," Janice said. "It wouldn't have worked."

"I'm human," I reminded her.

"Only half," Lynette said. "Your mother was a sorceress."

"Yes, she was, but we all know I take after my father." I had his height, his hair, and his humanness. There wasn't the slightest bit of magick about me and there never had been. I couldn't see into the future or shapeshift or bend spoons with the power of my mind. I was as solid and earthbound as one of the maple trees in Willard Grove.

"Nothing good happens when magick meets human," Janice went on. "Don't tempt fate, honey. Stick with your own kind."

What they meant was, "Your mother fell in love with a human and see what happened to her."

I was six years old when my parents died in a car crash not far from the Toothaker Bridge. The car skidded on black ice and slammed into a towering maple tree. My human father had been killed instantly. My sorceress mother lingered for two days while Sorcha and Lilith and all the people who loved her did everything in their power to convince her to stay, but in the end Guinevere chose to leave this world to be with the only man she would ever love.

My memories of that time were all in soft focus. Mostly I remember Sorcha, who had opened up her life and her home to me and made me her own.

Sometimes I hated my mother for making that choice. What kind of woman would choose to leave her daughter alone in the world? Depending on the time of day and how much wine I'd consumed, I either found her decision achingly romantic or the act of a supremely selfish woman.

"You're not listening," I said to my friends. "I don't have magick and I probably never will."

"You never know what might happen," Janice said. "You always were a late bloomer. You were the last in your class to start wearing a bra."

I was also the last in my class to score a date to the senior prom, something that still stings even now, thirteen years later. If it hadn't been for my pal Gunnar, I wouldn't have gone at all. "And your point is?"

Lynette leaned forward, all dark-eyed intensity. "My mother told me that your mother didn't come into her full powers until she fell in love. Maybe—"

"But she had some powers before she met my father," I reminded my friends. "I remember the stories. Why can't you both accept the fact that I'm never going to be more than I am right now?"

They exchanged another one of those knowing glances that reminded me of the housewives of Wisteria Lane.

"No matchmaking," I said, barely stifling a yawn. "Absolutely, positively not. I am way too old for matchmaking." Okay, so I was only thirty, but blind dates aged a girl in dog years.

"But he's perfect for you."

"That's what you said about the last one."

Janice had the decency to look a tiny bit sheepish. "I'll admit Jacob was a mistake."

"Jacob was a troll."

Literally.

"Midge Stallworth forgot to mention that. We thought he was a vampire like the rest of the family."

"If the Universe wants me to find someone, they'll send me a hot alpaca farmer who likes to spin."

"Honey, you know we're only thinking about your happiness." Lynette patted my hand.

Maybe they were thinking about my happiness, but they were also thinking about the accident just before Christmas last year. A bus carrying a high school hockey team en route to Brattleboro blew a tire and careened down an embankment near the Sugar Maple town limits, killing the goalie and the coach.

Things like that weren't supposed to happen here. Accidents, crime, illness, all the things that plagued every other town in America, didn't happen here. Or at least they hadn't up until recently.

Over three hundred years ago one of my sorcerer ancestors cast a protective charm over the town designed to shield Sugar Maple from harm for as long as one of her line walked the earth and—well, you guessed it. I'm the last descendant of Aerynn, and if you thought your family was on your case to marry and produce offspring, try having an entire town mixing potions, casting runes, and weaving spells designed to hook you up with Mr. Right.

"The accident was random chance," I said, trying to ignore the chill racing up my spine as I remembered the crowd of reporters who had flooded the area. "The weather was terrible. It could have happened anywhere."

"But it didn't happen anywhere," Janice said. "It happened here and it shouldn't have."

"Jan's right," Lynette said. "The spell is growing weaker with every year that passes. I can feel the difference."

Janice nodded. "We all do."

I didn't but that was no surprise. I could only take them at their word on this, same as I did on everything else I couldn't see or hear or understand.

"Cyrus met a charming selkie named Glenn at the Scottish Faire last week," Lynette went on.

"She already dated a selkie," Janice reminded her. "It wasn't a good match."

"I dated a selkie?" The parade of recent losers had mercifully blurred in my memory.

"You said his breath smelled like smoked salmon."

I shuddered. "I'll skip the selkies, thanks."

"You'd skip them all if we let you," Janice said.

She was right about that.

"Just keep Saturday nights open," Lynette said. "That's all I'm asking."

As far as I could tell, my Saturday nights were open from now until the next millennium. I nodded and stifled another yawn. "No trolls, no selkies," I said. "And he has to be at least six feet tall *before* the magic kicks in."

"Not a problem," Janice said. "Tall is good."

"Human might be nice for a change."

They looked at me, then at each other, and burst into raucous laughter.

"Honey," Lynette said as she patted my arm, "around here human might not be your best choice."

I wasn't usually prickly about their wariness about humans, but that night it got under my skin. It wasn't like I actually thought Mr. Right was going to show up at Sticks & Strings one snowy winter day searching for the perfect ski sweater to wear on the slopes. But I did think love was possible. It had happened for my parents, hadn't it? Maybe they hadn't managed the happy ending part of the equation, but for a little while I saw what real magic was all about and I didn't want to settle for anything less.

Now you know why I had five cats, one TiVo, and a stash of yarn I couldn't knit my way through in six lifetimes.

I mean, what were the odds that the perfect man would not only show up in Sugar Maple, but also be okay with the fact that the town wasn't the picture-postcard New England town our Chamber of Commerce would have you believe, but a village of vampires, werewolves, elves, faeries, and everything else your parents told you didn't really exist?

Or that he would be okay with the fact

that the woman he wanted to spend his life with had a few surprises lurking in her own gene pool?

Ten million to one sounded about right to me.

Besides, Sugar Maple was doing fine without my help. We had a thriving tourist trade and zero crime. What other town could make that claim? It seemed to me that Aerynn's protective blessing was still getting the job done even if we had had a few close calls over the last year or two.

The blessing's strength might be weakening, but we still had time to figure this out before it vanished altogether. All we needed was a frothy little protective charm to cover us until I either found the man of my dreams or came up with a Plan B.

And maybe things would have worked out that way if, just a few hours after she left my shop, Suzanne Marsden hadn't been murdered.

2

CHLOE

It was around eleven when we locked up the shop. I said good night to both Lynette and Janice then waited until they drove away before I cut across the tiny yard that separated my store from the empty pet shop next door and headed straight for the Inn.

It was one of those crystal-clear winter nights that made me glad to be a New Englander. Moonlight bounced off the snowy sidewalks, doing a better job of illuminating my path than our treasured gas lamps. The

gas lamps had been converted to electricity some years back, but they still imparted
a glow rich with nostalgia. The air was crisp
and cold, and it carried with it the scent of
woodsmoke and pine and something else,
something I couldn't identify but understood deep in my bones. It was the smell
of my childhood, of home and family, of the
place I knew I would never leave.

There had been a time back in our village's early days when someone like me
wouldn't have set foot outside after dark.
The energies had been wilder then. The
scent of human flesh triggered visceral
hungers that could be satisfied only one
way. The old way.

But that was a long time ago. Originally
our town had provided a safe harbor for
the hunted creatures of this world. While
towns like Salem waged an ugly war against
perceived witchcraft, our early citizens had
opened their homes to strangers whose
very appearance would strike terror in
most hearts. The risk had been great and
there had been losses along the way to
understanding but we had not only survived: we had thrived.

Sugar Maple had sheltered Aerynn and

her family when they fled Massachusetts, and to show her gratitude, Aerynn vowed that as long as females of her line walked the earth, the protective charm would keep the villagers of Sugar Maple from harm. Before she pierced the veil, she had poured all of her secrets into the Book of Spells, which would be passed down, along with her magick, through her female descendants.

For almost three hundred years the Book helped an unbroken chain of Hobbs women keep Sugar Maple safe from harm, and if my mother hadn't fallen in love with a mortal human, there was every reason to believe the chain would have remained unbroken for another three hundred years.

But not even Aerynn had been able to foresee the birth of a half-mortal girl who hadn't a drop of magick in her entire body.

When my mother died, she left both the Book of Spells and her six-year-old daughter in the capable hands of Sorcha, the town healer. Sorcha knew that the magick on those pages was powerful and needed to be hidden away. Until a Hobbs woman with magick at her command claimed the Book, it was vulnerable to darker forces, who would use it in ways Aerynn never intended.

"But how will I find it?" I had asked Sorcha when it was her time to pierce the veil. "Where should I look?"

"Have faith, daughter," she said, placing a tender kiss on my forehead. "When you're ready, the Book will find you."

It hadn't been looking very hard if you asked me. Except for a short-lived college career at BU, I've been in Sugar Maple every day of my life. When someone like Suzanne Marsden came to town, the event had my full attention.

I'm not a stalker by nature or even all that nosy about other people's lives, but that night I couldn't seem to control myself. It was like I was starving for a glimpse of how it could be when things were right between a woman and a man. I wanted to see the sparks flashing between them with my own eyes, not read about them in a book.

Osborne is a long avenue that runs parallel to the park. Back when the town was first incorporated, the park had been part of a forest that had long since given way to the demands of modern life. Somehow we had managed to hang on to enough wooded acreage to provide a healthy buffer between Sugar Maple and the next town.

Which, all things considered, wasn't a bad thing.

What moon there was that night splashed a silvery glow across the snowdrifts lining the sidewalk as I neared the Inn. The faint sound of laughter floated toward me and I imagined Suzanne Marsden in her naked dress with the shimmery shawl slipping off her shoulders as she flirted with her boyfriend.

Okay, so maybe I was really imagining myself in that naked dress and the shimmery shawl, perfectly lit by the glow of a half-dozen candles, smiling up into the eyes of a handsome Homo sapiens who couldn't keep his hands off me.

I never said I didn't have a few issues of my own. (Not to mention some fantasies that were frequently fueled by a box of Chardonnay and sappy old movies on DVD.) Sometimes I had to concentrate very hard to remember my parents' faces, the sound of their voices, but the memory of how it had been between them was crystal clear.

And I wanted that. I wanted to love someone so much it hurt. I wanted someone to
love me so deeply that I would believe in
forever even if forever could never be.

I knew that sooner or later I would have
to do whatever was necessary to keep
Sugar Maple and her own safe from harm,
but I couldn't help hoping that love would
be part of the solution. Not just the friendship kind of love I felt for Gunnar, but the
real can't-live-without-you kind that turned
your world upside down.

But in a good way.

A handful of cars with out-of-state plates
were parked in the lot behind the Inn.
Two Massachusetts, two New Hampshire,
one Wisconsin. Soft gray puffs of apple-
scented smoke rose from the twin chim-
neys on either side of the sloped roof. I
moved closer, careful to stay in the shadows, and watched as the Weavers delivered the ultimate country inn experience to
their unsuspecting guests.

Renate poured wine for a middle-aged
couple and said something that made
them both laugh. A trio of businessmen in
dark suits talked intently over thick porter-
house steaks. Colm, the patriarch of the

Weaver clan, danced attendance on a white-haired woman in vintage Chanel. Bettina, the Weavers' married daughter, sat on a ladderback chair near the hearth, playing the harp while her kids, Athens and Ithaca, bused the tables.

The diners hadn't a clue that the owners were faerie who lived under the first step of the center hall staircase when they weren't playing innkeeper. Part of Aerynn's protective charm was the way outsiders saw only what they expected to see in Sugar Maple, not what was right there in front of them.

One of the businessmen glanced toward the window. His eyes widened in surprise when he saw me and I hit the snowy ground face first, praying he would blame it on too many vodka tonics and not a dangerously lonely knit shop owner with too many cats.

Talk about a YouTube moment.

"Chloe?" A familiar voice sounded above me. It just kept getting better and better.

Gunnar, my best friend and occasional movie date, was bending over me. The shimmer of Transition still clung to him like a fine web of silver-blue stars. Even though I had known him my entire life, there were still times when his Fae beauty shocked me into reverent silence.

This, however, wasn't one of them.

I took his outstretched hand and rose to my feet, shaking off the snow like a dog spraying water after a bath. "If you say one word about this, so help me, I'll tell everyone about that time down near the lake when you—"

He gave me that smile of his, the one I wished made my toes curl. He knew his secrets were safe with me. "You want to tell me why you were spying on Renate?"

"You're here too," I pointed out. "Who were you spying on?"

"They had a full house tonight. I helped in the kitchen."

I shook my head in bemusement. "I never understood why Samantha let Darrin talk her out of witchcraft, and I don't understand why Renate doesn't just conjure up those delicious meals of hers." She was Fae. Her whole family was. They had powers and magick I couldn't even imagine. "If I had even half Renate's powers, I'd never block another shawl." A twitch of the nose, a blink of the eye, and voilà! Perfection.

"Magick isn't all it's cracked up to be," he said, brushing glitter from his golden blond hair. "Sometimes I envy you."

"Sure you do," I said with a grin. "Tell me that next time you magick yourself out of paying for bagels at Fully Caffeinated."

"So why are you spying on Renate?" he asked again. For a nice guy, Gunnar could be remarkably determined.

"I wasn't spying on Renate." I brushed snow off the front of my coat. "I was spying on someone else."

He glanced toward the window and grimaced. "Not the guy in the brown suit."

"Give me a little credit." The whole thing sounded so foolish I couldn't wrap my words around it. "A customer locked herself out of her car while she was waiting for the Inn to open. I wanted to see if she found her keys."

"You can do better than that."

"I wanted to get a look at her boyfriend, okay?" I kicked a fine flurry of snow in his direction.

I told him about the naked dress and the Orenburg and the way she lit up the room the moment she stepped into the shop. "And it's not just that she was drop-dead gorgeous or that she had magick like Simone or your mother. I'm telling you, Gunnar, when she was in the room, you couldn't take your eyes off her."

"It's called star power," Gunnar said. "Dane has it too."

I managed to keep my grimace to myself. Gunnar and Dane were twins, but believe me, the likeness was purely physical. They shared astonishing good looks and one set of full Fae powers that were unequally divided between them. As beautiful as Gunnar was, his brother was even more so. But fate hadn't been entirely unfair because Gunnar had claimed the lion's share of powers, a fact in which I took wicked pleasure.

The town matchmakers had done their best to turn our friendship into a love match, but finally even the most hopeful of the lot realized we were fatally platonic and tried to hook me up with his brother. I'm not proud of myself but Dane knew how to work that whole faerie/beauty/sex thing, and one long-ago night I had come close to taking a walk on the wild side. (Believe me, you don't know what seduction is until a faerie turns up the wattage.) Fortunately I came to my senses before I had to disinfect my entire body with Lysol. Call me strange but I like my men a tad less sociopathic.

Still there was something to be said for the chase. Being pursued had its charms. If Gunnar had been able to channel his energies the way his brother could, we would probably be married right now and expecting our fourth or fifth child. And I guess you could say if Dane had been even one-quarter as decent as his brother, I might be living an entirely different life right now.

But cruelty had never been a turn-on for me and I was glad when Dane started spending more time in the faerie realm than the earthly plain doing his mother's dirty work. Their mother, the terrifying Isadora, wielded enormous power in their world and craved it in ours as well.

Dane was hot-tempered and selfish. Gunnar was easygoing and loyal. Janice once said that I made him sound like a golden retriever but that wasn't how I meant it. He had a good heart and a good soul, and I would have given all my hand-painted silk to find a way to make it work between us, but the hard truth of the matter was I didn't love him the way he loved me and I probably never would.

As the only nonmagick taxpayer in Sugar Maple, I pretty much operated on a need-to-know basis and that position had served me well when it came to navigating the tricky waters between the real world out there and the world our ancestors had created. They called it plausible deniability in Washington. Up here we just called it common sense.

"Come on," Gunnar said, glancing back toward the Inn. "We'd better get out of here before Colm comes out for a smoke."

We quickly moved across the yard and driveway, then fell into step when we reached Osborne.

"This is getting to be a habit," I said lightly as I pulled my scarf more closely around my neck. "Third night in a row you've walked me home from work."

"Not that you're counting or anything."

"So what's up, friend?" I asked. "Why the escort service?"

Unlike most Fae of my acquaintance,

Gunnar wasn't good at emotional camou-
flage. "I heard the banshee wail."

I couldn't help it. I laughed out loud. "You
did not." It sounded like something from a
cheesy horror movie.

"Last night. Three minutes to midnight."

"After a few margaritas I usually hear
U2." He didn't laugh with me so I regrouped
and tried again. "You probably were having a bad dream."

"I was wide awake."

"I told you to quit reading Stephen King
before bed."

Again nothing. He didn't even crack a
smile.

Call me a wimp, but I wasn't a big fan of
banshee talk. Things that went bump in the
night, horror movies, your average circus
clown could all give me the screaming
heebie-jeebies. Which, considering where I
live, was pretty ironic. "Come on, Gunnar. I
know this is Sugar Maple but I don't think
anyone here has ever heard a banshee. I
mean, are you even sure banshees exist?"

"I heard one the night before your mother
died."

"I really wish you hadn't told me that."

"I wish I hadn't heard it." He unwound the cashmere scarf I had knitted for him from around his neck and draped it across my shoulders.

"How far away was it last night?"

He hesitated. "It was windy. I couldn't—"

"Tell me, Gunnar."

"Close," he said. "Very close."

I pulled in some icy air. "Okay, so let's say for the moment that you did hear a banshee's wail. Nobody dies in Sugar Maple, at least not in the mortal sense. That would mean it has to be an outsider."

"Not necessarily."

My heart was pounding so hard I could barely speak. I knew the answer in my bones but I needed for him to say it. "Who else could it be?"

"You're half-mortal, Chloe."

I flexed an imaginary bicep. "I'm healthy as a horse," I said. "I don't ski. I almost never drive. Unless I fall onto a stash of double points, I think I'm good for a few more years." I waited for him to laugh or smile or at least acknowledge my attempt at humor but his expression remained grim. "Okay," I said, "now you're really scaring me."

A train whistle blew in the distance, followed by mournful hooting from somewhere nearby.

"Maybe you heard an owl," I said. "The woods are filled with them."

"Or a lovesick fisher," he said, forcing a smile. "I spotted tracks last week in the woods."

"Lilith said they were repopulating. I'll bet that's exactly what you heard."

He made an upbeat comment about conservation and forestry. I answered with an even more upbeat comment about wildlife and the environment. We both ignored the fact that it wasn't mating season. We were practically back to our prebanshee comfort level until we locked eyes and a terrible certainty moved between us.

Change was coming. You could smell it in the air.

He walked me to my cottage at the edge of the woods, where we exchanged awkward good-byes. I wanted to throw my arms around my best friend and hug away the worry in his eyes, but when your best friend was also in love with you, a woman had to think twice. I squeezed his hand instead.

"It's nothing," I said even though we both knew I was lying. "This time tomorrow we'll laugh about it."

But once I closed the door behind me, tomorrow seemed a very long time away. This was one of those nights when the loneliness cut through me like a well-sharpened knife.

I was glad when a loud meow rang out and my feline family materialized from their various hiding places. After an initial burst of excitement, they assumed their usual looks of disdain and I hurried to do their bidding like a good human.

I spent the next forty-five minutes cuddling, cleaning litter boxes, and opening cans of Fancy Feast. Once I had Lucy, Pyewacket, Dinah, and Blot settled down, I popped a Lean Cuisine into the microwave, pumped myself a glass of red from the box on the counter, then plopped down onto the sofa to get pleasantly buzzed while I waited for my meat loaf with whipped potatoes to be ready.

I guess I must have dozed off somewhere between my second glass of wine and the bag of Chips Ahoy I'd sworn I wouldn't open until Saturday night because the next thing I knew I was startled awake by one of Renate's beautiful daughters.

Calliope was balanced on the rim of my wineglass, all teeny-tiny tattoos, piercings, and hot pink iPod permanently set on Stun.

"Wake *up*!" she said. "You have to get to the Stallworths' place right now or else."

"Calli?" I stifled a yawn. "What's going on?"

She shrugged and faerie glitter left over from Transition sent the cats running for cover. (That's the thing about the Fae: no matter how hard they try, they can't always cover their tracks.) "My mom says you'd better get there fast."

She vanished in another shower of glitter I would be vacuuming up for days.

The temperature had dropped considerably in the last few hours. A wicked northerly wind slashed through my heavy down-filled coat and penetrated three layers of wool and quiviut sweaters. As much as I hated the thought of driving the icy half mile between my cottage and Town Hall, I hated the thought of walking it even more.

It took forever to warm up my ancient Buick, long enough that I started wondering if maybe I needed Janice to devise a protective charm to keep the engine running one more year. Finally I shifted into drive and white-knuckled my way down Osborne Avenue. I slid to a shaky stop at the corner of Carrier and Osborne and saw the lights blazing at the Stallworth Funeral Home.

Beads of sweat broke out along the back of my neck and I yanked off my scarf and tossed it onto the seat next to me. I told myself that the Stallworths were nocturnal by nature and 2 A.M. was midday to them, but the knot of cars in their driveway wasn't a good sign. I mean, we weren't all vampire in Sugar Maple.

Gunnar's banshee talk swooped in on me like a swarm of bees. Was it possible he had been right and we had lost one of our own? I refused to wrap my mind around the concept. The death of my father was the last true death I could remember. Sorcha didn't die in the traditional sense; she literally passed from this dimension of being into another one. I had been present at the moment she left us, and while I had been unable to actually see her pierce the veil, there was no denying the fact that in the blink of an eye, her physical self was gone.

That was how it was with most of the villagers. When they moved into another realm, their physical selves moved with them, and there was nothing for the Stallworth Funeral Home to do but organize a gathering in their name.

Maybe one of those businessmen I had seen choking down porterhouses the size of my Buick had keeled over at the table after Gunnar and I left. It could be anything, I told myself as I turned into the circular driveway and glided to a stop behind our only school bus.

Janice, wearing a plaid flannel nightgown and Uggs, was waiting for me at the door. "The blond woman who bought your Orenburg is dead."

I stopped unbuttoning my coat. "What?"

"She's dead." A blaze of color stained her cheeks. "Paul Griggs and his sons were coming out of the woods on the north side of the skating pond and they saw something on the ice—"

Janice kept talking but her words were lost to me. I felt like the oxygen had been sucked out of my lungs. "It's a mistake," I said. "You saw her: she was meeting her boyfriend for dinner at the Inn. She wasn't exactly dressed for ice skating." The skinny heels. The naked dress. That beautiful, vibrant woman . . .

"Colm said she waited two hours for the guy to show up but he never did. She paid her bar tab then left around nine o'clock. That was the last time anyone saw her alive."

"You don't know that. You're guessing. You don't know anything."

"She's here, honey. She's in the—" She stopped and looked away, clearly searching for the right words, but there weren't any.

Slowly the rest of the room came into focus. Paul and his sons Jeremy and Johnny were slumped on the sofa against the far wall. They still bore the marks of Transformation on their forearms and along their jaw lines, dark wiry tufts of gray-brown fur that always reminded me of steel wool. His normally rambunctious sons stared down at their bare feet. The powerful claws were almost fully retracted, but what remained glittered brightly in the overhead lights. All three were swaddled in huge white blankets with bright yellow daisies embroidered in each corner. I had tried repeatedly to woo Midge Stallworth over to knitting, but she was staunchly in the embroidery camp, as evidenced by the profusion of daisies on every textile she owned.

"What are we going to do?" Midge cried the second she saw me. She was a small, round, motherly woman whose high color was the result of a recent feeding and not blusher. "We haven't ordered supplies in at least ten years. By the time we get a delivery, she'll be so stiff we won't be able to—"

The next thing I knew, I was looking up at the ceiling through a grayish mist. The voices were familiar—Janice and Paul and Jeremy's croaking adolescent tenor—but the faces weren't. I closed my eyes again, willing myself to pull the disparate images back into focus. When I opened them this time, everything was as it should be.

Except for the fainting part, that is.

"It's her blood sugar," Midge was saying as she drizzled Dr Pepper into my mouth. "They're always having trouble with their blood sugar." Midge blamed all my problems on being a nonmagick human.

"It's not my blood sugar." I pushed the

soft drink away. "And don't talk about Suzanne like that. She's not even cold yet."

"Oh, she's cold," Paul volunteered from the sofa. "She was near frozen when we pulled her out of the water."

The room started to spin again, but this time I managed to keep myself from fading.

"I want to see her."

They exchanged looks.

"I want to see her," I repeated, rising to my feet. "We can't just leave her alone in that room while we try to figure out what to do next."

The rituals surrounding human death were alien to all of us, but I knew her passage had to be marked even if the thought of actually seeing Suzanne Marsden's corpse was making it hard for me to breathe.

Midge led me down a flight of carpeted stairs and through a maze of dimly lit corridors painted an eerie silvery gray. Every ten feet or so a huge steel door with a tiny electronic locking system broke the monotony. Music, so quiet it was almost subliminal, softened the hard edges, but as we moved deeper into the core of the house, my fear of the unknown began to override my sense of what was right.

When Midge stopped in front of the last door and pressed a series of numbers on the keypad, it was all I could do to keep from running.

Stay, daughter. Sorcha's voice filled my head. *You are doing what you are meant to do.*

I turned to Midge. "Did you hear that?"

Midge frowned as the keypad beeped its disapproval. "You made me punch in the wrong number," she chided me.

"Are you sure you didn't hear anything?" I persisted.

"Only my creaking knees," she said as she punched in the code again.

There's nothing to fear. Sorcha's dear, familiar voice hummed against my breast-bone. *Do as I would do and with a full heart.*

But what would Sorcha do? She had left me on the night of my twenty-first birthday and not a day went by when I didn't think of her with love. She had taught me many of the healing arts but not how to cope with the end of human life. We had never faced anything like this before. No tourist or non-villager had ever died within our township limits. Aerynn's spell had made sure of it. Everyone was looking to me for answers but I hadn't a clue.

If I had ever doubted that the spell was spinning to the end of its life span, I didn't doubt it any longer.

I couldn't turn to Midge and her family for help. Most of what the Stallworths knew about the mortuary business they had gleaned from repeated watchings of *CSI* and *Six Feet Under.* Faced with reality, they were as much in the dark as the rest of us.

Janice. Renate and Colm. Manny and Frank from Sugar Maple Assisted Living. Lilith. Lynette and Cyrus. Not even my best friend, Gunnar. There wasn't a single soul in town who would be able to guide me through this maze. I was going to have to trust myself and pray that Sorcha's wisdom would somehow give me strength to make the right choices for all of us.

The keypad emitted a series of three beeps then swung open. Midge took my hand and squeezed. "Not to worry," she said. "It happens to all of you sooner or later."

Suzanne lay face up on a gurney in the middle of the room. A harsh puddle of fluorescent light washed over her, leaching out what was left of her color. Midge had wrapped her body in a pale pink blanket edged with embroidered violets and pansies. The naked dress was draped over the back of a metal chair in the corner. The Orenburg scarf lay in a sodden heap on the floor.

"Isn't she beautiful?" Midge made one of those clucking noises that reminded me of a brood hen about to lay an egg. "If only Paul and the boys had come out of the woods a moment earlier." She shook her head. "Such a shame. We could have helped."

I knew what she was thinking. There was life as Suzanne and I experienced it, and there was life the way the Stallworths knew it. If there had been time, they could have offered Suzanne the kind of choice most people believed existed only in fiction.

Eternal youth and beauty were powerful incentives, but I didn't think a shadow life would have been enough for a woman like Suzanne.

Then again, maybe she would have jumped at the offer. I had to remind myself that I'd known Suzanne Marsden for maybe ten minutes. There wasn't much you could learn about a woman in six hundred seconds.

Midge took my hand and squeezed. "Honey, don't be scared. There's nothing to fear."

Easy for her to say. She had been part of the living dead since 1793. But even Midge had her limitations, and sunlight was one of them. Dawn wasn't far away. We needed to get on with it.

I forced myself to really see what was in front of me.

"You're right," I said as I approached the body. "She's still lovely."

"I told you." Midge gave me one of her fifties TV mom smiles. "It's all a part of the Great Plan."

Whatever that was.

Someone had smoothed Suzanne's wet hair back from her face, exposing her perfect bone structure. She looked like a porcelain doll. All of the fire and flash she had brought with her to Sticks & Strings existed only in my memory.

"It's the soul," Midge said with a sigh. "It makes all the difference."

Surprising talk from a vampire, but this was Sugar Maple, where nothing was as it seemed.

I struggled to find words to convey what I was feeling but I failed. The realization that if I had magick, this wouldn't have happened filled me with remorse.

I stayed with Suzanne until daybreak. I tried to think deeply spiritual, philosophical thoughts about life and death and the hereafter, but my mind was a blank. I wished I had brought some knitting. Would Suzanne have minded? I didn't think so but I was only guessing. Had she been a churchgoing Catholic, a lapsed Episcopalian, an observant Jew, a questioning agnostic? What prayers or rituals were part of her heritage? I had nothing to offer her but my physical presence, no blessings or incantations meant to ease her way between worlds. Her own people would have to see to that when they came for her.

I wondered who her people were. Did she have a family whose hearts would be broken when they got the news? What about the boyfriend she had worn the naked dress for—how would he feel when he heard? Did she have children, a job, friends who depended on her for laughter and support? Who was out there waiting for the call I would make as soon as the sun rose?

I didn't have any answers, only the certainty that, like it or not, we were going to have to let the world in, if only for a while.

3

LUKE
BOSTON, MASSACHUSETTS—LATER
THAT SAME DAY

I was up to my ass in dead matter when I finally got the call.

"Luke MacKenzie." I balanced the receiver against my shoulder while I fed more paper into the shredder under my desk. Forget *CSI* and all those TV cop shows. Most of a real cop's day was spent figuring out what the hell to do with all the paper the job generated.

"Are you still looking to leave us?" Fran, the chief's admin assistant, asked.

We both knew the question was rhetorical. I had been looking to leave Boston PD for two years, three months, and eleven days, but up until now nobody in the contiguous forty-eight had work for a cop who wanted to disappear and still get paid for it.

"I have something for you." I heard the click of computer keys in the background followed by one of those hacking coughs that said winter in New England. "It's temporary and I know you're looking for permanent but when I saw who and—" She stopped. "I'm sorry, Luke, but there's no easy way to say this. Your friend Suzanne is dead."

༜

Ten minutes later I was standing near the window in the chief's office, trying to focus in on the printout from Stallworth Funeral Home in Sugar Maple, Vermont.

According to the statement from the guy who had found her body, Suzanne had apparently fallen through the ice and been unable to pull herself out of the semifrozen pond. She had left her car parked at the curb about fifty feet away. Her purse was on the passenger's seat. Skis were strapped to the roof and they found an overnight bag in the trunk. There was no sign of a struggle.

The victim was wearing figure skates when she was recovered.

A pair of pricey heels were found on a bench at the edge of the lake, along with a pack of cigarettes and a gold lighter.

I could almost hear her laugh as she kicked off her shoes and laced up her skates to take the ice. We grew up loving the ice. We loved the smell, the sound, the way it sometimes kicked our asses.

She understood the ice. She knew how to read a frozen lake better than I did. She knew you didn't test the center alone in early December, not even up there in northern Vermont. I was glad she had been taken while doing something she loved and pissed as hell that she hadn't been more careful.

I'm a homicide detective. I've been trained to rein in my emotions and concentrate on the facts of a case. But I've seen drowning victims. I know what happens to the human body after exposure to

icy water and no oxygen. It wasn't something you would want to see twice.

Fran was watching me closely. "You
okay over there, MacKenzie?"

I wasn't but I grunted something meant
to divert her attention from my struggle to
pull it together.

"Where's the police report?" I asked
when I trusted my voice again.

"There isn't one."

That got my attention. "They have a
body and no police report?"

"It's a small town. Things are different
up there."

"No town's that small," I said. And no
town was that different. Even small-town
cops generated enough paper to destroy a
few forests. "Anything from the coroner?"

"They sent the body to Montpelier but
the autopsy was canceled and the body
was rerouted to family in Connecticut."

"On whose orders?"

She leaned forward and motioned me
closer. "You didn't hear it from me, but Dan
Sieverts has been calling in favors all morning."

"The congressman with the hair? The
one who—"

Her eyes widened. "You didn't know they were seeing each other?"

I shook my head. "You sure?"

"I'm sure," Fran said. "I was in the room when the chief got the call."

Dan Sieverts was a very publicly married politician from Cambridge who was being prepped by the machine to make a run for governor next year.

I had heard the buzz around Sieverts. One of those golden boys destined for bigger and better things, he had the pedigree, the résumé, and the connections needed to climb the ladder. He also had the arrogance that came with the package. Apparently for the last two years that package had also included Suzanne.

Suzanne had been part of my life since grade school. We weren't what you would call close friends. I didn't tell her my secrets and she didn't tell me hers. But we shared a time and a place and for a little while we even shared a family. She had been married to my ex's brother for about five minutes, and looking back, the only surprise was that any of us had ever believed she and Andy had a chance in hell to make it work. They were over before they brushed the rice from their hair. Suzanne said good-bye to our small Massachusetts fishing village and set out to conquer the world.

I last saw her around this time a year ago. She was running a major PR campaign for a chain of upscale hotels looking to gain a foothold in Boston, and she showed up at the station house with two pastramis on rye and some Guinness. I passed on the Guinness, but we shared the pastrami near the Swan Boats and spent a good three or four minutes catching up on the old days.

"That's it?" she had said, laughing as the trickle of nostalgia ran dry. "That's all you've got?"

The sky was blue. The sun was shining. It hadn't snowed in at least four or five hours. I let her think my life was the equivalent of a fistful of Super Bowl rings. She let me think her life was the female equivalent.

At the time I thought only one of us was lying but now I wondered.

Suzanne was dead and the only thing I knew for sure was that it wasn't from natural causes.

I keyed back into what Frannie was saying. ". . . Sieverts was supposed to meet her at some inn last night but he didn't show. The owner said she waited two hours, paid the bar tab, then took off alone. Next thing, some hardware store owner and his sons were pulling her out of the water by her scarf."

I pushed back the image. "CPR?"

She shrugged her shoulders.

"Did they call 911?"

"All I know is what they told me on the phone."

"Have them fax you a police report."

"No cops, no police report."

"You mean no cops on the scene?"

"I mean no cops at all. Sugar Maple doesn't have a police force."

"They have to have some kind of police presence."

"Why?" She glanced at her computer screen. "According to this, they don't have any crime. No burglaries. No shoplifting. No fender benders. Their kids don't even TP the trees on Devil's Night. This drowning is the first incident of any kind reported within town limits for over eighty years."

"Bullshit. Even the Amish have their problems."

She spun her monitor around to face me. "Look for yourself."

I scanned the Chamber of Commerce web page she had pulled up. I skimmed the history of maple sugar and its importance in breaking down the nation's reliance on the West Indian slave trade and scrolled past postcard-perfect photos of a tiny Vermont town nestled in the Green Mountains. Skiing. Shopping. Picturesque views. A four-star restaurant in the middle of nowhere. Great-looking people straight out of central casting. Sugar Maple pretty much had it all.

Except crime.

"They probably cheat on their taxes," I said, spinning the monitor back into position. "Where's this going, Franny?"

"Sieverts's people are leaning on Montpelier to tie up all the loose ends about your friend's death before it has a chance to hit the media, and Montpelier's red-faced about letting a town slip between their sticky bureaucratic fingers." Both sides needed someone on the ground in Sugar Maple to put an official stamp on things.

Go in, snoop around, make sure there was no foul play, no nasty surprises to come back later and bite Sieverts on the ass. Once things were wrapped up to everyone's satisfaction, the boys in Montpelier would install one of their own and I'd be out.

"It's not permanent," Fran said, watching me. "I want to make sure you know that. You'll be cutting ties with us for something that isn't going to last."

"Nothing lasts forever, Franny."

I said yes.

4

CHLOE
SUGAR MAPLE, VERMONT

As it turned out, we didn't have to go looking for trouble. Two days later it found us and the whole town seemed to go crazy at once.

"It is what it is," Joe Randazzo from the County Clerk's Office said when he broke the news to me over the phone. "That pet shop next door to you is vacant. We'll put him there."

"You can't," I said, trying not to let him

know I was on the verge of a total melt-down. "I was thinking of expanding my business into that space."

I heard him take a long drag on a ciga-rette. "Like I said, Ms. Hobbs, it is what—hold on."

I said something entirely inappropriate.

Janice, who had stuck with me through my morning of ugly phone calls, looked up from the Baby Surprise Jacket she was knitting, "What's going on? You've been talking to him forever."

"You're the one with the powers," I said, a tad snappishly. "You tell me."

Janice shot me a look over her bam-boo needles. "I'm a witch, not a fortune-teller."

Which made me laugh, something I didn't think I would be doing again for a very long time. Janice was descended from a long line of women who revered Mother Earth and understood her ways. She was also understandably proud of her lineage and ready to do battle with anyone who didn't show it the proper respect.

"Don't blame me," I said as Muzak'd Barry Manilow assaulted my eardrums. "I'm only human."

It was Janice's turn to laugh. "That's okay, honey. I like you anyway."

"They're sending a cop to Sugar Maple."

"To ask questions? That makes sense. They have all those forms to fill out up there in Montpelier." She paused for a second but started up again before I could jump in. "I'll have to wax the Griggs boys and give them pedicures. Did you see them last night? The shock stopped Transformation just before the finish line." She pretended to shudder. "It wasn't a pretty sight."

All I had noticed were the bristly hairs piercing their skin and the tips of their pearly claws. Janice was acting like it was a scene from *An American Werewolf in London.* We never used to sweat the small stuff in Sugar Maple. Aerynn's spell would have taken care of everything, smoothing strangers' perceptions and creating the illusion of the expected even when the expected was nowhere to be found. Now we had no way of knowing when or where the protective charm might let us down. More and more, we were on our own.

I took a deep breath. "They're not sending a cop just to ask questions, Janice.

They want to open a police station in the shop next door."

Despite our tourist town popularity we had managed to fly below the scan of bureaucratic radar. We followed the letter of the law. We sent our kids to school. We voted. We paid our taxes on time. We were an asset to the state, and in true Yankee fashion, they had let us do our thing without interference. But I was afraid we were about to find out how much of that laissez-faire attitude was the New Englander's love of freedom and how much was courtesy of Aerynn.

The Muzak'd Manilow stopped abruptly and I motioned for Janice to be quiet.

"Got a pencil?" Joe Randazzo barked and then started rattling off a to-do list that made my head spin. "And one more thing," he said over a noisy slurp of liquid. "Pull together town records from 1946 to the present and make sure to include death certificates."

Uh-oh.

"Death certificates?" I asked in my best who-me-worry tone. "What do you want with death certificates?"

"I'm telling you what they're asking for."

He took another loud swallow of either coffee or single malt. With Joe you never
knew for sure. "They haven't been able to
find anything up there in Montpelier since
they decided to digitize the archives. They'll
probably want birth and marriage, too, but
right now death is all they're asking for."

The only death certificate we had that I
knew of was my father's. This was going
to be a problem.

"What's the rush?" I asked. "I mean,
we've been doing fine without help for a
long time." Almost three hundred years,
but who was counting.

"Get the paperwork lined up," Joe repeated. "They want it, and between us,
you'd be smart to provide it. In fact, maybe
you should knit the new guy one of those
fancy sweaters of yours while you're at it."
He laughed. Joe Randazzo was a fan of
his own humor. "You want to make both of
our lives easy? Do what they want and
don't ask questions."

"Don't ask questions?" A bead of per-
spiration slid down into my hairline over
my right ear. "What does that mean?"

"It means what it means. This isn't my
idea. I've got enough on my plate right

now without opening another precinct up there in the mountains. Don't fight it because this goes all the way to the top."

"The top?" I asked but I was too late. Joe had already hung up.

"What's going on?" Janice demanded when I turned to her. "You look like you've seen a ghost."

I couldn't help it. I laughed until I cried.

❧

News travels fast in a small town. By lunchtime everyone in Sugar Maple knew about the police station and they were up in arms. I was flooded with so many phone calls and anxious visits that I finally had to shut down the shop and call an emergency meeting at the Town Hall for 8 P.M.

Gunnar came by the cottage around seven thirty to drive with me over to the abandoned church we used as our central meeting place. The girls loved Gunnar and they converged at his ankles like a furry Welcome Wagon. You could barely hear yourself think over the roar of purrs.

"Tell the truth," I demanded as I offered him one of my precious Chips Ahoy. "You rub catnip on your ankles before you come over here."

He laughed but it was clear his heart wasn't in it. I suddenly realized my friend looked tired and more than a little distracted.

"Are you okay?" I asked as I grabbed a cookie for myself. I had never seen him look so drained, not even the time Dane found himself stranded beyond the mist and needed to access Gunnar's powers in order to return to this dimension.

I tried very hard not to think about that time. For a brief while I had thought we were going to lose Gunnar, and the deep sorrow I had felt at the prospect scared me even now, years later.

In the world of the Fae, twins were a rare occurrence that happened every five hundred years or so, an event shrouded in mystery and speculation. Much of it sounded like one of those dark and twisted Grimm's fairy tales, complete with fierce battles and grisly death. The only way a Fae twin could obtain full powers was upon the death of the other. Out of all the fantastical stories I knew to be true, this was the one I refused to believe. The thought of my world without Gunnar was too awful to consider.

Gunnar bent down and scratched Pye behind her right ear.

"Gunnar." I forced him to meet my eyes. "What is it?"

He rose slowly and I knew he was delaying the inevitable. "I heard the banshee wail again."

I went cold from my bones outward. "When?"

"About an hour ago."

Where was my inner Pollyanna when I needed her? "It's probably for Suzanne. You've heard about letters arriving years after they were mailed. Maybe—"

"That's not how it works," he said with a wry smile. "You'd better look up banshees."

"I know how it works." I didn't tell him I had searched banshees on Google while waiting for the men from Montpelier to come and take Suzannne's body away. "I'm just saying there could be an exception."

He handed me my coat. "You've had a long day. Why don't I drive?"

The last time Gunnar had driven a car was when we went to the senior prom. "Why would you—" I stopped as the realization hit me. "Now you're really scaring me."

My parents had been killed on a crisp, clear December night just like this. I had been asleep in the back at the time, snug beneath a fuzzy mohair blanket and safely tethered by my seat belt. If only they had been so lucky.

I had no conscious memory of the accident, but I had never been able to shake my dislike for cars. My knuckles went all white before I even put the key in the ignition. Driving on ice made me break out in a cold sweat.

"Let's walk," I said.

I tried not to notice the look of relief on Gunnar's face.

Abbey Church, our combination Town Hall/all-purpose meeting place, was a brisk ten-minute walk on a sunny day, but a forty-minute struggle on an icy night. We were the only ones on the street but that didn't mean we were alone. Even I could sense the energies swirling all around us. Have you ever seen a pavement appear to shimmer during a heat wave? That was what this looked like, except in Sugar Maple it wasn't an optical illusion. The cold night air practically vibrated with possibilities.

Gunnar looked both ways before he hurried me across the quiet street, even though the only vehicles in sight were parked right in front of the church.

"You're late!" Lynette said with a pointed look at her watch. "I was afraid you might have—"

Janice jabbed her in the ribs. "She's here now. That's what matters."

"How big a crowd?" I asked as Gunnar swung open the enormous wooden door.

"It's like a class reunion," Lynette said happily.

Janice leaned closer. "Simone swirled in but Midge shooed her out again. She still hasn't forgiven her for seducing Donald behind the bandstand during the solstice celebration last summer." She inclined her head toward Gunnar, who was now talking to Lilith from the library. "His mother's here."

"Isadora?" I groaned. "Where is she?"

"She's flirting with Manny and Frank and the other old guys from the Home. I know she's older than dirt but really . . ."

Nobody knew exactly how old Isadora was; the guesses ranged anywhere from over one hundred human years to I-can't-count-that-high. She was hot-tempered, clearly partial to Dane, sexually voracious, and so beautiful that none of the rest seemed to matter. Her faerie charms were turbocharged, and when she aimed them in your direction, it was like being Tasered.

Not that I knew firsthand. Isadora usually gave me a wide berth. She had made it clear on more than one occasion that she would rather see her sons gelded than hooked up with the likes of me. And I'll be honest, the thought of Isadora as a mother-in-law made my Still Life with Cats look pretty darn good.

The old Abbey Church had been deconsecrated in 1842 when the Episcopalians decided to head west to become pioneers. Except for two stained glass windows featuring Saint George battling various dragons and the fact that the ceiling vaulted heavenward, you would never know our Town Hall had been a spiritual gathering place. Okay, maybe the organ in the loft and the church bells didn't exactly scream local government but waste not, want not. After all, this was New England.

Lynette was right. It did feel like a reunion of sorts. The entire Pendragon crew.

The Weavers from the Inn. The Harris boys and the Souderbush family were fading in and out near the coffee urn. Even the elusive Simone, who had broken up three marriages last year without even materializing, had taken on more corporeal form for the occasion. She was the wisteria-scented cloud of azure blue drifting lazily overhead.

Isadora was holding court beneath the American flag near one of the Saint George windows. Just as Lynette had said, she had woven a spell around poor Manny and Frank and the other vampires of a certain age. Isadora was smiling at them like they were Brad's and George's better-looking older brothers, but trust me, there is nothing sadder than a vampire with a removable upper plate and a subscription to *Modern Maturity.*

Isadora shot me a look when I took my place behind the desk and adjusted the microphone, and I flashed an insincere smile in return. It wasn't that Isadora made me nervous exactly, but there was something about her presence that made me understand how a butterfly felt just before a collector pinned her wings.

Lilith waved to me from across the room. She was our township librarian/historian/ secretary, a good-natured troll of Norwegian heritage with hair so red that fire alarms tripped spontaneously when she entered a room. Her husband, Archie, also a troll, ran the electronic repair ship at the foot of Toothaker Bridge.

I gave Lilith the signal and she joined me at the desk then led the crowd in the Pledge of Allegiance. The Pledge was followed by a spirited rendition of the Sugar Maple anthem.

There was no denying the fact that we were a patriotic bunch. I waited while various villagers dabbed at their red-rimmed eyes with wadded-up Kleenex and then I rapped the gavel down on the maple desktop. "The fourteenth emergency meeting of Sugar Maple Township is called to order."

And that was when all hell broke loose.

"It's unconstitutional!" Paul Griggs's wife, Verna, was the first to weigh in. "What gives the county the right to force a police station down our throats?"

"Our charter," I said, pointing toward the framed document on the stand near the flag. "Once we incorporated, we gave certain rights to the county. This is one of them."

That statement didn't win me any friends.

"Too many rules and regulations if you ask me," JoJo, a poltergeist of dubious reputation, said. JoJo had an unfortunate habit of spitting small stones when he talked, which explained why Mamie Ferguson was holding her purse over her head. "Since when do we just lie down and let them boss us around? Last I heard, this was a free country."

"You're going to take this lying down?" Manny maneuvered his Rascal to a stop in front of me. Someone really needed to tell him to ease up on the Whitestrips. His fangs were practically blinding me. "We've been incorporated over three hundred years and now those idiots decide we need police protection?"

"Someone died within our township limits," I reminded them. "They take death seriously in Montpelier."

"They take taxes seriously in Montpelier," Manny's sidekick Frank bellowed. "Death is just an inconvenience."

"Manny's right." It was Janice's turn to chime in. "This is about money. They're probably looking for a way to raise our taxes."

If you ever want to incite a riot north of New York City, mention raising taxes and see what happens.

"This isn't about taxes," I shouted into the microphone. "This is about the fact that we have less than forty-eight hours to figure out how we're going to live with a cop next door to Sticks & Strings."

"There's a full moon coming up on Saturday night," Johnny Griggs reminded us. "We can pay him a visit he won't soon forget."

"Good thinking," Midge Stallworth volunteered. "There are ways to make a stubborn man see reason." And most of them involved a puncture wound and a blood draw.

Lilith was in favor of some involuntary herb therapy while Verna thought a well-considered hex involving bladder control and uncontrollable truth-telling might just be what the doctor ordered.

"I've been in touch with the Mothers,"

Janice said, "and this is only the beginning of our bad luck. We are in trouble, people."

Thanks a lot, Janice.

Isadora suddenly appeared in front of me in a dazzling display of faerie glamour. A shower of royal purple glitter rained down on us, thick as mountain snow. "It's your fault," she said, pointing a long, graceful finger at me. "They might be too polite to say it but I'm not. You're the one bringing the troubles to our town."

"No offense, Chloe, but she might have something there." Colm Weaver and his family materialized atop the lighted globe on the far end of the desk. "It's been thirty years since a Hobbs woman bore a female child. The primal energy is starting to fade."

"Just because someone fell through the ice after too many margaritas doesn't mean the protective spell is wearing off." I sounded a wee bit defensive but can you blame me? The thought that I was somehow responsible for Suzanne's death hit me hard. "It was just an accident."

"Are you really that selfish?" Isadora leaned closer. "Have you given no thought to what you owe this town?"

Only every waking minute of my life, but I refused to give Gunnar's mother the satisfaction.

"Give me the Book of Spells," she demanded. "Let me do for this town what you can't seem to manage."

Everyone knew what Isadora wanted to do: drag the entire town into the Fae realm beyond the mist, where her power would be supreme. I was gratified to hear an eruption of hisses and catcalls from the back.

"If you care so much for Sugar Maple, why don't you devise a spell of your own to keep us safe." Bless Lynette for having the guts to put it out there.

Isadora's glance was withering.

"We don't have time to worry about Aerynn's spell," I told the assembled villagers with a pointed glance toward Isadora. "We're going to have a cop strolling down Main Street, grabbing a cappuccino at Fully Caffeinated, picking up his mail at the post office. How long will it take before he figures out this isn't your average Small Town, USA?"

Lilith's Archie emitted a cross between a snort and a guffaw. "You watch too much TV."

No argument there. I singlehandedly kept him in business with emergency calls every time my satellite dish went out.

"Chloe's right." All eyes turned toward Lilith. She didn't speak very often, but when she did, we always listened. "I did a little research this morning and found out Suzanne Marsden was seeing a married politician in Massachusetts."

For the first time all evening the room fell silent.

Renate slid off the globe and landed on the floor with a thud as she expanded to human size. "Please don't tell me she was seeing Teddy Kennedy."

"His name is Dan Sieverts," Lilith went on. "According to my sources, he plans to announce his run for the governor's office in March and his people want to make sure there's nothing about Ms. Marsden's death that can derail his campaign."

"Seems to me a dead mistress would be a whole lot less trouble than a live one," Cyrus Pendragon observed.

A swirl of blue smoke floated down. "Never underestimate the dead, darling," Simone whispered as she entwined herself around him. I hadn't seen anything like that since my free preview of *Naughty After Dark.*

"Get off my husband, you slut!" Lynette launched herself across the room but Simone was too fast for her. By the time Lynette reached Cyrus, only Simone's mocking laughter remained.

"Ow!" Cyrus yelped as Lynette's beringed fist made contact with his upper arm. "She's gone, Lynnie!"

"I know." Lynette whacked him again. "Next time don't enjoy it so much."

I'm not prone to headaches but a wicked bad one was building behind my right eye. Isadora was watching me with a combination of pity and amusement that set my teeth on edge. She didn't like me, and the feeling was mutual, but her criticisms had found their mark just the same.

"Come on, people," I said, rapping the gavel again just for the heck of it. "Let's get back to our rent-a-cop problem."

Herding my cats was easier than trying to bring everyone back to the matter at hand after Simone's display.

According to Lilith's political contacts,

once the rent-a-cop was sure that Suzanne's death was nothing more than a tragic accident, he would be replaced after a decent period of time by someone local who would be voted in by Sugar Maple residents at a special election.

"Six months," Lilith said. "That's the time frame they're looking at in Montpelier."

Janice shook her head. "The spell will be broken by then. Three months is all we've got and even that's dicey."

Sharp-edged purple glitter rained down on me.

"Stop it," I snapped at Isadora. "Even if I got pregnant tomorrow, I wouldn't give birth in time to make a difference."

"The Book is wasted on you as it was wasted on your mother," Isadora said, favoring me with the kind of withering glance that destroyed lesser mortals. "You'll never be more than you are today."

"Take that back," Lynette demanded.

Isadora was undeterred. Her attention was riveted to me.

"You owe us." Fae anger was spoken about in whispers and it was easy to see why. The air around Isadora shimmered crimson and purple. It crackled with electricity seeking ground. A dark mist loomed behind her then disappeared as quickly as it had come. I drew back instinctively and she smiled. "We didn't have to take you in."

"You didn't take me in," I reminded her. "Sorcha did."

"Only because we allowed it. The last thing this town needed was Guinevere's half-breed daughter."

"Isadora!" Lilith sounded distressed. "Enough!"

"It's not enough. It's not nearly enough. Am I the only one who remembers that her own mother didn't love her enough to stay here?" Her words seemed to circle my head, pounding to get inside my brain. "Am I the only one who remembers what it cost Sorcha to stay?"

I saw myself as a terrified six-year-old. I felt Sorcha's love all around me like an embrace. The thought that I might have caused her pain was almost unbearable and I looked away.

"Chloe was a child," Janice said in my defense. "She didn't ask Sorcha to stay in this realm. Sorcha stayed to protect her until she came into her powers."

Isadora dismissed her with a glance. "Which hasn't happened."

"She's right," someone called out. "What if Chloe never gets her powers? What happens to us then?"

"Then we're in trouble, that's what." Henry from Fully Caffeinated stood up on his chair and waved an angry fist. "Maybe Isadora has had the right idea all along. I say it's time to think about moving the whole shebang beyond the mist."

"Sorry, Chloe, but Henry's right." Colm Weaver shot me another apologetic look. "Truth is you haven't been getting the job done. I grew up beyond the mist. If you can't keep us safe, I don't see where we have a choice but to listen to Isadora."

"You're nuts," Archie shouted. "They're a bunch of fascists in there. I'd rather take my chances and stay right where we are."

"But we can't stay here if we're not safe." Hiram was one of the itinerant house sprites who wintered in Sugar Maple. "I'd trade freedom for safety any day."

"You're a horse's ass," Archie, the diplomat, shot back.

Lilith, always the peacemaker, stepped

between them and quelled the dustup with a stern look.

But the damage had been done. I looked out at the crowd of familiar faces and saw that Colm and Hiram weren't the only villagers who were beginning to believe Isadora might have the right idea.

Isadora saw it too. The expression of triumph on her face cut me to the quick.

"Give her time," Janice said, staring down Isadora. "I know Chloe won't let us down."

"We've given her thirty years," Peggy Whitman called from the back of the room. "How much time does she need?"

"It's not Chloe's fault," Isadora said in a mock-sympathetic tone of voice. "She can't help that she'll never be more than she is at this moment: a nonmagick human who can do nothing to save us from ruin."

Recreational crying wasn't my thing, but my eyes were starting to well up with tears I hoped no one noticed.

Gunnar, however, noticed everything, and he sounded a warning.

"Let it go, Mother. There's no crime in being human."

Nervous laughter erupted like tiny brush-fires and was quickly extinguished.

"But being selfish is." She swung around to face me, and it took every ounce of courage I had to meet her eyes. "Be warned: the clock is ticking. Until you claim your powers, the Book of Spells is mine for the taking."

I opened my mouth to say something but Gunnar stepped in front of me.

I had known Gunnar all my life but I had never seen him like this. He seemed bigger, taller, more powerful. More dangerous. Nothing like the gentle friend I loved. His words were mild, his manner controlled, but anger flew from his body like thunderbolts. For a second I almost believed I could see them heading straight for his mother. Neither one of them uttered a word, but the room started to shake with the force of their silent battle, and just when I thought the very air between them was going to split in two, Isadora vanished in an explosion of red and purple glitter that sent Gunnar crashing into the back wall of the church.

The sound as he hit the wall sent chills up my spine, but that was nothing to the sense of dread when I realized he wasn't moving.

"I hope he's not dead," Archie said. "The way things have been going around here . . ."

"He's not dead," I snapped as I ran to him, our talk of banshees screaming inside my head. "He can't be."

I bent down over him and placed two fingers against his wrist. Nothing. My heart thudded hard inside my chest. The first time Gunnar heard the banshee wail, my mother died. The second time Suzanne Marsden drowned in Snow Lake. The third time—

I repositioned my fingers and held my breath. *Please, please* . . . A tiny pulsing, faint and thready, but there! My knees went weak with relief when his eyes opened and he groaned loudly.

"My mother?"

"Your mother," I confirmed.

Janice handed me a bottle of water. I uncapped it and held it to his mouth.

"She put on quite a display," I said as he gulped down some of the liquid. "I think you got caught up in the afterburn."

"Collateral damage." He rubbed the

back of his head and winced. "Maybe we should hand out crash helmets when she's around." His sense of humor was back. That was a good sign.

"And Kevlar vests," I said, helping him to his feet. "She's formidable."

"She's a bitch," Renate said, hovering in the air between us. "I know she's your mother, honey, but I went to school with her. She was a bitch then and she's a bitch now."

Nobody argued the point. Isadora was all of those things and one other: she was right. Sugar Maple had opened its collective arms to me years ago, and magick or no magick, it was time for me to repay the debt before it was too late.

5

LUKE

It was like being trapped inside a snow globe inside a Hallmark ad inside a Disney movie.

The Chamber of Commerce information Fran printed off the web had mentioned the "old-fashioned charm" and "wonderful New England ambience" of Sugar Maple, but those descriptions didn't even come close to the town spread out before me. The place belonged on a Hollywood soundstage from the 1940s. Maybe the 1840s.

Gas lamps lined the main street. Candles burned in front windows. Wreaths of holly and pine decorated front doors. Even the snow drifts looked like someone had airbrushed them until they were ready for prime time. I could almost hear Bing Crosby singing "White Christmas" in the distance.

The only thing missing was a flyover from Santa and his reindeer.

Perfect?

Definitely.

Weird?

Just weird enough to bump my cop's curiosity up another notch. The original plan was to do a quick drive-by on my way to the motel north of town where I'd be staying, but maybe a closer look wasn't a bad idea.

The bridge let me off at the corner of Osborne and Bishop. I made a right on Osborne and rolled past a bank, an apothecary, and a candle store before I rounded the curve that led me to the lake.

Snow Lake was more like Snow Pond, a perfect oval that I would have guessed was man-made if I hadn't skimmed a few paragraphs about Sugar Maple's geographical features over a Big Mac earlier in the day.

I was a New England kid. I'd grown up playing hockey on the lake behind our school. You didn't have a Zamboni maintaining the ice. You learned to skate over tree trunks, broken branches, divots and pits and soft spots. And you did it on hockey skates, not three-inch Manolo Whoevers.

What the hell had Suzanne been thinking? The guy who found her body said she had been wearing some kind of scarf, a cocktail dress, and her skates. She must have been drinking. Nothing else made any sense. I walked the perimeter, trying to see it with Suzanne's eyes, but my attention was drawn to the cracked portion left of center from where I was standing.

That was where she had gone in. I could hear the cracking sound the ice made when she broke the surface. Her yelp of surprise as she dropped into the shockingly cold water. I knew the gut-twisting despair she must have felt when she realized it was too late.

A small wooden bench was positioned near the skate rental shack. The bench was piled high with snow except for two long indentations. On closer inspection they looked like prints from a pair of women's high-heeled shoes.

Suzanne's.

Reading about Suzanne's death had been tough enough, but seeing this last reminder of her vibrant, complicated self punched it home. I felt like I had been Tasered. I stood there for a few seconds, looking down at the snow prints, letting my mind spin back through the years.

Trips down memory lane aren't all they're cracked up to be.

I turned away from the bench and scanned the terrain. Mostly I saw trees. Sugar maples with a few pine, spruce, and fir thrown in to keep it interesting. Nothing out of the ordinary.

I scanned the rest of the area as I started back to the truck. Not that I expected to find anything, but without a police presence in town, it was possible major pieces of evidence might have been left behind. Suzanne's death was probably accidental but there was a five percent chance it wasn't. And that five percent was where I needed to put my energy.

There was no pattern to any of the vegetation, at least not as far as I could see.

Except for the rental shack and the bench, humans had walked softly on the land, which was why the tree caught my eye. A scruffy maple flanked by a pair of stubby Douglas firs, it had suffered its share of lightning strikes and all-you-can-eat deer buffets. The bark had been stripped in spots, gnawed in others. The surprising thing was that the tired old tree was still standing.

Scratch that. The really surprising thing was the circle gouged into the bark on the north side. I'm no naturalist but even I knew that deer weren't into decorative munching.

In a way I was glad to see a sign of teenage rebellion in Sugar Maple. Maybe it was cop humor, but there was nothing like a little defacement of public property to humanize a town, and from what I'd read, this town needed it.

It took two tries to get the engine to turn over, but it finally caught and I headed back toward Osborne Avenue and went east. The stores were shuttered. The streets were empty. Nobody out walking the dog. Nobody on a quick run to the convenience store for milk and bread. I had a strange sense of déjà vu as I drove around but chalked it up to the fact that there was a built-in sameness to all northern New England villages. It was part of what made people love them the way they did.

Certain things were nonnegotiable and Sugar Maple had them all. The village green. The skating pond. The old whitewashed church with brightly painted red doors and stained glass windows with lights blazing from inside.

At ten o'clock on a Wednesday night in December?

I cut my lights and rolled down my window as I moved closer. A blue and white school bus with the words SUGAR MAPLE ASSISTED LIVING painted across the side was parked in the no-parking zone along with a beat-up VW van. Tomorrow that might be a problem but tonight I was still a civilian. I let it slide.

Loud voices spilled out into the street. It didn't sound like a religious service to me unless liturgical language had changed a hell of a lot since my days at Saint Aloysius. And it definitely wasn't a party.

I made a left and parked along the dark side of the narrow wooden structure. Snow drifts lined the cleared sidewalk and the path that led around to the front of the building. I slipped into the shadows and made my way toward the small window near the rear door.

I melted a small circle of ice beneath my thumb then peered inside. I couldn't see much, but my line of sight landed on a knot of people who stood where an altar would have been. They were all vying for the attention of a tall, skinny blonde, one of those disheveled types who always seemed on the verge of a meltdown. A taller, blonder man stood next to her, nodding in agreement at everything she said.

I melted a larger circle and zeroed in on the skinny blonde. I know a fair bit about body language, and it was easy to see she was in charge and the tall guy with the six-pack was probably riding shotgun. A Julia Roberts type with long red hair was talking animatedly while a Catherine Zeta-Jones curvy brunette texted someone on a Blackberry. Even the old guy in the wheelchair looked like an aging Cary Grant. The skinny blonde was the plainest one in the group and she would rate a second look just about anywhere.

What the hell was in Sugar Maple's water anyway?

The meeting, or whatever it was, finally came to an end. The blonde started bulking up beneath layers of sweaters and scarves while the tall guy waited patiently. Poor bastard. It was clear he was the beta in the mix. I felt sorry for them if they were a couple, because she'd be wearing his balls as earrings before they hit their first anniversary.

Not that I was interested in her—skinny blondes didn't do it for me—but he seemed too comfortable in her shadow, like a politician's spouse during campaign season. People drifted in and out of my line of vision as they offered their good-byes to the blonde, a constant stream of villagers who seemed to think she had all the answers.

I heard the front door of the church swing open some thirty feet away and footsteps moving closer.

Shit.

I did what any other cop in my position would do: I ducked behind one of the huge snow-covered bushes and tried to become invisible.

The footsteps stopped abruptly. I heard

muffled conversation. Then the footsteps retreated back across the ice-encrusted snow. A chorus of voices called out "Good night," and a bus engine turned over with a clunk. The VW van I'd noticed added its distinctive high-pitched whine.

The night fell silent in a way it never did in Boston, and I was counting off a full two minutes of it before breaking cover when I got that old familiar feeling, the one that made the hackles on the back of my neck rise.

I was being watched.

I turned toward the church. The windows were dark. No telltale condensation on the glass. No movement. I scanned right, then left. Nothing. But the prickling sensation along the back of my neck was still there and it was never wrong.

And then I saw it. A quick flicker of darkness in my peripheral vision. The kind of thing only a cop would notice. I turned quickly but there was nothing there. No footprints. No broken branches. Just the familiar knot in my gut that signaled trouble.

The place was lousy with wildlife. When had I become a city dweller who could be thrown by country noises? People were trouble after dark. Owls weren't. Raccoons foraged for food at night but they usually gave humans a wide berth. An entire segment of the animal world came alive when the sun went down, and most of them managed without acknowledging the presence of man.

Still the feeling that I was being watched persisted. I scouted around some more then finally chalked the whole thing up to the fact that I hadn't slept in two nights. It was time I got my ass to Motel 6 and crashed for a few. Stifling a yawn, I climbed behind the wheel of my truck and headed back toward the bridge that led to the highway.

It would all make sense tomorrow in the daylight.

It always did.

6

CHLOE

Janice drove Gunnar and me home after the meeting. We told Gunnar it was because Janice needed to borrow a set of US1 double point needles to finish a sock she'd been knitting, but the truth was we didn't think Gunnar was steady enough on his feet to be left alone.

We would have taken him back to his own place but neither one of us had a clue where his place was. Gunnar was my best friend and I didn't know exactly where he lived or how he lived. So much of his life was shrouded in the whims and mysteries of the Fae that there were times when I wondered how well I really knew him.

"I know what you're doing," he said after Janice drove off with her knitting needles. "I'm fine. I just had the wind knocked out of me."

I put the tea kettle on the stove to boil. "You were blown across the room into a wall," I reminded him. "And no offense, friend, but you haven't been looking so good lately."

He didn't meet my eyes and the light dawned.

"Dane?" I asked.

He nodded. "He must be in some kind of trouble. My powers have been leeching away faster than I can replace them. It's been a bad couple days."

"Maybe that's why your mother was in such a contentious mood."

"Contentious?" He lifted a brow.

"Okay," I said. "Bitchy. You have to admit she was in rare form tonight." I set out two big mugs and an assortment of tea bags. "I really wish you could find out why she hates me so much."

He pushed back his chair and stood up. "I'm going to skip the tea and head out. It's late."

"You look hungry. Why don't I make you some scrambled eggs?"

"Chloe, I—"

I felt Dane before I saw him. A sharp, almost metallic presence in the room that set my teeth on edge, like biting down on a piece of aluminum foil. The cats emitted high-pitched meows of surprise then fled from the room as Dane appeared in a shower of steel blue glitter that smelled like the air just before an electric storm.

He said something to Gunnar that I didn't understand, in a language I had never heard before, and then I screamed as a bolt of lightning shot from his right forefinger and pierced Gunnar's right eye. Gunnar whirled, both arms extended, and shimmering silver ropes encircled Dane's ankles and pulled him off his feet.

Dane's roar of rage as he crashed to the ground sent me reeling backward against the kitchen counter. The air felt jagged. The sharp edges of their anger stabbed at my exposed skin. A deep, almost primal, terror started building inside me as the lightning bolt vanished and Gunnar's eye healed itself while I watched.

Everything I had ever believed about belonging here, about being the same as everyone else, disappeared as I found myself scrambling atop the counter like a terrified field mouse. The power in the room almost sucked the oxygen from my lungs. I could feel it swinging wildly like the tides from Gunnar to Dane and back again. I wanted to help but had never felt more clueless, more helpless, in my life.

Dane placed his hands on the silver ropes around his ankles, and tongues of flame leaped to life. The bonds vanished in a shower of silver ash and the smell of burning leaves.

My small kitchen wasn't big enough to contain their rage as they crashed together in an explosion of broken dishes, spilled water, and body blows. A hideous creaking noise sounded overhead and I looked up in time to see the roof of my cottage tear away from the structure and rise slowly into the icy night air as if lifted by invisible hands. Moonlight flooded the room as Gunnar and Dane, locked in what seemed to me to be mortal combat, spun upward past the roofline, glowing like hot embers.

How was I going to explain this to State Farm?

The thought was so ridiculous I started to laugh out loud. The kind of nervous braying laughter that had nothing to do with humor and everything to do with the fact that the only thing that kept me from grabbing the cats and my mother's stash of roving and running away was that I had nowhere else to go.

Plates and cups and glassware swirled around my kitchen in a Martha Stewart tornado. My best friend and his brother were trying to kill each other in the airspace over my house while my roof floated down Carrier Court like a David Copperfield magic trick gone bad. You could keep sibling rivalry. For the first time in my life I was glad to be an only child.

I thought I had pretty much seen it all. In Sugar Maple, villagers appeared and disappeared at will. I didn't think twice when a teenage faerie appeared on the rim of my wineglass or I had to design a special ski cap for a troll. Grown men transformed into wolves, bears, and other forest creatures every full moon. Retired vampires polished their dentures then rolled out after dark in motorized wheelchairs.

But this anger-fueled violence was new to me. Sure there had been family squabbles and disagreements, but until tonight I had never witnessed anything like the mayhem swirling over my head.

Under normal circumstances, Gunnar would have been able to deflect his brother's blows and retain dominance. But Dane had been steadily draining his resources, and his confrontation with Isadora earlier in the evening had compromised him further. A member of the Fae with full powers was impervious to anything a mortal could do to harm him. Neither Gunnar nor Dane had full powers. The fact that the balance between them shifted almost daily was proof of that. It was possible that somebody could be hurt, even killed, and the fact that Gunnar had heard the banshee wail again only heightened the urgency.

Even if I dragged a ladder in from the garage, I wouldn't be able to get close enough to either one of them to make contact. And to be honest, I wasn't sure how close I wanted to get to the battle. I could dial 911 but it would still take Leonard and his crew of sprites and hobgoblins ten minutes or more to assemble themselves on the fire truck and—

My gaze landed on the fire extinguisher hanging from its holder near my back door. What was it Paul Griggs had said when I plopped down almost fifty bucks for it? "This bad boy has a longer reach than the tax man."

Well, now was as good a time as any to see if he was right. I slid carefully off the counter, where I'd been cowering like some horror movie chick, and held my breath as I skirted the domestic whirlpool wreaking havoc with my kitchen. Lucy poked her nose into the kitchen, saw the kitchen tornado, then turned and ran back to safety.

Smart cat.

Stupid woman.

I probably should have taken my cue from Lucy and fled the scene. Instead, I slowly eased my way around the perimeter of the room, careful to keep from offering up any part of my person to the example of Mother Nature Gone Wild that was currently turning my maple kitchen table into toothpicks.

I had never liked being the skinny girl with the small boobs, but tonight it seemed like a blessing from the gods. Finally I made it to the other side of the room. I grabbed the fire extinguisher from the wall, aimed, and pulled the trigger.

At least I tried. The second my finger touched the metal, I screamed in pain and it crashed to the floor at my feet.

"You fool!" Isadora appeared before me in a violent explosion of color and sound. She retrieved the fire extinguisher and heaved it into the whirlpool and I watched with a combination of horror and wonder as centrifugal force held it captive. "Are you trying to destroy us?"

Destroy us? Wasn't I the one with the removable roof? If anything was being destroyed, it was my home.

Before I could say anything, she flicked her narrow wrist in the direction of her warring sons and they froze in place, locked in deadly combat. Suspended in midair, they looked like Greek statues from the mind of a mad genius.

Suddenly I was the center of her attention, not a place anyone with a passing grasp on sanity would ever want to be. As she aimed the full power of her green-eyed gaze in my direction, I finally understood the depth of her hatred. If she ever dragged Sugar Maple beyond the mist, I would be left behind.

"Get rid of the stranger before you bring destruction to this town." Her voice was a sharp blade against my skin. "I meant what I said, Chloe. Your mother broke the chain of protection and it's up to you to put it together again. If you can't save Sugar Maple, I will and soon."

She didn't wait around for my response. As I watched, Gunnar was enveloped in a pocket of black mist that slipped through a tear in the sky and vanished from sight. A long plume of purple mist swooped around Dane then unfurled itself around Isadora's bare feet. The next moment they vanished through a sky tear the same as Gunnar had.

I looked at the kitchen tornado and the starry night sky where my roof used to be. My place had been trashed. My cats would need therapy. My best friend got the crap beat out of him by his brother, and I had made an enemy of a faerie woman whose powers made Wonder Woman look like a wimp. And as if that wasn't enough, the entire future of Sugar Maple rested in my hands.

That was the bad news.

The good news?

Things couldn't possibly get any worse.

7

LUKE

I rolled into Sugar Maple a little before eight the next morning and parked my Jeep in the small municipal lot across from the church. A Santa Claus clone in a bright red sweater gave me a time-stamped ticket and a coupon for a free cup of coffee (regular only) at Fully Caffeinated. You had to wonder if central casting had a hand in populating the burg. So far it had been a parade of supermodels, movie stars, and now Saint Nick.

I was starting to feel like a gargoyle.

I tucked the ticket into my pocket. "Where do I find Town Hall?"

He considered me with twinkling blue eyes. "You looking for a hunting license?"

"Nope."

"Fishing license?"

"Not in this weather."

His blue eyes twinkled brighter. "Marriage?"

"Actually I'm trying to find your mayor." Googling hadn't turned up the names of any municipal officials, and Fran hadn't been able to turn up anything through her sources either.

"Then you're looking for Chloe Hobbs." He pointed over my left shoulder. "You'll find her in the knitting shop across the street from the library."

I pictured a roly-poly gray-haired woman in sensible shoes, the kind who would knit baby booties for a stranger's new grandkid. A rosy-cheeked Aunt Bee type who would spill everything she knew about Suzanne's death in the first three minutes of conversation, then hand over names and addresses of everyone in town who might be able to help me.

That déjà vu feeling I'd experienced last

night reasserted itself as I headed down the main drag, but I chalked that up to having watched too much TV as a kid. Sugar Maple was Mayberry R.F.D., Bedford Falls, and a New England version of Innisfree all rolled up in one.

Even the town meeting or whatever it was that I'd observed last night in the old church had had the feel of something from another era. I had almost expected Jimmy Stewart to amble into the room and make an impassioned speech that swept the skinny blonde off her feet and into his arms.

Frank Capra would have loved this place.

A group of down jacket–clad women were decorating the village green for the season, stringing lights, hanging huge glass balls from the branches of a giant fir tree next to the band shell. It was easy to imagine the green ablaze with flowers in the spring or welcoming a brass band for a Fourth of July celebration. It was classic Americana seen through postmodernist eyes. I wasn't sure if the ten-foot-high replica of a lighthouse was a touch of kitsch or symbolic of some aspect of Sugar Maple's history. Especially since the ocean was at least one hundred miles away.

The smell of freshly brewed coffee drifted from Fully Caffeinated at the corner of Nurse and Bishop. Bringing Mayor Hobbs a cup of something warm and sweet would go a long way toward ingratiating me with her. And assuming she still had her own teeth, a toasted bagel wouldn't hurt.

Five minutes later I hit the street again with two cups of coffee light and three toasted sesame. I passed a young mother wheeling an infant in a black lacquer carriage. Her smile was bright, her hair was shiny, her face pretty and fresh-scrubbed in an all-American kind of way. The Gerber baby gurgled at me. I smiled back at them both. Back home in Boston I would have been brought up on charges but here it felt natural.

There wasn't much street traffic. Two cars, both late models, drove by without incident. A man in a navy blue ski jacket jogged past with a pleasant nod of his head. A little girl with a giant golden retriever on the end of a Christmas green leash flashed me a guileless smile.

I pushed all thoughts of Stepford from my mind.

Sticks & Strings was on the east side of Carrier, wedged between a pet shop with an OUT OF BUSINESS sign posted on the door and a pizzeria. Lacy scarves and sweaters shared window space with baskets of brightly colored yarn that probably had a fancy name and cost a week's pay. It was the kind of place I could walk by ten times a day and never notice until someone committed a felony.

I'd introduce myself to the mayor, schmooze her over coffee and bagels, then get the key to the makeshift police station I'd be calling home for the next few months. And the whole time I would be painlessly extracting information that would start me on the road toward piecing together the last few hours of Suzanne's life. Hell, I'd have Mayor Hobbs's social security number and e-mail password before she finished her coffee.

After all, I was a big-city cop and she was a small-town mayor with a knitting jones. How tough could it be?

The shop was dark but the WELCOME sign was in place. I opened the door and stepped into what had to be moth heaven. Wool was everywhere. Baskets of yarn hung from the ceiling. Floor-to-ceiling cubbyholes of the stuff lined the walls. More baskets over-flowed onto the floor and on chairs and ta-bletops. An old-fashioned spinning wheel was set up by the display window.

The only thing missing was Chloe Hobbs.

I stepped deeper into the store, past a polished maple worktable piled high with pointed sticks and scissors and things that would never make it past airport security. The place smelled of lavender and licorice and a hint of mint. Lots of magazines with sweaters on the cover were stacked in neat piles on one side while an equal number of unfinished knitting projects were stacked on the other. I noted a ball of something blue and fluffy and picked it up. I squeezed it and the price tag jumped out and I quickly put it back down again. For *one* ball of yarn? This was worse than crack. Get ad-dicted to this stuff and you would be living in your minivan.

"Hello," I called out.

Nothing.

She had to be here somewhere. I lis-tened for the sound of water running or a radio tuned to a local station, but the room was still except for an odd rumbling noise followed by a low whistle. I stopped and listened harder.

There it was again. Same pattern, same rhythm.

I peered around the tall free-standing display case adjacent to the worktable and saw her.

The tall, skinny blonde from last night was curled up on a tiny love seat tucked into an alcove near the crackling fireplace. She wore a black sweater that looked like it had been put on backward and faded jeans that had seen one too many spin cycles. Her long legs were tucked under her. Her hair, gathered into a messy pony-tail, cascaded over her right shoulder. A bright red blanket lay pooled on the floor. Next to the blanket the fattest, blackest cat I had ever seen slept in a basket of what looked like pale gray fluff.

Did I tell you she was snoring?

Not the cat. The woman.

It wasn't a wake-the-dead kind of snore but a pretty damn good one, all things considered. You wouldn't think such a small nose could create such a loud noise.

Actually the cat was snoring too, but so far the blonde was winning hands down.

I took another look at her. Her nails were bitten to the quick. She sported pale violet circles under her eyes. Small breasts. Long, elegant feet. Her toenails were painted fire engine red.

Cops notice things. It's an occupational hazard. Noticing details about a woman's appearance was part of a detective's job description. It didn't mean anything.

Not even if the cop in question found himself standing there with a stupid grin on his face.

As far as I could tell, I had three options.

I could use the opportunity to turn over a few balls of yarn there in her shop and see what I could uncover before she woke up.

I could leave and come back later.

Or I could pull up a chair and wait to see what happened next.

CHLOE

Remember when I said things couldn't get any worse?

I was wrong.

Maybe it was the heat kicked out by the old furnace or the fact that I had been up all night while twelve of Sugar Maple's most powerful villagers combined their magick to reassemble my cottage. I'm not sure what it was, but I guess I fell asleep not long after opening Sticks & Strings for the day.

One second I was deep into a dream about a gorgeous guy who could knit, purl, and cable without a needle and the next second I was looking into his eyes. Dark green eyes, bottle green to be exact, with flashes of gold like Fourth of July sparklers. I mean, what were the odds?

"Not funny, Lynette," I mumbled, squeezing my eyes shut again. "Shift back *now.*" I really hated it when she started that mind-reading stuff and messed with my head.

I waited a handful of seconds then opened my eyes again.

The man of my dreams (literally) was sitting in the overstuffed chair catty-corner to the sofa. A big broad-shouldered stranger with one of those faces that gave away nothing at all. Dark, slightly shaggy hair. Dark green eyes. A thin white scar ran across his left cheekbone. A Fully Caffeinated travel tote sat on the tabletop next to him, and a copy of *Vogue Knitting* lay opened to a sock pattern next to it.

This time my friend had gone too far.

"I'm not kidding, Lyn," I said, glaring at my shapeshifting friend. "Shift back now or else."

"Shift what?" he asked. "Are you talking in your sleep or should I be scared?"

I was the one who should be scared. That wasn't Lynette playing a practical joke on me. Unless I missed my guess, it was our brand-new rent-a-cop and I might have blown the town's cover in the first five seconds.

"Who *are* you?" I demanded and probably not in the friendliest tone of voice. For the record, I don't wake up each morning brimming over with the joy of life. The joy of life pretty much arrives around the same time as my third cup of coffee and the fourth round on my latest sock-in-progress. "What are you doing in my shop?"

"Your door was unlocked. The open sign was in place. You're lucky I didn't clean you out."

"You're lucky you didn't try. I have an excellent security system."

"Up until today you didn't even have a police presence."

"We didn't need one. We take care of our own."

He looked down at Penny and grinned. "Yeah, she could cause some serious damage."

"You should have knocked or something." The thought that he had been watching me sleep made me shiver.

"I knocked," he said, "and I said hello. You probably couldn't hear me over the snoring."

I gave Penelope a protective scratch behind the right ear. "Penny's snoring isn't that bad."

"I wasn't talking about the cat."

I felt myself launching into one of those full-body blushes that end up embarrassing me more than whatever faux pas triggered it in the first place.

"You're the cop, aren't you?" Playing dumb had never worked for me. Neither had flirting, for that matter. I had been cursed with a blunt, straightforward personality that, coupled with my half-human bloodline, probably ensured permanent spinsterhood.

"Luke MacKenzie," he said, extending a huge paw of a hand. "I'm looking for Chloe Hobbs."

What was wrong with me? I couldn't seem to find my voice. "Y-you've found her." I sounded like an addled frog.

What was it about cops anyway? Don't they ever blink? His hand was hanging out there like a catcher's mitt, but something I didn't understand was holding me back from making the connection.

"They told me Sugar Maple wasn't too happy about my appointment but even boxers shake before they come out fighting." He kept his tone light but I could see curiosity behind his green-eyed gaze and something else. Something even more unsettling.

What choice did I have? I had come close to exposing our town's secret to him in the first thirty seconds. I couldn't risk making him any more curious than he already was.

My hand touched his, and we both jumped back as silver-white sparks crackled through the space between us.

"What the hell—?" He looked at me as if I had pulled a gun on him.

"Static electricity," I said, even though I had never seen anything like that before in my life. "It's the wool."

"Impressive."

I just smiled. For all he knew, we were shooting sparks and tongues of flame around here every hour of the day.

He reached down and pulled an extra-large cup of coffee from the Fully Caffeinated bag. "I got this for you."

I refrained from telling him we always keep a pot of coffee brewing at Sticks & Strings. "Thanks."

"Light with sugar."

"Perfect," I said, even though I drank mine black. "Do all big-city cops deliver takeout?"

"Only the ones who are trying to get a smile out of the mayor."

I glanced at the grandmother clock against the far wall. "Come back in three hours," I said. "My smile doesn't kick in until noon."

"So you're not a morning person."

"So you're not just a cop, you're a detective too."

"You read my résumé."

"Lucky guess."

Lucky? Who was I kidding. If there was anything worse than having a cop next door to Sticks & Strings, it was having a cop who was a detective next door.

A horrible thought popped into my head.

"What time did you get here?" I asked.

He shrugged. "I don't know . . . seven thirty, eight o'clock. Something like that."

He couldn't possibly have seen the team of sprites carrying my roof back from Procter Hill, where they had found Forbes the Mountain Giant using it as a snowboard. That was the kind of thing most humans would mention.

I tried to mask my relief with a business-like attitude. "We weren't expecting you until tomorrow."

Again I had the sense that he saw more than he let on. I didn't particularly like the feeling.

"Is that a problem?" he asked.

"The place isn't ready yet."

"Define 'not ready.'"

"Well, I haven't been in there lately but I know we need to get the power turned on, a phone line activated . . ." I let my voice trail away. The truth was I didn't have a clue what was going on in the empty pet shop next door and I hadn't been overly worried about it. Janice had arranged for the same household elves and construction sprites who had repaired my house last night to whip the old pet shop into shape tonight. In fact, it would have been done by now if Dane and Gunnar hadn't staged a throw-down in my kitchen.

"How long has it been empty?" he asked.

"Maybe three months."

"I thought this was a popular town," he said. "I'm surprised another store didn't move right in."

"Actually it wasn't on the market. I was planning to buy it."

He glanced around my crowded storefront. "Business is that good?"

"Better."

He looked like he was about to say something but thought better of it.

It took every ounce of self-control I had to keep from pushing the issue. In this case, less was definitely more, in every sense of the phrase.

"Why don't you give me the key for next door and I'll get out of your hair."

I rummaged through my desk, the basket of unfiled correspondence next to my desk, the box of clippings and magazines under my desk, and came up empty.

"I know I have it somewhere," I said as I started dumping baskets of yarn across my already overburdened desk. Paul had given me a copy so I could let the guy from the phone company in to do his thing.

"What's that on the corkboard?"

I glanced up at the knitting patterns, notes, photographs, and charts pinned to the corkboard over my desk. "I don't see anything."

He moved closer. He smelled like the ocean. Or at least the way I remembered the ocean. Don't get the wrong idea. I don't go around sniffing strangers, especially strange men, but he was standing very close and sometimes breathing has fringe benefits you don't expect.

His hand dipped under a stack of charts for Aran cable designs I was playing around with and popped a key dangling from a pushpin.

"So you have X-ray vision," I said. "I'll have to remember that."

"Don't worry." His tone was easy, light, probably deceptive. "I don't have any other superpowers."

"Good to know." I held out my hand for the key.

"I don't get one of my own?" he asked as he dropped it in my palm.

"I'll make a copy for you at the hardware store."

"Why don't I make a copy at the hardware store?"

"Because until the power is on, the utilities are up and running, and we receive signed papers from Montpelier, you're nothing more than a tourist with an agenda."

Which was probably not the best thing to say to a cop, but like I told you before, I'm not myself before my first three or ten cups of coffee.

"That's cold, Mayor Hobbs."

"You think so, Detective MacKenzie?" I favored him with my best precoffee smile. "And it's only December."

He looked at me.

I looked at him.

We looked at each other.

He laughed first.

I kind of liked him for that.

"Come on," I said, reaching for one of my mohair wraps. "Let's take a look at your new digs."

8

LUKE

"Sorry," Chloe said over her shoulder as she fiddled with the door lock. "It seems to be stuck."

"No problem." I wondered what the hell was so hard about unlocking a simple Quikset.

"There!" She straightened up and pushed open the door. "After you."

"I wouldn't use that lock on a bathroom door," I told her as I stepped into the darkened storefront. "You need to make a few upgrades."

"You're lucky you even have a lock," she said. "We don't have a lot of crime in Sugar Maple."

"You don't have any crime in Sugar Maple."

"Which is why we don't need a police force."

I inhaled and wished I hadn't. "Damn, it stinks in here. Did the last tenant keep monkeys?"

"Actually he did." She lifted the shades and pale winter light flooded the place. "Macaques. It was a pet shop."

My olfactory system was threatening to pack up and head back to Boston. "Did they keep goats too?"

"Stuart had an eclectic inventory."

She looked around. "This is awful," she said, meeting my eyes. "I'm really sorry."

"Unless you put the claw marks on the wall, you have nothing to be sorry about."

"You can't possibly work in here until we Lysol the whole place."

"Either that or an exorcism."

"What?" Her expression shifted so swiftly it was like a magic trick.

"I said it was either Lysol or an exorcism." I waited a moment. "That was a joke."

The last time I saw eyes that guarded they had belonged to a man with an addiction to wearing shoplifted Victoria's Secret panties under his Armani suits.

Which was another joke she probably wouldn't like any more than she had liked the first one.

"Where are you staying?"

"A Motel Six on the other side of the highway until I find something else."

"Better hang on to it," she said quickly. "We don't do rentals."

"I could stay at the Inn."

"They don't have any vacancies."

"I'll get on a wait list."

"They're booked through to the spring."

"You handle their reservations?"

"What's that supposed to mean?"

"You sound pretty sure they're full up."

"They're always full up," she said. "That's just the way it is."

Defensive. Confrontational. Argumentative.

My kind of woman.

"I'm not here to cause trouble," I said. "I'm

just here to tie up a few loose ends. Hell, I'm not even going to ask why you call yourself mayor when Sugar Maple hasn't held an election since 1814."

Her throat and cheeks reddened. "It's an honorary position. My mother was mayor before me."

"You don't deal very well with authority, do you?"

"Are you implying you have some kind of authority over me?"

"I'm no fan of Joe Randazzo's, but I'm starting to feel sorry for the poor bastard. You'd probably burn your records before you'd turn them over to him."

If she had been armed, I would have been reaching for my gun. The look she gave me was lethal.

"Don't look so worried. I'm from New England too. I get the whole Live-Free-or-Die thing."

" 'Live Free or Die' is New Hampshire's state motto. Vermont's is 'Freedom and Unity.' "

"Same difference."

"You must be from Massachusetts," she said. It didn't sound like a compliment.

"Bradford, between New Bedford and Salem."

"Those are cities compared to us."

"I've seen a hundred towns just like this," I told her. "Don't worry. I'm not going to rock your boat. Hell, once this space is set up, you won't even know I'm here."

CHLOE

Two hours later I was back in my shop unloading a huge box of Koigu yarn from Canada while Janice and Lynette assembled craft kits for my annual Last Minute Holiday Gifts workshop later that afternoon. We had fallen into the habit of spending our lunch breaks knitting, gossiping, and occasionally eating.

Today, however, I bribed them with chocolate then put them to work while I told them about the unexpected arrival of Sugar Maple's newest resident.

"Tell me you're kidding," Janice said as she counted out six buttons then slid them into a plastic envelope.

"I'm not kidding," I said, fondling the

gorgeous hand-painted yarn. "I almost blew our cover in the first few seconds."

"That's no surprise," Lynette said, up to her elbows in pattern sheets. "All of your bodily humors are in disharmony. I mean, look at you. You look terrible!"

"You actually told him to shift back?" Janice let out a muted howl of anguish that sent the pile of circular needles spinning crazily across the tabletop. "What were you *thinking*?"

"I wasn't thinking, Jan. I must have fallen asleep on the couch, and when I opened my eyes and saw the same face I'd just been dreaming about, I figured Lynette had dipped into my dreams and was pulling one of those shapeshifting practical jokes that makes me crazy." I still hadn't forgiven her for the time she pretended she was Johnny Depp (in full Captain Jack drag) in search of a skein of Noro Kureyon #40.

"You've been working too hard, honey." Lynette leaned across the worktable and patted my hand. "You were hallucinating. It happens to the best of us."

In Sugar Maple it was hard to tell hallucination from reality but I let it pass. I was in enough trouble already without adding *smart ass* to my list of transgressions.

"You're sure he didn't pick up on it?" Janice prodded.

"I dodged a major bullet. He thought I was talking in my sleep."

"Where is he now?"

"He walked down to Griggs Hardware." I took a deep, steadying breath. "There's more."

Lynette shrank down into a childlike version of herself then swiftly reassembled as a grown woman.

I plunged ahead. "I told him he could use my office until we get the pet shop ready."

"Don't make such a big deal out of it," Janice said. "In a couple of hours our magick will be back to full capacity and we already have the extra work crews in this dimension. We can have his office set to rights by tomorrow morning."

There was a lot to be said for taking the magick way out. Last night was the perfect example. The Harris boys heard about what happened in my kitchen through the Spirit Trail grapevine, and they added their one hundred fifty years of carpentry experience to the mix. A trio of household sprites who wintered at the Inn with the Harris and Souderbush families and the other travelers on the Spirit Trail teamed up with the band of elves who lived on the other side of the park, and together they restored my house by the time the sun rose.

But clearly this was one time when I would have to get by without a little help from my friends.

"He saw the place. He'll probably need to have his sinus cavities fumigated. He'll be suspicious if it smells like rosebuds tomorrow." I refrained from telling them about the claw marks on the walls, the parrot damage to the windowsills, or the other less appetizing mementoes left behind.

"Wait a second," Janice said as the light dawned. "Are you saying we can't use magick?"

"No magick, no elves, no sprites. We'll have to do it the old-fashioned way."

"But that *is* the old-fashioned way," Janice said.

"The old-fashioned *human* way with mops and brooms and Lysol and vacuum cleaners. I can handle some of it myself and get high school kids to do the rest."

"Oh, honey!" Lynette's look spoke volumes. "These kids don't know the first thing about mops and brooms. If it's not magick or music, they don't want any part of it."

I stared at my friends in disbelief. Between them, their offspring could staff a football team. "You mean your kids wouldn't—"

I had never seen them laugh quite so loud or so long.

"I'd help out," Janice said, "but between the salon and the kids and my knitting, when would I have time?"

"I'm heartbroken I can't help," Lynette said, "but we're rehearsing *Carol.* We open Saturday."

Considering the fact that they had been performing Dickens's *A Christmas Carol* every season for over fifteen years, I had trouble imagining there was anything left to rehearse.

"Ask Gunnar," Janice suggested. "You know he would do anything for you."

"You didn't see him last night. He was pretty banged up. I don't think he'll be fit for manual labor anytime soon." In typical fashion, Isadora had ignored Gunnar's cuts and bruises and whisked Dane away to wherever faerie mothers from hell took their injured offspring.

"What about Dane?" Lynette asked. (I had always wondered if she had a mild thing for him but never had the guts to ask.) "He's big and strong too."

"Big and strong and crazy," Janice said, and I nodded in agreement. "She's better off doing the work herself."

Actually I was better off not doing the work at all but that option was now officially off the table.

"Why did he have to show up early?" I moaned, burying my face deep into a mountain of sweet worsted weight wool. "One more day . . . that's all we needed . . . just one more—"

"Whoa!" Janice pointed toward the front window. "Is that him?"

I looked up, bleary-eyed from lack of sleep, and saw Luke standing out there on the sidewalk, chatting up Martha Blayney, our mail carrier. "That's him."

Janice popped on her glasses for a better look. "You forgot to mention he was gorgeous."

"That's because he isn't. His hair is shaggy. He has crow's feet. And he has a scar on his left cheek."

"Not that you noticed or anything," Lynette said with a wink.

"Green eyes," Janice said, staring out the window. "Dark hair and green eyes. Yum!"

"He's not a jelly donut. Stop—"

Except I was the one who stopped midsentence as a wave of dizziness broke over me, sending the room spinning like the minitornado in my kitchen last night.

"Chloe?" Janice's voice came toward me through a long tunnel. "What's wrong?"

It was over as quickly as it had started. "I must be coming down with something. Esther Greenberg was sneezing all over the place last night. I'll bet she—"

Janice kicked me hard under the table. "We have company."

LUKE

The Julia Roberts look-alike smiled at me as I approached.

The Catherine Zeta-Jones clone looked up and aimed a dazzling smile of her own in my direction.

And then there was Chloe.

She was slumped in a folding chair, her long frame folded in on itself like origami gone bad. The redhead kicked her under the table, and she muttered something I probably didn't want to hear and turned in my direction.

Let's just say I'd received warmer welcomes from suspects in a lineup.

"Door's locked," I said, nodding to her two friends.

"Well, that was stupid," she said.

I grinned as the redhead kicked her again.

"You didn't lock the door?"

"Why would I lock it?" she countered. "You only went to the hardware store."

I had the feeling we were on the verge of an Abbott & Costello "Who's on First" riff.

"So do you want to open it for me or just toss me the key."

"Why go in there at all until it's cleaned up? You'll need a gas mask."

"I want to take some measurements."

"Planning to hang curtains, are you?"

Her friends laughed and she seemed pleased, which pissed me off.

"Montpelier is sending down some furniture."

"Nice to know our tax dollars are being put to good use." She swung toward her red-haired friend. "Kick me one more time, Meany, and so help me . . ."

The redhead stood up and extended her hand to me. "Janice Meany. I own the hair salon across the street."

"Luke MacKenzie." I glanced toward Chloe then back again. "You probably already know my name."

We shook hands.

No sparks.

The brunette was named Lynette Pendragon. She and her husband owned and operated the community theater I'd noticed on my drive through town.

No sparks there either.

And there had been no sparks with Paul at the hardware store or with Martha the mail carrier. The only sparks had been with Chloe, giant sparks that made me think of the Fourth of July. My palm still burned from them.

Chloe unfolded herself from her chair and plucked the key from the corkboard for the second time that day. She tossed it to me and I pocketed it.

"I cleared a spot for you in the storage

room," she said. "You can set up when-ever you want to."

"Do you have a fax machine I can use?"

She pointed toward a setup in the cor-ner.

"And a high-speed connection."

"The connection is wireless but not all that fast. I'll give you the password."

"One more thing," I said as I turned to leave. "I'll need a list of everyone who was here the night Suzanne Marsden died."

"I was giving a workshop that evening so some of them were out-of-towners."

"Addresses, phone numbers, e-mails?"

"No problem."

"Are the locals available for question-ing?"

She gestured over her shoulder. "The locals are sitting right there."

Janice and Lynette winked and waved at me.

"I have an opening tomorrow between eleven and twelve," Janice said. "I can talk and give you a haircut at the same time."

Lynette whipped out a planner bulging with inserts, Post-its, and index cards that sprayed across the table when she opened it. "Before nine in the morning or after ten at night," she said, "except on Fridays, Saturdays, and Sundays between now and New Year's Day."

"They're staging *A Christmas Carol* at the playhouse," Janice explained.

"My fifteenth year as Mrs. Fezziwig," Lynette said with obvious pride. "We open Saturday night. I'll leave a pair of tickets for you at the box office. You can bring your wife or significant other."

I thanked her and sidestepped the veiled marital status question.

"What's the problem?" I asked Chloe, who was glaring in the general direction of her dark-haired friend. "She's being friendly, not offering me a bribe."

"You're a cop. I thought you weren't supposed to accept freebies."

"Until that paperwork you mentioned comes through, I'm just a random tourist."

"If you're just a random tourist, why should I give you the names and addresses of my customers?"

We locked eyes. "You must be one hell of a chess player."

"I play Scrabble."

"Listen, I—"

"I shouldn't have—"

We laughed and some of the tension in the shop evaporated.

"You first," I said.

"We got off to a bad start," she said. "How about we declare a truce and start over again."

"Sounds like a plan."

We shook for the second time that day, and just like the first time, silver-white sparks leaped into the air between us.

"Next time we'd better ground ourselves first," I said, my right palm crackling from the static electricity.

Chloe laughed but her two friends didn't.

Something had changed in the room. It was as if the molecules had rearranged themselves into a pattern that was almost but not quite like the one that had come before and the three of them knew how and why.

9

CHLOE

The holiday gift-giving workshop started at three o'clock, the same time Luke Mac-Kenzie chose to move his stuff into the store room. We had a large crowd that included six knitting friends from upstate New York, an architect and his life partner, a quartet of nurses from Vermont General, and Renate's harpist daughter Bettina and her daughter Maeve.

Every time he walked by, their heads popped up like a whack-a-mole as they followed his progress from doorway to hallway.

"Ladies," I said quietly, "no drooling on the yarn."

"Who *is* that anyway?" Bettina whispered as she struggled with the Star Toe on a pair of Christmas socks.

"Our new police chief," I said.

"Looks like Montpelier finally got it right."

"We'll see."

"You don't think he's hot?" The usually composed Bettina sounded astonished.

"I'm trying not to think about him at all." Every time I did, my right palm burned, a reminder of the explosion of sparks that occurred when we shook hands.

The New York knitters started speculating about his marital status while the architect and his partner wondered out loud about his sexual orientation. When the quartet of nurses started to muse about certain anatomical possibilities, I excused myself to brew another pot of coffee for the crowd.

That's what I told them and it was partially true, but I also wanted to make sure the door to the store room was closed. I really didn't want him to know there were knitters in the next room fantasizing about his package.

Everything seemed under control and I was about to head for the kitchen to start the pot of coffee I'd promised the paying customers when the overwhelming urge to see him came over me. I mean, it was like one of those irresistible forces you read about, a force so strong and powerful that there was nothing I could do but give in.

I knocked twice, softly, on the door and he opened it before I could change my mind and flee.

The deep green of his eyes startled me anew and it showed.

"I'm putting up a fresh pot of coffee and thought maybe you'd like some . . . I mean, I know you like coffee . . . you brought me a cup this morning . . . mine's not as good as Fully Caffeinated but it's not bad . . . maybe you want something else . . ." What was wrong with me? The words spilled from my mouth like overflow from a dam. "Sorry . . . you're busy . . . I have to get back to the workshop . . . anyway you know where the coffeepot is, right . . . just . . ."

One second I was backing away and the next I was propelled forward into his arms.

Was he surprised? He didn't act like it. He acted like he had been expecting it— no, like he had been waiting for this moment.

My knees buckled but I didn't fall because he held me close. Nobody had ever held me that way before. I could feel his very human heart beating beneath the rough fabric of his store-bought sweater. (I'm a knitter. I can't help noticing things like that.)

Oh God, he smelled good. Even better than he did earlier that morning if it was possible. His body was hard and muscular and so warm. His warmth seemed to pour into my body, warming me from the inside out, filling the empty spaces.

Maybe this was Janice's doing. Or Lynette's. Maybe they had put a love potion in my coffee. I didn't care. Whatever it was, it was spectacular. The feel of his hands along my rib cage. The smell of his skin. The warmth of his mouth as he brought it closer and closer to mine and—

"Chloe?" His voice seemed to rip through layers of warm, sweet mist. "What's wrong?"

I was standing in the hallway by the storeroom.

He was leaning against the jamb, an expression of curiosity on his face.

We weren't touching. We weren't even close to touching.

"I—uh, I—" What was I doing there? I couldn't remember.

"You knocked on the door," he prodded. "Did you want something?"

The gears in my brain clicked back into place. "Coffee," I said, grateful I didn't have to tell him what I really wanted from him. "I'm putting up a new pot if you're interested."

"Great," he said. "Thanks." He leaned closer and met my eyes. "Are you sure you're okay?"

"Just tired," I said. "It's been a long day."

"It's only four o'clock."

"I was up most of the night with a . . . household emergency." Which was twice as much as I should have told him. "Give me five minutes and there will be coffee in the kitchen if you want it."

Luke MacKenzie had been in Sugar Maple for less than twelve hours and I was already coming apart at the seams. Isadora was right. They all were. We had to get rid of him.

And the sooner, the better.

LUKE

Joe Randazzo from the County Clerk's Office faxed me the signed paperwork, which I countersigned and faxed back to him.

It was official. I was now the temporary police chief (and the entire force) of Sugar Maple, Vermont. After more than two years of trying to escape Boston and start over somewhere else, Suzanne's death had provided the way out. I liked to think she would have appreciated the irony even if I was having a tough time with it.

Chloe had provided me with the contact information for the knitters who had been in the shop the night Suzanne died and I started making calls.

"I can't believe she's dead," the rocket

scientist repeated for the third or fourth time. "She was the most beautiful woman I've ever seen!"

The teacher from New Jersey said pretty much the same thing. "I can still see the way she looked when she was peeking in through the window. She was like a cross between a movie star and a supermodel!"

I left messages for the sisters from Pennsylvania.

There was no denying Suzanne had been one hell of a good-looking woman, but as smoking hot as she was, in Sugar Maple she blended into the crowd.

So far there had been no surprises. Influenced by too many margaritas and a bruised ego, Suzanne had made a bad decision and paid for it with her life. I had more questions to ask but I didn't expect the answers to be any different. If the man who stood her up at the Inn had been a plumber and not a politician, I would have marked the case closed right now.

But the rules were different for politicians. Dan Sieverts and his group wanted to make sure the candidate's name wouldn't be dragged into the story. Montpelier wanted to make sure the lack of a police presence didn't cloud the issue. Sugar Maple wanted it all to go away.

And I wanted to make sure an old friend got a fair shake.

Chloe was running some kind of knitting workshop up front so I decided to hang out in the storeroom and do a little web surfing. If she had anything to hide, she was doing it in plain sight because the storeroom where I had set up my laptop was packed floor to ceiling with file folders and banker's boxes begging to be riffled.

I looked her up on Google instead.

There were one thousand seven hundred thirty-six references to Sticks & Strings in Sugar Maple and over two thousand for Chloe Hobbs. Her shop was a top link on websites and blogs from neighboring New Hampshire to Malaysia with all stops in between. Okay, so maybe it was like reading Sanskrit (apparently knitters had their own language), but I was able to translate enough to know Chloe's shop was something special.

I flipped through screens of praise for the shop.

Chloe could teach a cat to knit!
                    —Nancy H., New Jersey

I'd been trying to master a picot bind off for ten years. Chloe showed me once and suddenly it all made sense.
                    —Laura P., Missouri

Sticks & Strings is a magical place for knitters and spinners.
                    —Fran B., Kansas

According to the posts I read online, Chloe was Elvis and Sticks & Strings was Graceland, which I would probably chalk up to being a suburban legend if it weren't for the fact that the noise level at the front of the store could cause hearing loss.

Definitely Elvis.

Headphones sounded like a good idea.

I photocopied a simple map of Sugar Maple and had started overlaying Suzanne's actions on the grid when Margaret Hansen, one of the Pennsylvania sisters, returned my call.

"How terrible," Margaret said when I told her about the accident. "She looked just like Sharon Stone."

"Did she say or do anything out of the ordinary?"

"You mean besides wearing a red carpet kind of dress in the middle of winter? Let me think . . . well, she said she had skis and skates in her car." She laughed. "Skis and skates! I mean, you should have seen her. She looked like the type who would hire other people to ski for her."

I asked a few more questions but mostly the woman kept circling back to Suzanne's dazzling good looks. I thanked her for her help and was making a few notes in my log when I heard a knock on the door jamb.

"You can come out now." Chloe poked her head into the room. I had left the door ajar after her last visit. "They're gone."

I stood up and stretched. "It sounded like a revival meeting out there. I thought knitters were a quiet bunch."

"You have a lot to learn about knitters, Detective."

"So what happens after they leave here? Do their sweaters unravel or something?"

She gave me an odd look. "Nothing

happens," she said. "They go home and build on their new skills."

I fished around on the makeshift desk for the faxed contract. "The paperwork came through." I handed her a copy.

"Great." She glanced at it quickly then folded it in half. "We're going to try and have the place usable by Monday morning."

"Don't bother," I said. "Paul and his sons are going to help me." We planned to start first thing in the morning and power through.

She looked startled. "We'll take care of it for you. I don't think disinfecting your office is in your job description, do you?"

"I like working with my hands," I said. "It helps me think."

"I get some of my best ideas while I'm knitting."

"I get my best ideas when I'm installing a new transmission."

"Same difference," she said with her first real smile of the evening.

"I have help. Paul's kids want to earn some extra cash and Paul said he wouldn't mind pumping up his bottom line."

"And how much will this cost the town?"

"It's not going to cost the town anything. The state picks up the tab."

"I'm liking this more every second."

"So where's the best place to eat around here?" I asked as I followed her out the back door.

"The Inn," she said as she locked the flimsy glass door behind us. "No contest."

"How about joining me?"

She shook her head. "Thanks but all I want to do is go home and crash."

"You're not hungry?"

"I'm too tired to be hungry."

"You still have to eat sometime."

She stifled a yawn. "I'll warm up some soup."

"It's a business dinner. You get a good meal, I get some answers about Suzanne. Win-win."

"Suzanne?" I had her attention. "Did you know her?"

A smarter cop would have lied. "We grew up together."

She had one of those faces that broadcast every emotion. Surprise, sympathy, and a fleeting wariness that seemed out of character for a woman who lived in a town without crime.

"I'm sorry," she said finally. "Were you close?"

"We were friends," I said carefully. "She was married to my brother-in-law for a little while."

She nodded, deep in thought. "If the offer still holds, I'd like to join you at the Inn."

A fierce wind smacked us in the face as soon as we rounded the corner of the building.

"My truck's in the lot across town," I said. "Where's yours?"

"In my driveway." She gave a little laugh. "I walked to work."

"You Vermonters are tough."

"Tougher than you Massachusetts types, definitely."

"Ouch," I said as we navigated our way around a huge patch of ice. "We hold our own."

We fell into step together. I'm usually pretty good at reading people but Chloe Hobbs kept eluding me. She was smart, beautiful, and funny. She ran a successful business that she seemed to love, and she was loved in return by her customers and friends. No arrests, no DUIs, not even a parking ticket. As far as I could tell, she was a model citizen living in a postcard-perfect town.

But something didn't fit. There was a puzzle piece missing, and I was determined to find out what it was.

10

CHLOE

I experienced a momentary jolt of apprehension when it looked like Renate was steering us toward one of the cozy lovers' tables, but I should have known better. She quickly gauged the situation and found us a table near the window.

"Perfect," I said as she handed us our menus. "Thanks, Renny."

"What's good?" Luke asked me after Renate went back to her station up front.

"Everything," I said then laughed. "I know that's not much help but it's true."

Neither one of us spent much time poring over the menu. We ordered quickly then settled down to the reason why we were there.

He leaned back in his chair and settled his gaze on me. "So tell me how you met Suzanne."

There wasn't much to tell. It sounded like nothing more than another adventure in retail but with a very unhappy ending.

"She locked herself out of her car?"

"That's what she told us," I said carefully. "Why else would she be walking around town in a cocktail dress and no coat?"

"Was she drunk?"

"I don't think so." I told him that she had planned to wait at the bar for her boyfriend but the Inn didn't open early for anyone.

"Did you smell alcohol on her breath?"

"I'm not sure."

"How did she get her car open?"

"She was going to phone Triple A but Lynette—" I stopped and regrouped. "This is going to sound terrible but Lynette volunteered her daughter Vonnie to open Suzanne's car for her. She said Triple A would take forever and Vonnie could do it in a flash."

"Lynette's daughter opens locked cars for a living?"

I couldn't help smiling. "Vonnie's a senior at Sugar Maple High. She just happens to have a talent for mechanical objects."

"Like locks."

"Yes," I said. "Like locks." I explained about the Sugar Maple Arts Playhouse and how the Pendragon kids had grown up knowing how to do a little bit of just about everything, same as their parents.

I also congratulated myself on leaving out the fact that the "everything" included shapeshifting, psychokinesis, and just plain screwing around with electronic equipment for the hell of it.

"So Vonnie Pendragon opened the car door for Suzanne?"

"I guess so. I don't really know. I never saw Suzanne again and I never thought to ask Lynette."

Death had taken everything else off the table.

"Take me through the whole thing, Chloe,

from the moment you first saw her until the moment she disappeared from your sight."

"Shouldn't you be writing this down or taping it or something?"

"People are more comfortable if you're not playing court reporter."

"TV cops write everything down."

"TV cops do a lot of things real cops don't always do."

"Like take a witness out to dinner?"

"An efficient use of time and resources."

I looked down at my beautiful (and expensive) plate of Caesar salad then back over at him. "Whatever you say, Detective."

I told him everything I remembered, from the first sight of her face at the window to the last sight of her, draped in my Orenburg shawl, as she dashed down the salted street on her stilettos toward the Inn.

"Can you characterize her mood for me?" Luke asked. "Happy, sad, pensive?"

"Happy," I said. "Excited. A little annoyed that her boyfriend was running late but nothing serious."

"Would you say she was suicidal?"

"God, no! Absolutely not! I mean, I didn't know her or anything, but there is no way she was contemplating suicide. Not that night. Definitely not."

"Why do you think that?"

"I don't know," I said finally. "Women's intuition maybe. She seemed too strong a woman to take her life just because some guy didn't show up for dinner."

There was something in his eyes, a kind of acknowledgment that swiftly came and went.

"Did you know what kind of car she was driving?"

I shook my head. "I think she told Lynette the model and year but I don't remember."

"Did she mention where she was staying?"

"Not here," I said. "That's all I know for sure."

"Can you think of anyone else she might have spoken with?"

"She probably spoke to Renate and the wait staff. Beyond that—" I shrugged.

"Anything else you want to tell me?"

I hesitated. I hadn't told him about my little side trip to the Inn that night or how

Gunnar had caught me peering through the window like one of the orphans in *Oliver!* It was embarrassing, pathetic, and as far as I was concerned, totally irrelevant.

"No," I said. "That's it." I felt a little guilty but that was okay. I could live with guilt.

Renate's cousin Felix delivered our entrees and a complimentary bottle of Barollo, which he opened for us with a great flourish.

Suddenly I saw myself standing outside in the snow two nights ago, peering through the window at the happy humans breaking bread together. Now here I was, sitting where I had imagined Suzanne would sit, across from a man who lived in the real world. If you ignored the fact that we had spent most of our time discussing Suzanne Marsden's accidental death, you might even think it looked like a date.

Which it wasn't. I swear to you my subconscious leaped up and hit me in the head in its eagerness to remind me of that fact.

No problem. I knew it. I got it. I wasn't about to forget it.

On the short list of impossible soul mates for a sorcerer's daughter, a human cop was right there at the top.

But it felt so good to be connected to someone who was exactly what he seemed to be. No magick. No spells. No tricks. Someone who was like me in ways nobody in Sugar Maple could ever be. I didn't even care that it wouldn't last beyond the time it took us to eat dinner. I could live off the memory for a very long time.

I've been lonely for most of my life. After my parents died, Sorcha had done her best to keep me from feeling the full weight of my separateness, but as I grew older, the truth of it had become unmistakable.

And with it came the kind of loneliness that sometimes took my breath away.

If the pharmaceutical companies really wanted to pump up their bottom line, they would create a pill to eradicate loneliness. Even though I had been raised by Sorcha, a healer who took her cures from the natural world around us, I would be their first customer.

Tonight, however, I didn't need a magic pill to make the loneliness disappear.

I didn't care that the only reason we were sharing a meal was so he could interrogate me about Suzanne Marsden's death. I wanted the night to never end.

Luke asked about the town and I had just launched into the Chamber of Commerce version of our history when I realized he wasn't listening.

"Hey," I said, "you're the one who wanted the history lesson."

He gestured with his wineglass. "I think someone is trying to get your attention."

I swiveled around in my chair and saw Gunnar walking slowly in our direction. For a second I wasn't sure if it was Gunnar or Dane—they had both been banged up pretty badly last night—but then he smiled and I knew.

The poor guy looked terrible. A dark bruise decorated his right cheek. The circles beneath his eyes were darker than they had been yesterday and that was saying something. He seemed frail, breakable in a way he had never seemed to me before.

"Renate said you were here." He bent down, wincing with the movement, and kissed me on my cheek. He aimed an easy smile in Luke's direction. "I'm Chloe's friend Gunnar."

Luke clasped his hand. "Luke MacKenzie. Good to meet you."

"What are you doing here?" I asked.

"I got my wires crossed," he said with a self-deprecating laugh. "I thought tonight was the Green Mountain Lawyers Association Christmas party."

"You're a lawyer?" Luke asked.

Both Gunnar and I laughed out loud at the question.

"I help out in the kitchen," Gunnar said.

"So you're a chef." Luke was a cop. Cops needed to find labels for people.

"Cook," Gunnar said with a shrug of his shoulders. "Sommelier. Busboy. Whatever they need."

"This isn't Boston," I reminded Luke. "We don't stand on formality here."

Gunnar cast an eye to the wine bottle resting in the bucket adjacent to our table.

"Barolo." He gave me a look. "Since when?"

"Since tonight," I said. "Renate and Colm sent it over."

"Chloe usually buys her wine by the box," Gunnar told Luke with a small smile.

Luke said something about being a Guinness kind of guy, and Gunnar said something about single malt while I tried sending Gunnar "go away" signals with my eyes. He just smiled back at me in that maddeningly noncommittal way he had and kept on talking.

Finally Luke said, "Pull up a chair," and to my horror, Gunnar did exactly that.

I wanted to kick his Fae butt from one side of the room to the other. What was he *thinking*? Hadn't Gunnar heard about the virtues of keeping a low profile?

Luke stood up. "Back in a few," he said. "I need to set up an appointment to speak with the waitstaff."

"What's going on?" Gunnar asked as soon as Luke was out of earshot.

"I was about to ask you the same thing."

"Renate told me you needed reinforcements."

"What I need is for you to get out of here before the cop comes back to the table."

If Gunnar had a flaw, it was the fact

that he lacked the emotional armor most people needed to get through the day with their heart intact. He didn't have to say a word for me to know I had hurt his feelings.

"He's human," Gunnar said. "There's no future."

"Future?" I almost laughed out loud. "The only future I'm interested in includes dessert."

"I know you're lonely, Chloe. Don't let it blur the lines."

"You're way off base," I said, wondering who else had been reading my mind these days. "This is a business dinner. He asked his questions about Suzanne Marsden, I answered them, and now we're just talking." Gunnar was my closest friend but right then I could have happily hit him over the head with Felix's serving tray.

"No problems?"

"Why would there be any problems?" I countered. "I mean, it's not like I have anything to hide."

It took a second but he started to laugh, and just like that everything was back to normal between us.

"I called this afternoon," he said, "but your cell phone's off."

"I forgot to charge the battery." I had a rocky relationship with all things electronic.

His smile was sweetly familiar but he said nothing. Once again I found myself wishing with all my heart that I loved him the way he deserved to be loved.

"And since when do you call my cell phone anyway?" Sugar Maple villagers had far more interesting means of communication available to them.

"If we're going to have a human in our midst, we have to do as the humans do."

"You think I'm going to screw up, don't you?" I said as the light dawned. "I didn't plan to be caught off guard this morning. I fell asleep on the sofa with the door unlocked and there he was."

"That's the point," Gunnar said. "We have to guard against the unexpected."

I picked a piece of silver-blue glitter from his shoulder. "I'm not the one shedding sparklies, friend."

"Hey," he said, reaching across the table to squeeze my hand in his, "we're friends, aren't we? Friends have each other's back."

"Did Isadora put you up to this?" I loved Gunnar dearly but he was his mother's son and her power was absolute.

"You heard her last night," he said as a chill ran up my spine. "She wants the Book of Spells."

"But why now?" I asked. "She's had all these years to make a run for the Book. Why pick now to get serious?"

He looked uncomfortable.

"Tell me," I said. "I need to know."

"According to Isadora, the same charm that's protected the town all these years also keeps the Book of Spells safe."

"So if the town is in danger, so is the Book."

"Once you possess full powers, you'll be able to lock in your claim on the Book of Spells and it will be too late. The time for her to strike is now."

Each and every descendant of Aerynn had faced a challenge from outside for ownership and each time we had won the day. The magick contained within the Book was powerful and demanded an equally powerful woman who would use that power to protect the town and all who lived there.

And to make matters worse, if I died without powers and without a daughter of my own, the Book of Spells would be absorbed into the Universe and Sugar Maple would be on its own.

So how did a twenty-first-century woman with no magick prove herself worthy of a seventeenth-century Book of Spells anyway? Dragons were in short supply in Sugar Maple. Maybe I was supposed to thwart a demon or, better yet, sit around and wait for Prince Charming to lend a hand.

I hadn't a clue.

I started to laugh. Unfortunately it was one of those near-hysterical laughs that made people turn around and shoot you a look. "Gunnar, this is me you're talking to: the woman with no powers. The woman who is never going to have any powers."

"She's not usually wrong about these things."

"The only way I stand a chance to get my powers is if I fell in love and I don't see that happening anytime soon."

He met my eyes. "Unless it's already happened."

LUKE

The Weavers said they would be happy to give me a list of employees who were on duty the night Suzanne died.

"I distinctly remember her," Renate said. "She was sitting alone right over there." She pointed toward a cozy corner table near an elaborately embroidered screen. "I think she was drinking margaritas while she waited but I could be wrong."

"Did you enter into a conversation with her?"

"Nothing but the usual welcome speech, the list of specials." She paused, thinking. "Actually, that's not entirely true. She dropped by earlier and wanted to sit at the bar and wait. I told her we opened at six sharp and not a second sooner. I don't think she liked that very much."

Renate was being kind. The Suzanne I had known would have hated it, and she wouldn't have hesitated to let the world know just how much.

"Was she alone?"

"Yes."

"Both times?"

"Yes." She gave me a friendly but professional smile. "I need to get back to work now, Detective MacKenzie, but I'd be happy to talk to you tomorrow."

So far tomorrow was shaping up to be one hell of a busy day.

"By the way," she said, "you should ask Gunnar over there if he saw anything. He was helping out in the kitchen that night."

I walked back to the table. Chloe looked a little edgy as she noted my approach. Her golden-boy friend seemed distracted. On him it looked like moody introspection. He probably spent a good three or four hours a day staring at his reflection in every mirror he passed.

Not that I was jealous or anything. In a town of great-looking people, he was just another pretty face, but there was something about the guy that got under my skin.

I reclaimed my seat. "You saved me some whiskey cake," I said. "Thanks."

Chloe smiled at me. "At great personal sacrifice, I'll have you know."

I took a bite and decided I probably wouldn't have been that generous. The stuff was amazing. "I owe you one."

I wasn't ignoring the guy next to me but I wasn't exactly pulling him into our circle either. She didn't treat him like a boyfriend. There was no touching, no hand-holding, no lingering glances. If anything, she seemed pissed with him.

"So what's that all about?" I asked, gesturing toward his right eye.

"Family disagreement," he said, wincing. "Things got out of hand."

"Speaking as your local law enforcement provider, anything I should know about?"

"My brother likes the Pats. I'm a Dolphins man. They play each other next Sunday."

"Got it," I said. I was a Patriots fan too. Hand-to-hand combat seemed to come with the territory.

I settled down to the whiskey cake.

CHLOE

By the time Gunnar said good-bye, I had fallen into a football coma. I suppose I should have been grateful to him for taking Luke's mind off his investigation, but the sense that we had dodged another bullet was strong.

"I love him," I said to Luke after Gunnar had left, "but I thought he would never leave."

Luke's eyebrows shot skyward. "You love him?"

"No, no!" I started to laugh. "I don't love him that way. I love him like a brother."

"Does he know that? Because I wasn't picking up brotherly vibes heading your way."

"We tried dating years ago," I admitted, "but we're better off friends."

"Are you seeing anyone?"

"I see lots of men," I said airily. "I just don't see any of them a second time."

Maybe you had to be there (or be brined in fancy wine), but we started laughing and we couldn't stop. Felix refilled our coffee cups and we laughed harder. Renate strolled casually by to see if everything was okay, but we couldn't answer her through the gales of laughter. Have you ever had one of those nights when absolutely everything was funny? Every sight, every sound, doubled us over with the kind of hilarity I'm not sure I had ever experienced before.

When the cute little snifter of Cour-voisier I'd been nursing slipped from my hand and somehow flew across the table and upturned itself in Luke's lap, I was almost relieved to be interrupted by magick.

Almost being the operative word, of course. Right then I was praying he didn't notice that the brandy snifter had a bet-ter jump shot than Michael Jordan in his prime.

"What the—?" He leaped to his feet, Courvoisier sluicing down his muscular (I wasn't too drunk to notice) thighs.

"I'm sorry!" I grabbed for a clean napkin and leaped unsteadily to my feet too. "I don't know how that happened. Let me—"

He took the napkin from my hand. "I'll do it."

Renate hurried over with ice water and more clean napkins, and except for the delicious smell of brandy, he was as good as new in record time.

"That was some trick," he said.

"I don't know what you mean."

"That glass hung in midair before it tipped over. How the hell did you do that?"

Funny how quickly a girl could sober

up. "You must have had too much wine. It slipped out of my hand."

Very funny, Gunnar. I pictured him standing outside the window laughing his butt off. He knew the rules. When it came to practical jokes, outsiders were off-limits. We hadn't managed to keep our true story hidden all these years by taking chances.

Renate and Felix hovered over us as if we were small children in need of supervision. I eyebrowed Renate to back off but she blithely ignored me and encouraged Felix to do the same. This was probably part of the "Let's Keep Chloe from Screwing Everything Up" campaign under way in Sugar Maple.

"Would you like anything else?" Felix appeared at our table, all smiles and bristling with curiosity. I wouldn't have been at all surprised if he had been eavesdropping on us and reporting back to Renate.

"Just the check," Luke said.

I made an attempt to pay my half of the bill but he waved me off.

"Business expense," he reminded me.

"Even the wine?"

"Renate comped it."

I had no idea whether or not he was happy, but suddenly I realized that I was. Embarrassingly happy, to be precise. When the Barolo-and-brandy buzz wore off, I would remember that we had spent half the evening re-creating some of the last moments of a woman's life, but at that moment on that particular night I was about as happy as I had ever been in my life.

For the first time in my thirty years on the planet, I wasn't wishing I could step into someone else's shoes, someone else's life. I was happy just as I was. Too bad it couldn't last.

We said good night to Renate and Colm then stepped out into another dazzling Vermont night. The snow-blanketed mountains glowed silver-white beneath the waxing moon. An owl hooted softly in the distance. The air was so crisp and sweet I wanted to take a bite out of it, and I pulled in a long, deep breath.

"Oww!" I clutched at my head.

I could hear a chuckle in his voice. "Oxygen will do it to you every time."

"You drank as much as I did. Why aren't you having trouble?"

"I'm driving," he reminded me. "I only had half a glass."

I babbled something about the great food and great wine and God knows what else. We must have walked to the parking lot because the next thing I knew I was strapped into the front seat of his truck, shivering while we waited for the engine to warm up.

"You don't really have a pine tree hanging from your mirror, do you?" I tapped it with the tip of my index finger.

"You've got something against pine trees?"

"Yes, I do," I said, happily tipsy. "They belong in the forest, not dangling over your dashboard."

I launched myself into a goofy riff on pine tree air fresheners, furry car seat covers, and satellite radio that probably didn't make any sense at all.

"So where do you live?" he asked as he drove out of the lot.

I had to think for a second. "You know where Osborne and Nurse intersect? I'm east of there, right near Proctor Park." He punched some info into a GPS and it recited instructions in one of those creepy robotic voices that weirded me out even when I was stone cold sober.

"I could have walked home from the Inn," I said. "You're going out of your way."

"No problem. I need to learn my way around town."

Was I too buzzed to walk home? I didn't think so. Our town was safe, we had no traffic, and I had a homing pigeon's sense of direction. But I was very glad he thought I was because it meant we had more time together.

He turned off Wilde Way onto Osborne and I found myself wishing I lived on the other side of the galaxy. My eyes were getting all teary and I pinched myself on the inside of my arm. What was wrong with me? I never cried. But suddenly I was overflowing with feelings that had no place to go but out in a maudlin display of tearful self-pity.

I felt dizzy, disoriented. This wasn't like me at all. I wasn't used to emotional turmoil. It gave me the same queasy, white-knuckled feeling I got the one time I tried ice skating. That was exactly how I felt right now. Out of control, skidding helplessly across the ice toward a giant tree with my name on it that—

I blinked and the haze of wine and brandy cleared long enough for me to realize it wasn't my imagination. We were spinning across Osborne like an amusement park ride gone bad, heading straight toward a stand of maples.

11

LUKE

"Hang on!" I yelled and I swear we went airborne there for a second. Black ice stretched from one side of the roadway to the other. We couldn't break free of it. I steered into the skid and managed to turn the wheel to the left just before we would have slammed head-on into one of the maples. Instead the right front fender hit the nearest tree with a sick thud, spun us around, and sent us careening off in the other direction. I hung on to the wheel, and every prayer I had ever known came rushing back to me as I eased down the brake and brought us to a shuddering stop inches away from disaster.

For a second the world went silent. The sound of my heart pounding in my ears drowned out everything but the squeak of the back wheels as they spun crazily in the ice-encrusted snow.

I turned to Chloe. Her face was ashen, her hands braced against the dashboard. "Are you okay?"

"I don't know . . . I think so . . ." She met my eyes. "W-what happened?"

"Black ice," I said. "By the time I realized it, we were already fishtailing." I leaned closer. "Are you sure you're okay? You don't look so good."

"Story of my life," she muttered. "Just give me a minute to get myself together."

"No problem." I got out and spent a few moments inspecting the damage to the Jeep while she did whatever it was she had to do.

I was leaning against the back of the truck when she joined me a few minutes later. She looked a little shaky on her pins but more like herself.

"Much damage?" she asked.

"Mostly cosmetic. Another couple inches and it would have been a different story. I couldn't seem to steer clear of the ice." I gestured toward the back wheels, which were mired in snow. "Right now our biggest problem is digging our way out."

"You did a great job back there."

"I grew up in Massachusetts," I reminded her. "I'm not a stranger to winter driving." I was still riding a wave of adrenaline that had me feeling euphoric.

She looked anything but.

"That's how my parents died," she said quietly. "A patch of black ice near the bridge."

"Jesus," I whispered, reaching out to her. "I'm sorry."

Her voice was clear and steady. She told her parents' story without embellishment or self-pity. The six year old who had been left orphaned by the tragic accident was standing there with us too, and I realized it was the first time in years that I had listened as a man and not as a cop.

"Who took you in?" I asked. "Family?" I imagined a large and loving extended network of grandparents and aunts and uncles and cousins who opened their collective arms to her and held her tight.

"I have no family," she said. "A friend of my mother's took me in and raised me as her own."

"In Sugar Maple?"

She smiled. "You know how they say it takes a village to raise a child? In my case it was true."

Her mother-lioness defense of the town suddenly made sense. So did the deep affection everyone seemed to have for her. These people were her family.

When you're a cop, you learn early on to compartmentalize. You need a hell of a lot more than a bulletproof vest to protect you on the street: you need to find a way to bulletproof your emotions as well.

I was pretty good at that. During my years in Boston I had acquired a reputation as a clearheaded cop who didn't get sidetracked by emotion. I dealt with facts. My world was filled with brokenhearted children, lonely widows, hollow-eyed men who had lost everything that mattered. They could take you down with them if you let them, but I never did. I got tougher.

My heart grew harder. After a while I forgot where the cop ended and the man began.

Until tonight.

And it scared me more than that stretch of black ice.

"So how long did you live in Boston?" she asked, breaking the growing silence between us.

"A little over eleven years." I was usually the one asking the questions. It felt strange to be on the other side of the process.

She gestured toward the line of trees and the open fields beyond them and the mountains beyond that. "I lived in Boston for a little while. Country life must be a big adjustment for you."

"I was a small-town kid," I reminded her. "I like the pace."

I didn't tell her that I had been looking for a town exactly like this where I could disappear. I didn't tell her anything. We stood there next to each other, leaning against the truck, while the night unfolded around us. Dark skies. Brilliant stars. Waxing moon. The same sounds that had freaked me out last night seemed familiar tonight.

"I'm okay," she said. "You probably want to get back to the motel."

Her words had barely faded when the sound rose up from nowhere and everywhere, a high, keening wail that made my hackles rise.

"What the hell was that?" I asked.

"I'm not sure." Her voice was low, her words almost inaudible.

The wail split the air again, longer and louder this time.

"That's straight out of a horror movie." I glanced over at her. "A wolf?"

"It's not a wolf." She wrapped her arms around her midsection and shook her head. I noticed that she had started to tremble. "It's probably a fisher over a kill. They're repopulating. Proctor Park gives way to protected forest acreage."

The sound was primeval. It sank its claws deep into some kind of tribal memory buried under centuries of civilized behavior and drew blood. She had lived here all her life, and if she couldn't stop her visceral reaction to the fisher's call, what chance did I have?

"If I didn't know better, I'd swear it was a banshee wail."

She spun around to face me. "Banshee?"

"My mother was first-generation Irish. She said they heard the banshee wail whenever a family member died."

"Do you believe that?"

"If you'd asked me an hour ago, I would have laughed. Now I'm not so sure."

Her expression was impossible to read even for a cop who made his living doing exactly that.

"You're going to hear a lot of strange sounds living in Sugar Maple and I can promise you they're not banshees wailing."

"Banshees keen." What the hell was wrong with me? I couldn't let it go. "That sounded like keening."

"And you sound like you've done your banshee homework."

Which was probably a polite way of asking if I had slipped a gear. Maybe I had.

"I grew up near Salem, where everyone believes in things that go bump in the night." I couldn't tell if she was amused or pissed off. "I take it you don't."

"Believe in banshees? I'm afraid not."

Which begged the question: What did she believe in? God. Ghosts. Santa Claus. Love at first sight. I might have asked if a car hadn't rolled to a stop and flashed its lights. I instinctively stepped in front of Chloe to shield her until the driver's identity could be ascertained.

"It's okay," she said, stepping forward. "That's Midge Stallworth's car."

"Stallworth?" The name sounded familiar.

"Funeral home."

I was beginning to wonder if I was on a Stephen King tour of New England.

A round little woman in a bright red down jacket bounced her way across the snowy divide toward us.

"Oh my! Oh my!" She sounded like she had been sucking helium. "What happened here?"

"Black ice," Chloe said, giving her a hug. "Detective MacKenzie managed to keep us from getting into real trouble."

Midge Stallworth frowned and glanced back toward the road. "Black ice? There's no black ice on Osborne."

"That's the point, Midge. You can't see black ice until it's too late."

"Honey, I just drove that same road. I'm telling you there's no black ice, white ice, or anything else ice. The road's dryer than a lizard's skin."

"You must have drifted out of your lane and missed it," Chloe said to the merry mortician. "Trust me, there was black ice."

Midge opened her mouth to say something else then shut it just as quickly. "I have kitty litter in my trunk," she told me with a cherubic smile. "Best thing ever invented and I don't even own a cat."

I followed her across the snow drifts to her car and found myself wondering if the woman was part mountain goat. She practically floated over the top of the same drifts I was slogging my way through. Talk about aerobic conditioning.

Midge unlocked her trunk and I whistled out loud.

"You have a better selection than they have at Griggs Hardware," I said as she started rooting through her trunk.

"I was a Girl Scout, honey," she said with a wink. "I always come prepared."

Midge was Barbie doll's slightly dirty grandma, a cross between Mae West and Betty Crocker.

I borrowed a shovel and a five-pound

sack of kitty litter and a handful of minutes later had the truck back on the street. It was a little worse for the wear but every-thing was in working order.

"Don't be a stranger," Midge said as I dried off the shovel and placed it back in her trunk. "We can always use new blood around here."

I could hear her laughing as she drove off down the street.

CHLOE

It was a good thing Midge was already dead because I could have killed her for that last stupid remark. *New blood?* Was she out of her mind? The last thing we needed was vampire jokes. Factor in her maniacal laughter and the banshee wail and I wouldn't be surprised if Luke aimed his truck for the state line.

Strangely, I had to admit he didn't seem particularly unnerved. I wasn't sure if that was a good or a bad thing. I had lied to Luke when I said the strange keening wail was the sound of a fisher over a kill. The truth was I had never heard a sound like that before and hoped I never would again.

The sound seemed to carry all the sorrow in the world within it. I had no idea what animal produced the keening wail but it was easy to see how it had come to be associated with death. No wonder Gunnar had been so shaken last night. I totally got it now.

"Midge is something else," Luke said as we climbed back into the truck and snapped on our seat belts. "That must be one rockin' funeral home."

"You don't know the half of it. Her husband thinks he's Elvis."

I made him laugh with a few carefully censored anecdotes about Midge, and we drove the rest of the way to my house without incident. No flying wineglasses. No more patches of black ice. No banshee wails. No middle-aged undead rescue squad. For six minutes and thirty-two seconds, it was all good.

He pulled into my driveway and stopped behind my Buick.

"An 'eighty-five?"

"Good eye."

"It's in great shape."

"It should be," I said. "It only has twenty-two thousand miles on it." Most of those had been clocked by the first owner, one of Archie's troll friends who lived in the subdivision beneath the bridge.

"Well," I said as I gathered up my things. "Thanks for dinner."

"Thanks for joining me," he said. "I had a good time."

I didn't mean to laugh. "Sure you did. Black ice, banshees, a bawdy mortician. What's not to like."

"You forgot the flying brandy." He flashed me a smile. "Someday you'll have to tell me how you managed that trick."

I gave what I hoped was an enigmatic smile while I made a mental note to give Gunnar a piece of my mind for that stunt. Harrier jets and helicopters hover in place. Stemware, not so much.

There was a long awkward pause where, if we had been on a first date and not a business dinner, the good night kiss would have happened. You know the kind of kiss I mean: long and slow and filled with heat and promise.

Yeah. That kind.

"Good night." I hesitated then extended my right hand.

He smiled and enclosed my gloved hand in his. "No sparks this time."

Maybe not, but I felt like I was floating ten feet off the ground just the same.

"You sound disappointed," I said.

"A little." His smile widened. "But this is good too."

This was better than good, better than Barolo and probably more dangerous. The warmth of his skin, his solid male strength. He wasn't going to vanish in a burst of golden glitter or a puff of scarlet smoke. He was as real as I was, just as earth-bound and mortal and alone—

A wave of dizziness swept over me. I closed my eyes and waited for it to pass.

"Chloe?" His voice floated toward me from a great distance. "Are you okay?"

"I'm fine," I said as the dizziness receded. "I guess I really did drink too much wine."

"I'll walk you to your door."

I didn't protest. I wanted the night to last as long as it possibly could. We started up the shoveled path to my front door and were laughing about Midge and her trunk load of kitty litter when I realized we were following a trail of royal purple glitter. There was only one person in Sugar Maple who left a trail like that behind her and that was Isadora.

I shot a quick glance toward Luke. He was happily relating a story about last year's Boston blizzard. He didn't seem to have the slightest idea that he was kicking up shimmering purple clouds with every step he took.

I took another look around me and my heart kicked into overdrive. Smudges of steel blue glitter, Dane's signature color, stained the windowsills and door frame. The sizzle and burn of major Fae powers unleashed had melted snow on either side of my driveway and singed the bark of the trees.

Luke was a sharp-eyed cop trained to be suspicious. It occurred to me that the only reason he hadn't strapped on Ghost Busters gear and started collecting forensic evidence was because the spell was still working. He didn't see what I saw but that could change any second.

I had to do something. We were less than ten feet from my front door. What if he wanted to come in for coffee? What if he needed to use the john? What if he suddenly decided to seduce me?

We were almost at the porch steps and I was up to my ankles in glitter. Lights glowed behind the curtains, psychedelic bursts of scarlet and magenta and acid yellow. My house glittered like a BeDazzled T-shirt. I could feel the energies building up toward some kind of crazy confrontation that would probably send my roof sailing back to Forbes the mountain giant.

Time was short and my options were limited so I did what any other red-blooded American girl would do in a similar situation.

I jumped him.

Considering Luke probably outweighed me by sixty pounds, the fact that he went down like a box of rocks was pretty amazing. Not even the element of surprise could have accounted for that. Aerynn and my ancestors must have been watching over me and I whispered my thanks.

Funny how many separate impressions you could register in the space of a moment. I mean, how long did it take to throw yourself at a guy? Maybe two seconds? But those two seconds were the best two seconds of my life.

The snow cushioned his fall. His body cushioned mine. I forgot about the banshees and the ransacking faeries, about vampires and spells and the kind of loneliness you could die from. I was crazy scared happy brave and everything in between. Who needed magick when life could be this good all on its own?

Did I mention that he smelled like the ocean on a spring afternoon?

Luke rolled us over so he was on top of me and life got even better. "What the hell are you doing?"

"I tripped."

"You tackled me."

"I was trying to break my fall."

"With my body?"

"I had to grab something and you were the only thing available."

The amazing thing was that I was able to form a sentence. We were close enough to share the same breath.

"Why, Chloe?" His words brushed my lips.

"I told you," I whispered.

"I don't believe you."

"I know."

"What are you hiding?"

"Nothing."

"I'll find out."

"No," I whispered against his mouth. "You won't."

His eyes were a deep green, a shade called bottle green that didn't exist anymore except in imagination. A clear green with flashes of gold near the pupil like bursts of light.

He said something but his words were lost to me the second his mouth found mine. Everything else fell away. *Everything.* Reason. Caution. The thousand and one reasons why this was a Really Bad Idea. There was only this moment, and because I knew this moment couldn't last, I melted into it.

Into the kiss. Into him. Into a future I knew I could never have, a life that could never be mine. I loved the weight of his body on mine. The heat growing between us. The hot, sweet taste of his mouth. The way time seemed to wrap itself around us.

But the sad truth about kissing is that sooner or later you have to stop and take a breath. I know better than most women just how fragile a thing magic really is. In the time it took to breathe, reality stopped us in our tracks.

He helped me to my feet. I brushed snow off the back of his jacket. He did the same for me. We plucked his cell phone out of a snow bank and found my keys beneath a wintering lilac. There was no sign of faerie glitter anywhere. The rainbow lights were gone and only a small blue lamp burned in my front window. I suppose I should have been relieved but all I felt was sad.

We faced each other near the front door.

"I'm sorry—"

"I shouldn't have—"

We laughed uncomfortably. He plunged his hands into his jacket pockets. I hung on to my bag as if it were the last lifeboat on the *Titanic.*

"I think I can take it from here," I said. "Thanks for driving me home."

"No problem."

He turned and walked back to his truck and he didn't look back.

I got what I wanted: our secrets were still safe.

I just wished I felt happier about it.

12

LUKE

I waited a few minutes after Chloe went inside her cottage then slowly drove away.
Nothing like slamming into a stand of maples to make you rethink your driving skills.
We'd skidded on a patch of black ice. I was
sure of it. The tires lost traction and not
even all-wheel drive could compensate.

So why didn't the merry mortician en-
counter it too? She was only five or six minutes behind us on the same road, traveling
in the same direction. Ice didn't suddenly

evaporate when it was ten degrees Fahrenheit and dropping.

Midge wasn't a stupid woman. She had stared at Chloe and me like we were crazy when we told her about the black ice that had sent us spinning across Osborne.

This was winter in New England. Black ice could happen anywhere to anyone. It was a geographical hazard. It was the price you paid for the picture-postcard views.

Hell, black ice had taken out Chloe's parents. The look on her face after we slammed to a stop wasn't something I would forget anytime soon. I had some of Midge's kitty litter in the back of my truck. If I could find the ice, I could do something about it so nobody else got into trouble.

I drove slowly, carefully, down Osborne to the place where we'd hit the trees. The road was bone dry, just as Midge had said. I parked the truck on the shoulder and paced off sixty feet north and south. No ice anywhere. Not on either side of the road. No oil slick. Nothing that could cause a spinout.

But it had happened. The dent in my truck was proof of that.

Operator error? That was a possibility but not a probability. I had been driving slowly, not because there was a problem with the roadway but because I didn't want the evening to end. The slower I drove, the longer I would have with Chloe. If I'd had the guts I had as a teenager, I would have played the out-of-gas card, but I was thirty-four years old and Chloe was too smart to fall for it.

I climbed back behind the wheel and was about to pull out when I saw a shadow moving toward me from the woods. Sugar Maple might be a town without crime, but trust me, cops don't like seeing strangers pop out of the woods late at night on a deserted country road.

My gun was in the glove box. I probably wouldn't need it but it was good to know it was there. The shadow began to take shape as the woods thinned and it moved closer. It was a male. Tall. Broad-shouldered. Moving with the distinctive glide of a cross-country skier.

Chloe's friend Gunnar?

I beeped the horn as he exited the woods. He looked up, startled, and saw my truck, but there was no sign of recognition.

I climbed out again and called out a greeting. He looked at me across the snowy expanse, and I could see the wheels spinning inside his head as he tried to place the truck, the driver, into context.

"What the hell, dude? We just met a few hours ago." I waited but still no click. "Luke MacKenzie. You stopped at our table to talk to Chloe."

He glided over to where I stood. "You met Gunnar," he said with an easy grin. "I'm Dane."

Twins. Who knew?

I noted there wasn't a mark on him. Clearly I was talking with the winner of the sibling brawl. We exchanged pleasantries. He was easier to talk to than his brother, and I chalked that up to the fact that Chloe wasn't a factor.

"How long are you here for?" he asked. "This isn't exactly a hotbed of crime."

"A few months," I told him. "Once we close the Marsden case, they'll probably turn this over to the village to fill the position."

"Makes sense," Dane said. "Who else

could put up with this burg over the long haul?"

Spoken like a man who was looking for a way out but I kept the observation to myself. I had learned a long time ago that you found out more that way.

"I'm heading for the highway," I said, "if you need a lift."

"Thanks, but I'm in training for a race and have to get some more miles under me before I quit."

"A little late to be in the woods, isn't it?"

"Best time," he said with a grin. "See you around town, MacKenzie."

A second later he disappeared back into the woods. The darkness swallowed him and it was like he had never been here at all.

CHLOE

I had to hand it to Isadora and Dane. They had trashed my house like a pair of rocker faeries with an agenda.

Every closet, drawer, cabinet, and secret hiding place had been rifled and the contents spread from one end of my home to the other. Bookshelves had been toppled. Cushions and mattresses tossed. I found my terrorized cats hiding in the basement behind the oil burner. Even the stash of kitty litter had been searched.

Isadora's signature royal purple glitter was smeared on every available surface. Dane's steel blue glitter was scattered across my bed and bathroom and beyond. Did they really think the Book of Spells was tucked away in the lettuce crisper? I mean, tossing perfectly fine produce was just plain nasty.

I felt angry and violated and everything in between, and if I had been living anywhere but Sugar Maple, I would have been on the phone with 911 so fast your head would spin.

But 911 wasn't an option so I did the next best thing: I called my friends.

Lynette was the first to arrive. She flew down the chimney and into the room, shook out her feathers, then shifted back to her normal humanoid form. The bad news: she was on top of the china closet at the time, and both the closet and Lynette toppled to the floor with a resounding crash.

The good news: instead of stuffing my china closet with fragile dinnerware, I had stuffed it with Cascade 220, worsted weight, in every color of the rainbow.

"Let's hear it for one hundred percent wool," Lynette said as she checked herself for fractures. "That stuff is better than an air bag."

I considered giving her a lecture on looking before she landed but decided against it. Who was I to judge? I was the one with the trashed house, no powers, and a missing Book of Spells.

Janice arrived a few moments later in a spectacular explosion of emerald green smoke that smelled like spearmint and made the cats sneeze. She was wearing an old chenille bathrobe she had found in a thrift shop and her ever-present Uggs. She glanced around the room. "Where's Gunnar? We have work to do."

I motioned them into the kitchen. "I made coffee. I'm going to try Gunnar one more time." I pressed the redial on my cell phone and murmured, "Pick up, pick up, pick up," but it flipped immediately to voice mail. I repeated my earlier message and disconnected.

"The phone?" Lynette arched a brow. "Since when?"

"He said we needed to play by human rules as long as Luke was in town." I had to admit that our local phone company hadn't mastered the communications link between this world and Gunnar's.

"Screw that." Janice brought the tips of her fingers together in a pyramid shape, and I watched as a pure blue flame began to glow from the base. I had seen her do that many times but it never got old. Her people had been sending messages that way for longer than Sugar Maple had been around.

But there was still no response from Gunnar. I added one more worry to my growing stack.

Lynette glanced around at the mountains of purple and steel blue glitter all over my kitchen. "Isadora really has it in for you, honey."

I shot her a look. "You think?"

"Spill," Janice demanded. "Why did the Mother of the Year and her evil spawn trash your place?"

"In thirty words or less," Lynette said.

"I can do it in four: the Book of Spells."

"That woman needs a good family therapist," Janice said with an eye roll, "not the Book of Spells."

"I'm with Jan," Lynette said. "She's a bitch who's just trying to annoy you."

I took another swig of coffee. "What exactly do you two know about the Book?"

"Only that it's the Holy Grail for sorcerers," Janice said.

"And that it passes down through the female line of your family," Lynette added.

"Have you ever seen it?"

"Nobody has," Janice said. "You Hobbs women keep a pretty close eye on it."

"Sorcha never showed it to you?"

"She guarded it with her life," Lynette said.

"So you don't know what it looks like? I mean, if it's red or blue or leatherbound or—"

Janice clapped a hand over her mouth to hold back the scream. "Tell me you didn't lose it."

"I didn't lose it," I said quickly. "I never knew where it was in the first place. Sorcha said I would understand everything when the time was right."

"Meaning when you came into your powers," Lynette said.

"Exactly," I said. "And we all know how well that's worked out."

Janice shifted to her game face. "So what if Isadora gets her hands on it. It's not like she'd be able to use it or anything. She's not a Hobbs woman."

"It's not that simple, Jan. Until the Book is secured by a Hobbs woman with full powers, it's fair game."

Up until I came along, that minor detail had never been a problem. I waited while the bad news registered.

"Crap." Janice always got right to the point. "We're screwed."

Lynette leaned over and smacked her on the arm. "Don't say that!"

"We're not screwed," I said. "Compromised, but not screwed."

"Why is she so hot to get it now?" Janice demanded. "I mean, it's been floating out there for almost twenty-five years. She could have made her move anytime."

"According to Gunnar, the spell protects the Book as well as the town, and we all agree it's growing weaker by the day."

Janice was not about to be mollified. "If you don't know where the Book is, how will you know if it's missing?"

"We're talking about Isadora," I reminded her. "If she gets her hands on it, everyone in Sugar Maple will know."

"Good point," Janice said. "Terrifying, but good."

"Gunnar should be here," Lynette said. "I want to hear what he knows about this."

"Maybe he's duking it out with his brother again." Janice mimed a right hook. "And Mama Bear is refereeing the match."

"Maybe Isadora and Dane found the Book, and Gunnar is trying to get it away from them." Lynette has always had a flair for the melodramatic.

"He's probably sleeping," I said. "He really looked like hell tonight."

"He hasn't been looking well at all lately," Lynette, the tenderhearted, mused. "And that brother of his is probably going around like a well-fed cat."

"I saw Dane last night," I said. "He didn't look too great but he's in better shape than Gunnar."

Janice nodded her agreement. "That's exactly what Trixie told me when she came through the mist last week for highlights."

I took a deep breath and plunged in.

"Gunnar heard a banshee wail the night Suzanne Marsden died."

"Oh, please." Janice rolled her eyes. "If I had a nickel for every banshee wail I've heard, I wouldn't be waxing the Griggs family on a weekly basis."

"Banshees are nothing but a Vegas lounge act," Lynette said, laughing. "Lots of noise, not much substance."

"There's more," I said. "The cop and I heard it tonight. I told him it was a fisher over a kill but it wasn't."

"Since when are you an expert on banshees?"

"I'm not," I said, "but he seems to know a lot about them."

Lynette nodded. "It's that whole Celtic vibe he has going on. I mean, my Irish grandmother actually believed in leprechauns."

"We have a leprechaun living at Sugar Maple Assisted Living," I reminded her.

"Okay, bad example," Lynette said, "but you know what I mean."

"What if banshees do exist?" I persisted. "If you hear a banshee wail, does that really mean someone you know is about to die?"

"You're starting to get on my nerves," Janice said. "Listen to me: banshees are imaginary. They. Do. Not. Exist."

"But what if they do?" I couldn't let it go. "Most people think trolls and sprites and vampires are imaginary too but we know better."

"Point taken, but I still say you heard a fisher."

"I know what a fisher sounds like, and this wasn't a fisher." Fishers on a kill made a sound like the scream of a terrified child. The cry I heard tonight was different. Mournful. Filled with foreboding. "Gunnar heard the banshee and Suzanne died. I heard the banshee tonight . . ."

Lynette mimed a shiver. "I'm not crazy about banshee talk."

"Neither am I," I said, "but what if there's something to it."

"Call Pam at Sugar Maple Assisted Living," Janice said. "Ask her if anyone's about to tip over to the other side."

"I can't do that." I started to laugh despite myself. "I'll check the obituaries tomorrow."

"Wuss," Janice said, but she laughed too. "This place is giving me a headache. I can't think in this mess."

She reached into the felted tote bag she carried everywhere and pulled out two plastic baggies filled with dried herbs and flowers then placed a pinch from each in the palm of her left hand. Her incantation was low and melodic and utterly incomprehensible to me. She passed her right hand over her open palm, and right before my eyes the tiny pile of fragrant plant matter vanished.

Dishes pieced themselves back together and marched obediently back into the cupboards. Glasses unshattered and resumed their rightful places on the shelves. Cans, boxes, silver, they all stood up, brushed themselves off, and went back where they belonged.

Even better was the fact that the same thing was happening in the rest of the house.

When a freshly brewed pot of coffee magically appeared in the center of the table and poured itself into our waiting cups, I sighed with pleasure.

"I owe you, Janice," I said.

"I know," Janice said with a grin. "You can repay me when you crack that Book of Spells."

"How big do you think it is?" I asked. "Paperback? Hardcover? Coffee-table book?"

Janice shrugged. "I've seen them tiny as a grain of sand and big as the side of a bus. It all depends on the creator."

"We'll need to search the entire town," Lynette said.

"And we can't be obvious about it," I reminded her. "Not while Luke's living here."

We divided the search into three sections. I would tackle my cottage, the knit shop, and the pet store that was being turned into a police station. Lynette would take the east side of town, Janice the west.

"Don't tell anyone," I warned them. "Not even Lilith. If Isadora gets wind of what we're doing, she'll level the town."

Which would sound like an exaggeration if you didn't know Isadora the way we did. She made the Wicked Witch of the West look like Mary Poppins minus the edge.

"What about Gunnar?" Janice asked.

"First one who sees him clues him in," I said, a little miffed that he still hadn't answered my call.

"You're going to have to keep Duke busy for a few days," Lynette reminded me.

"Luke," I said. "His name is Luke MacKenzie." The minute I said his name, my stomach seemed to turn upside down. Not to mention inside out. "I need some water."

Janice was back in a flash with a bottle of Poland Spring. "What's wrong?"

"I don't know." I rested my head on the table. "I think I had too much wine at dinner."

Janice placed a cool hand against my forehead. "You're burning up."

It was Lynette's turn to check my temperature. "There's a flu going around. I'll bet you picked it up from one of those sniffling knitters the other night."

"I don't have time for the flu. I'm holding six more workshops between now and Christmas." I aimed a meaningful look in Janice's direction. "You're supposed to be connected to the natural world. Help me!"

"You should have asked me before you got crazy with the vino," she said, laughing in the face of my misery. "I could have set you up with a nice little charm that would have protected you but now . . ."

"Janice! That isn't helping."

"Take the potion anyway," Janice advised. "You can never be too careful."

The house had been set to rights. We had mapped out a plan to find the Book of Spells. The coffeepot was empty.

And Gunnar still hadn't called.

"You know what it's like beyond the mist," Lynette said with a wave of her hand. "God knows how we ever get a message through to any of them."

Actually I didn't have the slightest idea what it was like beyond the mist, and to be honest, I hoped I never would. If Isadora and Dane were any example of what went on when Fae were left to their own devices, I would rather take my chances with known felons of the human persuasion.

I hugged Janice and Lynette and thanked them for abandoning their nice warm beds to help me out.

"Oh, you'll pay," Janice said.

"Definitely," Lynette said, laughing. "I'm thinking cashmere."

"Cashmere's good," Janice agreed. "But quiviut's even better."

"We'll talk," I said. The truth? I was so thankful for their friendship that not even my mother's self-replenishing stash would be enough to show my gratitude.

Lynette was the first to leave. She slowly shrank down to a pinpoint of gunmetal gray and I watched, spellbound, as she just as slowly evolved into a sleek homing pigeon that circled my living room then whooshed up the chimney.

Believe me when I say it never got old.

"The girl knows how to make an exit," I said, shaking my head in wonder. My best exit was the time I tripped leaving Fully Caffeinated and spilled a mocha latte on my favorite ivory mohair scarf.

"Your cop is coming in at noon to question me. Anything I should watch out for?"

"He's not my cop, Jan."

"You're blushing!" She leaned closer and inspected my face. "I've never seen you blush before."

"I'm having a hot flash," I lied. "I told you I was premenopausal."

Her expression grew more serious. "Honey, listen to me: he's not for you."

"I don't know what you're talking about."

"You're looking for a future and that's

something you can never have with a human."

"I had dinner with him, Jan. A business dinner. Nothing more."

"You kissed him."

I felt like I had been sucker-punched. "Were you spying on us?"

She shook her head. "I didn't have to. Your aura changed. I saw it the second I arrived."

"It was a preemptive measure. I had to distract him from what was going on in here."

"Do you really expect me to believe that?"

"And do you really think I'm crazy enough to get involved with a human cop? Give me some credit, Janice."

The look she gave me was part wonder, part pity, completely annoying. "Sometimes a woman doesn't have a choice."

"This is the twenty-first century. We always have a choice." And mine usually involved wine and old movies.

"Just keep Saturday night open," Janice said. "My cousin Haydon said he would stop by on his way to the Wizards Annual

Winter Solstice Convention in Halifax. I think you'll like him."

"You wouldn't try to sneak another troll by me, would you?"

"Six feet two inches of pure wizardry," she promised. "You won't be disappointed."

I didn't have the heart to tell her that I already was.

13

LUKE

I hooked up with Paul Griggs and his sons in front of the old pet shop the next morning. The sun was just beginning to rise over the mountains to the east, and the boys already had five o'clock shadows.

"How old did you say your sons are?" I asked as they fell on the donuts and coffee I'd picked up at Fully Caffeinated.

"Fourteen and fifteen," Paul said. "They're big for their age."

That was an understatement. Both kids were taller than me and I'm six-three. They were also the hairiest pair of teenage boys I had ever seen. Their old man was no slouch in the body hair department, but clearly puberty had hit those kids hard.

"Sorry I'm late," I said as I grabbed a donut for myself. "Damn truck stalled out on the bridge. Took ten minutes to get it to turn over again." I didn't mention that my wipers went wonky and the radio kept blaring disco instead of the sports preset.

"I know a shortcut," Paul said. "You can avoid the bridge entirely. On icy days that's not a bad thing."

I thanked him.

"No problem," he said with a quick smile. "Bridge gives lots of folks trouble."

I gathered up the empty cups and donut bags and chucked them in the trash. "I should've picked up gas masks while I was at it."

"You sure nothing died in here?" Paul asked as we cranked open the windows and let the arctic air blow through.

"Good question," I said, gulping down the rest of my coffee. "You check the front, I'll check the back. The boys can start washing down the walls with the bleach solution."

The boys were good workers, same as their father, and I used the time we were together to ask my questions. All three told the same story about the night they found Suzanne's body in the lake. They had been cutting through the woods with their father on the way home from their grandmother's house on the other side of Snow Lake. They had just stepped into the clearing when the younger of the two saw a pair of women's shoes on a bench near the closed skate rental shack.

"Anything unusual about that?"

Paul shrugged. "Not really. Full moon's coming, lots of light. There's always somebody looking to skate off a big dinner or a little tension."

They were about to continue on their way home when Paul noticed something strange near the middle of the ice. When you grew up skating on lakes and ponds, you learned to read the ice. You knew the weak spots, the last areas to hard freeze. The places to avoid. In early December, the center of the ice was one of those spots you treated with respect.

Suzanne should have known better but those margaritas had probably blunted her judgment. By the time they found her, it was too late.

Jeremy and Johnny split for school around eight thirty. Paul went off to open the hardware store at nine. I cleared away an abandoned squirrel nest near the boiler and swept out the store rooms. The combination of bleach and fresh air began to erase the pungent reminder of monkeys gone wild.

I dragged a few loads of trash out to the Dumpster in the back and saw that the lights were on at Sticks & Strings.

I still couldn't figure out what the hell had happened between Chloe and me last night or why. It was either the most powerful sexual chemistry on the planet or she was playing one damn strange game and I needed to learn the rules ASAP.

The one thing I did know, however, was that she had something to hide.

Everyone did. That was one of the first things I'd learned when I joined the force. We all had our secrets. There was no reason to think Chloe Hobbs was any exception.

I cleaned up in the reclaimed bathroom then crossed the yard to the knit shop and let myself in the front door. Penelope the cat wrapped herself around my ankles like a furry boa constrictor with an attitude.

Chloe appeared in the doorway, arms laden with what looked like half of a very colorful sheep.

"There's coffee in the kitchen," she said. "I have to get this shipment ready for UPS. You can set up your laptop at my desk until the workroom is free. And a fax for you came in. It's in the machine."

"Great," I said. "Want me to pick up some bagels from Fully Caffeinated?"

"Not for me but don't let that stop you."

It wasn't easy to look cool with a fifteen-pound cat on your foot but I gave it my best shot. "Listen," I said, "about last night—"

"You don't have to say anything. It was a mistake."

"I shouldn't have—"

"I didn't mean to—"

We were in each other's arms before we had finished our sentences. Whatever it was that had happened the night before was nothing compared to what was happening now. Sparks of gold and silver careened off the walls around us, lighting the room with their glow.

I knew it wasn't real. The feel of a woman's mouth against yours didn't send sparks flying around the room like flaming confetti on New Year's Eve, but it was one damn fine hallucination.

I don't know how long we stood there in the middle of her shop making out like teenagers, but when a cell phone rang, it took us both a few seconds to emerge from the sex haze we were in.

"Yours," she said, her mouth red and swollen from kisses. "Mine's in the workroom."

I unclipped my cell and glanced at the display.

"It's Randazzo," I said to Chloe. "I've got to take this."

She nodded. Her sweater had slid off one shoulder. Her hair was tousled. The look in her eyes could have melted steel.

Joe wasn't in a good mood. I stepped outside to talk. "I thought we'd see something from you this morning."

"I had a long night."

"Did you find anything out?"

"So far it's looking pretty open and shut."

"Accidental?"

"The stories are all consistent and they all point toward too many margaritas and bad judgment."

"Sieverts and his people have been on my ass. Her family's decided to have her body autopsied."

"You're kidding me."

There was a long silence. I didn't know Randazzo well but I had the feeling I wasn't going to like what he had to say. "Sieverts sent some people to talk them out of it, but now they're threatening to escalate the investigation."

Which meant I had better get my ass in gear before all hell broke loose.

I made the usual promises, but beneath it I felt sad for Suzanne and how her life had ended.

Randazzo gave me the tracking number for the office furniture they were sending down and a contact for vouchers. I was about to hang up when he said, "Tell Hobbs to check her voice mails. They're bugging my ass for those death records I asked for."

That grabbed my interest. "Don't they have those things digitized in Montpelier?"

"For every place but Sugar Maple. No records of births, deaths, marriages, it's like the town slipped between the cracks a few hundred years ago and stayed there."

"Nothing as in zero?"

"They're on the tax roles. They vote. The town's featured in those fancy travel magazines all the time. But as far as the state is concerned, nobody has ever been born or died in Sugar Maple since the date their charter was granted. Tell her to get on it before Montpelier does it for them."

More proof that there was something weird about the town that went beyond the lack of crime and the extreme good looks of its residents. I couldn't shake the sense that I had wandered onto a movie set.

I went back into the knit shop. Penny the cat was sleeping in the basket of fluffy stuff. Chloe was with a customer. Her back was to me as she explained something knitterly to the young woman. I'd catch her later.

Paul was standing in front of the pet store, smoking a cigarette. "Gotta air the place out," he said. "Johnny knocked over a bottle of solvent that could take out a city."

"Monkeys and petroleum by-products," I said, shaking my head. "It just gets better and better."

We agreed to meet up again later that afternoon after the latest stench had cleared.

I remembered seeing a cemetery somewhere beyond the Sugar Maple Arts Playhouse during my first drive-through. I didn't know exactly what I expected to find there or how it would pertain to Suzanne, but Randazzo's agitation over those missing death certificates had set the wheels spinning. Papers went missing. Digitized data got corrupted. People were born and they died. Even in beautiful little towns like Sugar Maple, death was a fact of life.

But I would feel a whole lot better when I saw the proof.

The day was cold but sunny so I figured I'd walk. I could use the exercise. As far as I knew, Sugar Maple didn't have a gym or health club, which struck me as strange, considering the level of physical perfection I had encountered in town.

I had rounded the corner near the Playhouse when a male voice sounded behind me.

"Hey, Luke, I thought that was you. How're you doing?"

It was one of the golden boys from last night.

"Not bad," I said. "You?"

I didn't have any trouble figuring out which twin I was talking to. I was happy to note that bright sunlight wasn't his friend. He looked worse than he had last night in the restaurant. Dark purple shadows made the lines under his eyes stand out even more, and a multicolored bruise outlined his swollen left cheek. I'll give him one thing though: even battered and bruised, he had that whole chiseled thing down cold.

"Holding steady. Where are you headed?"

They didn't waste much time on chitchat in Sugar Maple.

"Thought I'd walk around and get a feel for the town."

"Not much to see where you're headed except for the cemetery."

"I'm a history buff. I like old cemeteries."

I started walking again. He fell into step with me.

"Sugar Maple must seem pretty tame

after Boston." It hadn't taken him more than a handful of seconds to get to the point.

"I'm a cop," I said. "Tame is good."

"You don't think you'll get bored?"

It took me a while but I finally got the subtext. He was marking his territory in a beta kind of way. "I won't have time to get bored," I said. "This isn't a permanent gig."

"Then what?"

"Don't know," I said with a shrug. "I'll see what comes up." It was my turn to ask some questions. "So what do you do when you're not subbing at the restaurant?"

"Starving artist."

"Painter?"

"Painter, sculptor."

"Ever sell anything?" I was in full-on cop mode.

"To my brother," he said.

We both laughed. Or at least grunted in unison. It's a guy thing.

"I met him last night." I told him about seeing Dane (Dean? Dino?) coming out of the woods on cross-country skis.

"He's the outdoorsman," Gunnar said. "He wanted to play pro hockey when we were younger but it didn't work out."

We passed a few minutes talking about the relative worth of the NHL's finest.

I gestured toward his cheek. "So what happened?"

He grinned. "My brother wanted his money back."

It was a good line and we both laughed. But I knew that was his way of saying, "Back off." He was right. His family squabbles weren't any of my business.

"They told me at the Inn that you were working the kitchen the night Suzanne Marsden died."

"One of the line cooks took the night off."

"Got time for a few questions?"

"Sorry, dude. I've got a meeting with a gallery owner two towns over. I'll catch you later."

He peeled off like one of those fighter jets in *Top Gun* and disappeared around the corner. No problem. That wasn't the last I'd see of him.

As it turned out, I couldn't get near the cemetery. A county work crew had the area blocked off while they repaired some downed wires.

I asked the foreman when he figured the job would be done.

"Hoping for tomorrow," he said, "but I said that two days ago and we still can't get the son of a bitch up and running."

Call me crazy but I was dead sure Chloe's pal Goober was laughing his golden ass off right about now. Score one for the local boy.

I had some time to waste before the appointment with Janice Meany at Cut & Curl so I settled in to watch the work crew do its thing while bits and pieces of information I'd gathered so far formed and re-formed patterns that still didn't make sense. But sooner or later they would.

"Hey!" the foreman yelled. "Look out!"

I barely had time to hit the ground as a cable sliced the air where I had been standing a half second ago.

"Holy shit," one of the workmen said. "Is he dead?"

"He could've been fried," another workman chimed in.

"Sorry," the foreman said as I cautiously stood up and brushed off the snow. "You've got yourself some good reflexes, pal."

I made all of those macho "no big deal" sounds that went with laughing in the face of danger, but the truth was Joe Randazzo

had come damn close to getting his second death certificate in less than a week.

I wondered if he would have appreciated the irony.

With the cable snapping and crackling
less than three feet away from where I
was standing, I wasn't sure I did.

CHLOE

Luke had been outside for a good ten minutes when I finally got tired of trying to
eavesdrop and went into the kitchen to pour
myself a cup of coffee. The same weird
feelings I had experienced last night were
back with a vengeance. A visit to WebMD
had reassured me that I wasn't approach-
ing an extremely early menopause, but
something was definitely wreaking havoc
with my equilibrium. I felt dizzy and un-
steady on my feet.

Then again, it was hard to breathe and
kiss at the same time. I was probably still
oxygen deprived.

I still wasn't exactly sure how it had happened. I mean, my arms had been piled

high with an outgoing shipment of kettle-dyed DK weight Blue-faced Leicester, and anyone who knew me knew that nothing short of nuclear Armageddon would make me sacrifice one fuzzy, fibery gram of the stuff for anything as fleeting and insubstantial as a kiss.

But when Luke MacKenzie walked into the shop this morning and looked at me with those bottle green eyes, I might as well have been carrying a load of acrylic for all I cared. The yarn went flying as I flew into his arms.

If Luke had been selkie or vampire or something normal like that, I would have suspected there was a spell at work creating the fireworks between us, the impossible-to-resist magnetism, but nobody in Sugar Maple, not even Isadora, would do anything to encourage a mortal to hang around any longer than necessary.

I poured a mug of coffee. I arranged some stale donuts on a platter. Today's edition of the *Sugar Maple Gazette* arrived, and I flipped it open to the obituary page, which was an obituary page in name only. The space had been sold to Griggs Hardware to advertise their Christmas extravaganza sale.

How long a lead time did they have at the paper? Six hours. Ten? Anything could have happened since press time.

I dialed Pam at Sugar Maple Assisted Living.

"I know this sounds crazy, Pam, but has anyone . . . left us in the last day or two?"

"Nobody's left us since Sorcha, and you know how long ago that was. They fade in, they fade out, but when all is said and done, everyone's still here."

Assuming they even existed, there had to be a statute of limitations on banshee wails. If you heard a banshee on the first Thursday in January and your Great-Uncle Harry died on the last Friday in March, did the banshee really deserve props or was it just coincidence at work? I came down on the side of coincidence.

Just thinking about the whole mess made my head hurt.

But then again, so did breathing.

No more Barolo. No more brandy.

Ever.

I opened a can of Fancy Feast for Penny. I searched three of the storage closets for the Book of Spells and came up empty each time.

Finally I couldn't stand it any longer and I went back up front to spy on him.

But there was one small problem: he wasn't there.

I opened the door and stepped outside. He wasn't on the sidewalk. He wasn't in the pet shop. I looked up the street toward Town Hall then down toward Snow Lake but there wasn't a sign of him anywhere.

Not that he had to check in with me or anything, but a quick "I'm off to look for some crime" might have been nice.

Lynette popped in around eleven thirty with sandwiches from the coffee shop on the corner.

"Where's Janice?" I asked, tucking into a huge tuna salad on rye.

"She shooed me out. The cop is on his way over to question her about that night."

We grabbed our sandwiches and took up our positions at the front window.

"Look," I said, gesturing with my garlic dill. "Is that him in the chair?"

"She's giving him a haircut," Lynette said. "I swear that woman could sell conditioner to a bald man."

"I would have figured him for a barber shop kind of guy," I said, watching as Janice drew a comb through his thick, dark hair.

"When in Rome," Lynette said with a laugh. "I wonder if I could convince him to understudy the Ghost of Christmas Present. We wouldn't have to worry about alterations. He's almost as tall as Gus Ekstrom."

We bantered back and forth as we watched Janice talk his ears off.

"She's finished," I said. "Do you think she'll charge him?"

"He'll be lucky if she doesn't tack on a surcharge for the Q and A."

My cell phone rang as Janice started to brush the back of his neck and unwind the protective collar.

Joe Randazzo. The last person I wanted to talk to.

"What's up, Joe?" I sounded easygoing, friendly, totally phony.

"Didn't MacKenzie give you my message? I've been waiting for your call."

"I haven't seen him since he stepped outside to take your call." I didn't have a good feeling about where this was going.

"I need those death certs yesterday."

"Listen, Joe, about those records. We started storing everything off-site a few years ago, but unfortunately the head of our Bureau of . . . Vital Statistics is the one with the information."

"So ask him."

"Ask her," I corrected him. "Lilith is on a religious retreat in India and can't be reached." I was making it up as I went along, praying Joe would swallow it whole.

"There must be some way to reach her. What if there was a family emergency?"

"That's the point of the retreat, Joe. You step away from the world and refresh your soul. No phones. No mail. No Internet. Just you and your consciousness."

"And when does Gandhi come home?"

"After the New Year." I knew enough about governmental bureaucracies to know that emergencies usually faded away after a few weeks. And if this one didn't, my fabrication would give me time to come up with a new excuse.

He wasn't entirely receptive, but at least he didn't threaten us with the National Guard for noncompliance.

"Not bad," Lynette said as I disconnected. "I didn't know you had it in you."

"Neither did I." I looked toward Cut & Curl. "He's gone!"

"And he didn't look happy," Lynette said. "She probably suggested highlights."

"Which way did he go?" I sounded like the sheriff in a bad Western.

"I don't know," she said. "I turned away to see what Penny was doing, and when I turned back, he was gone." She patted my arm. "Honey, you can't keep your eyes on him every second. He lives here now. You can't lock him up next door for the next few months."

"There you go reading my mind again."

We both laughed but Lynette was right. I couldn't track him 24/7, but as de facto mayor and resident human, I owed it to the town to give it my best shot.

"I'd better tell Lilith she's at an ashram in India before Randazzo tracks her down and blows our cover."

"Go," Lynette said. "I'll watch the store."

See what I mean? My friends always had my back.

Lilith looked up as I burst into the library and beamed the kind of smile that made you feel good for hours. I know trolls don't have the greatest reputation for hospitality and good manners, but Lilith, with her Norwegian background, was definitely the exception.

Sometimes I wondered if I had a little troll lurking in my DNA along with the (clearly recessive) sorceress gene. I didn't even take a second to say hello.

"Lilith, I don't know how to tell you this, but if Joe Randazzo from the County Seat calls, you're not here."

She blinked. "Where am I?"

"You're at an ashram in India and you won't be back until after New Year's."

"If I'm in India, who's answering the phone?"

It was my turn to blink. "I don't know. I haven't had time to think that far ahead."

"Any particular reason I'm in India?"

"You went to raise your consciousness and connect with a higher power."

"I mean is there any particular reason

why you want Joe Randazzo to *think* I'm in India?"

Bless Lilith, she got it before I was half-way through the story.

"No problem." She closed her eyes for a second, opened them, and started speaking in a rhythm and accent I had never heard before. "My Norse grandmother Dyrfinna will be happy to handle all phone calls."

It was all I could do to keep from leaping across the desk and grabbing her in a bear hug.

I was starting to think that maybe we would make it through this turmoil in one piece when Lilith gestured toward the Archive Room at the rear of the library. "Our new policeman has been back there for an hour. He's quite the cutie, isn't he?"

"Lilith!" I struggled to keep from shouting. "Are you crazy?"

"What choice did I have? He's the law, honey."

"How could you let him go back there alone?"

She leaned across the desk and drew me closer. "Don't worry," she whispered. "I ran a spell-check before I unlocked the door and it's in full force. He won't be able to see anything more than old newspaper clippings, census reports, some maps, that sort of thing."

In Sugar Maple, *spell-check* meant something Bill Gates had never dreamed of.

If you wanted to find out everything you needed to know about Sugar Maple, the library was where you'd do it. Giving Luke access to the original Town Charter (not the one we post for public consumption) and the List of Passages that contained records of every village birth and leave-taking was like striking a match next to a leaky gas line.

They say that in times of danger your entire life passes before your eyes, and at that moment, it was true. I was treated to a highlight reel of my thirty years on the planet as I raced down the hall to the Archive Room, praying Aerynn's spell would keep us safe a little bit longer.

14

LUKE

I heard Chloe before I saw her. In less than two days the sound of her footsteps had imprinted itself on me. She walked with a syncopated rhythm that was as unique to her as the smell of her skin or those huge, deep gold eyes.

Or the way her hair felt like spun silk between my fingers . . . or the warmth of her mouth or—

If there had been an ice bucket handy, I would have dumped it over my head.

She appeared in the doorway looking a

lot less friendly than she had a few hours ago, and I felt the molecules beginning to rearrange themselves around us.

"Why didn't you give me Joe Randazzo's message?" she demanded.

"Sorry," I said. "It slipped my mind."

"If you're looking for Sugar Maple's records, they're not here." She walked over to the table where I was sitting and glanced down at the array of books and papers spread out in front of me. "And you won't find birth or marriage records either." She gave me a wide, totally fake smile. "Just in case you were looking for them too."

"I wasn't but now you've got me curious. If they're not here, where are they?"

"They're being digitized at an off-site storage facility."

"Randazzo seems to have a bug up his ass about them."

"I know," she said, fingering the diagram of the cemetery I hadn't gotten to yet, "but he'll have to wait awhile longer. All these years and nobody ever once questioned our record-keeping abilities. Now he wants them yesterday."

Randazzo had learned his people skills at the Idi Amin School of Diplomacy.

Splotches of high color stained her cheeks. Her voice was tighter than usual. She kept twisting the gold band on her right index finger. A body language expert would have a field day with her.

I almost felt guilty for knocking her off-balance with my question. "Do you ice skate?"

"Not if I can help it. Where did that question come from?"

"Did you know that there had never been an accident of any kind at Snow Lake before Suzanne?"

She shrugged her shoulders. "I guess I never really thought about it."

That seemed to be the default answer to most questions around Sugar Maple.

"It sees a lot of traffic. Kids, hockey games, figure skaters practicing their spins. But until the other night, nobody so much as twisted an ankle on the ice. What's up with that?"

"Maybe we're amazingly agile."

"You don't think it's strange?"

"Whoa," she said, taking a step back. "You mean you really want an answer?"

"I'm a cop. I always want an answer."

"We've taken our share of tumbles," she

said, watching me closely. "We just don't feel the need to record them for posterity."

"Anything else you don't feel the need to record for posterity?"

"More questions, Detective?" She said it lightly but there was no denying the sharp edge behind her words. "Listen, I know what this is about. No judgment, but your friend was seeing a married politician and you've been sent here to clean up his mess so he can run for governor. I get it. But don't try to blame us for something that was clearly an accident."

"Where the hell did you hear that?" More to the point, how had she got it so right?

"Cops aren't the only ones with sources. We might be a small town but we have a long reach."

There was a cynicism to her words that stung, and I found myself wanting to explain myself to her.

"I don't know what else you heard, but I didn't come here to help Sieverts," I said. "I came here because it was Suzanne."

We looked at each other and the desire to take her right there on the cluttered tabletop started to burn away brain cells.

"I know that too."

"What else do you know?" I asked.

"That you'll be gone as soon as you wind up the investigation."

"Temporary's good," I said, "as long as everyone understands the rules."

"I don't do temporary," she said. "That's *my* rule."

Her hands were braced against the table. I placed my right hand on top of hers, and a quick burst of silver-gold sparks appeared right on schedule.

"Try to explain that," I challenged her.

She pulled her hand away. "Long winters, dry heat. I told you that last time."

"And I'm still not buying it."

"What do you want me to say?"

"That you know something's happening between us."

"How would that make a difference?"

"It would make me feel like I wasn't going nuts."

She was silent for a moment, then: "You're not going nuts."

I waited for the sense of vindication but it didn't come. Instead the room seemed to be growing smaller, bringing us closer together in a way I didn't understand.

"This isn't what I want," she said.

"Me neither."

"Then what are we doing? Why do we keep ending up—"

I stood and pulled her into my arms. "Like this?"

"Yes," she whispered. "Exactly like this."

CHLOE

I tried to tell myself this was another diversionary tactic, like taking the offense or tackling him to the ground, that I had designed to draw his attention away from digging deeper into Sugar Maple's secrets, but even I wasn't buying it.

The truth was I couldn't help myself.

And in case you were wondering, that wasn't hyperbole. I literally couldn't keep myself away from him. It had to be some strange offshoot of the protective charm at work because nothing this powerful, this core shaking, could possibly exist without magick.

In a perfect world, he might have been The One. Yes, I had known him only a handful of days. It was too soon. I knew too little. I wanted too much. But that didn't change the fact that he was The One I had been waiting for. The legendary Mr. Right you always hoped was just around the corner.

And how thoughtful of whatever magickal forces were at work that they picked a great kisser. If this was as far as it was going to go—and believe me, I was all about setting limits—this was just about as good as it gets.

I was sinking deeper into his kisses, getting lost in the heat, when I opened my eyes and saw Gunnar watching us from the hallway.

Luke and I leaped apart like guilty high school kids.

"Sorry," Gunnar said, looking both embarrassed and a little hurt. "I was in the back making copies. I didn't know you were here."

"I thought you had a meeting." Luke didn't sound very friendly.

"Canceled," Gunnar said. "I figured I'd use the time to knock off some paperwork."

"How do you know Gunnar had a meeting?" I asked Luke.

Gunnar was right there with the answer.

"I bumped into Sugar Maple's finest near Carrier and Martin. I think he was on his way to the cemetery."

"The cemetery?" I turned to Luke. "Why were you going to the cemetery?"

Luke turned to Gunnar. "I didn't say I was headed for the cemetery. I said I was going for a walk."

"Sorry," Gunnar said again. "I could have sworn you said you were headed for the cemetery."

"You were the one who pointed out I was headed for the cemetery," Luke said. "Not me."

"Did you go to the cemetery?" I asked Luke. I wouldn't have believed the human heart could beat so fast and not explode.

He glanced pointedly in Gunnar's direction. "The road was blocked. A power company crew was trying to fix some downed wires."

"That's news to me," Gunnar said.

"They told me they've been out there for two days."

Gunnar looked over at me. "Did you know?"

"No," I said through gritted teeth. "I didn't."

I don't know what they taught them in Boy School, but pissing contests weren't all that much fun to watch.

Gunnar didn't move. Luke didn't blink. It was like being trapped in a room with a pair of crash-test dummies. I knew that Luke was being all territorial and Gunnar was being protective, but enough was enough. Sooner or later a girl had to take a stand.

"You know what?" I said. "I have a business to run."

And it would have been a terrific exit line if I hadn't bumped into the table and sent all of the maps and graphs and extracts sliding to the ground.

I should have stopped and helped Luke pick them up but I didn't. I shoved past Gunnar, stormed past Lilith, and pushed my way out the door into a minor snowstorm and a sidewalk thick with tourists.

I dashed across the street and into Sticks & Strings, where I had left poor Lynette to hold down the fort.

"Thanks a lot," Lynette grumbled as she grabbed her coat from the hook near the door. "You missed a vanload of seniors from New Hampshire on a yarn crawl.

They'll be back around four. And that doesn't count the walk-ins."

I showered her with thanks and apologies, which she brushed off with good-natured humor.

"Just make sure you're front row center tomorrow night for the opening," she said, then raced off to the final dress rehearsal for this year's *A Christmas Carol.*

"I promise." She was my friend so I didn't tell her I had seen so many performances of her Mrs. Fezziwig that I could recite the lines with her.

I had lied to a county official, pissed off my closest friends, and left the man who could blow our cover alone in the library with access to everything he needed to destroy our way of life forever. And it wasn't even three o'clock yet.

I flipped through the pile of messages on the counter. A question about Fiesta La Boheme in the Alaska colorway. Two workshop requests. One very annoyed knitter in California demanding to know where her order was. If I returned the call now in the mood I was in, I would probably bite their heads off and leave 'em for dead.

One of my regulars popped in for a skein

of Debbie Bliss Cashmerino in a gorgeous mossy shade of green. Fortunately she wasn't in the mood to chat.

I rattled around the store, unable to settle down to any one task. I knew I should be tearing the place apart looking for the Book of Spells, but my hands itched to start another pair of socks. Penny was playing in the corner with a catnip-filled mouse one of my regulars had knitted for her so I used the opportunity to fluff up the roving in my mother's basket.

Usually the roving fluffed back to full abundance the moment Penny leaped out of the basket, but today, for some reason, it hadn't. I bent down and moved things around a little, but there was no denying that for the first time I could remember there was less roving there today than there had been yesterday, which was further proof that my entire life was spinning out of control and all I could think about was whether to cast on toe up or top down.

In my defense, it was a great pair of socks. I had used roving from my mother's stash, hand-painted it in the colors of a Hawaiian sunset, then spun it into a lovely (if I do say so myself) fingering weight yarn. I wasn't up for anything difficult, just a plain old cuff-down stockinette, but by the time I finished the 2/2 ribbing and had launched myself down the leg, the world was beginning to make sense again.

The thing about working a basic sock was the way it freed your mind to roam. If I were Sorcha, where would I have hidden the Book of Spells? Closets were too easy. Basements flooded. A safe-deposit box was too bureaucratic. Her cottage had been absorbed into the next dimension with her so I could scratch that off my list. Which pretty much left 98 percent of Sugar Maple to be searched.

"Are you speaking to me now?"

I jumped at the sound of Gunnar's voice.

"Quit sneaking up on me," I said, irritated. "Somebody should force Fae to wear cow bells." He was standing a few feet away from me, snow glittering in his hair and across his shoulders. He looked tired, uncertain, very much my dear friend, and my heart melted.

"So are you speaking to me?" he asked again.

"I shouldn't be but I am." I motioned for

him to take off his coat and hang it up. "There's coffee in the back. Help yourself."

He did, then sat down across the worktable from me. "Go ahead," he said with a weary smile. "Unload on me."

"That wasn't funny back there, Gunnar. That was the human equivalent of bearbaiting."

"Harmless male jousting."

"I'm not talking about the pissing contest," I snapped. "I'm talking about the phony road crew and the downed wires."

"I thought you'd thank me."

"Thank you?" My head was threatening to explode. "You were at the Town Hall meeting. We agreed we were going to stay away from magick tricks. The last thing we need is for him to start seeing Sugar Maple through curious eyes."

"Think about it," Gunnar said. "The state wants to see our death certificates and the new cop was heading over to the cemetery. Do you really want him to start matching names and dates?"

"How did you do it?" I asked. "Some kind of spell?"

"The Pendragon boys owed me a favor."

"What if he decides to go back to the cemetery tomorrow?"

"Then we come up with Plan B."

"I hate this," I said. "I wish Suzanne Marsden had never set foot in Sugar Maple."

"So do I," Gunnar said. "So do I."

There was something about his tone that made me shiver. The fact that he looked like he was in pain didn't help. We sipped our coffees in silence for a few minutes.

"Wait a second!" I put my mug down on the tabletop. "If you don't do spells, how do you explain the flying brandy snifter last night?"

He looked at me with a blank expression. "What flying brandy snifter?"

"The one that hovered over the dinner table like a helicopter then dropped into the cop's lap."

"I'd be glad to take credit for it but unfortunately I'm not responsible."

"You have to be. I mean, who else could have done it?"

"Maybe it was you."

I thanked him for my first laugh of the day.

"Something's different, Chloe," he said. "I think you're getting your powers."

"If I had powers, I wouldn't be tearing through the shop looking for the Book of Spells, would I?"

That got his attention. "What do you mean, looking for it?"

"If you'd bothered to answer my call last night, you would know what I'm talking about."

"You called?"

"Twice," I said. "And Janice used blue-flame."

He looked puzzled. "I didn't get any messages."

I gave him the abridged version.

He was up to speed in an instant. "I'll search the old church and the cottages in the woods. We have to find it as soon as possible. I've never seen Isadora this driven."

That was one of the many things I loved about Gunnar. When times were tough, I could always count on him.

"There's no way I'm going to let that woman get her—" An odd expression crossed his beautiful face, and I felt my own face grow hot with embarrassment. "I'm sorry. She's your mother. I should have—"

He reached for my hand. "No apologies. Not between us."

The touch of his hand was comforting and as familiar as the touch of my own. We were friends. Friends sometimes held hands or threw their arms around each other. Casual. Spontaneous. Not even remotely romantic.

But this was different. His touch was different. I tried to gently slide my hand out from under his but he increased the pressure slightly, just enough to let me know this was significant.

"Gunnar." My tone was light but regretful. "Nothing's changed."

"You have," he said. "I'm losing you."

I started to say that he couldn't possibly lose me because I had never been his to lose in the first place, but this wasn't the time for a semantics debate. He pushed back his chair and drew me to my feet next to him.

"I wish I felt the way you want me to feel, but I don't." And I never would. There weren't many things I knew for sure in this always-changing world, but the impossibility of Gunnar and me was one of them.

I also knew why this was happening now. Suzanne's death had set off a chain reaction in Sugar Maple that Luke's presence was intensifying to an alarming degree. We were all trying to hang on to the safe and familiar for as long as we could.

He moved closer and this time I didn't move away. I had to make sure or I would spend the rest of my life wondering. He was Gunnar. He was part of my childhood, part of my life. And if there was even the slightest chance for a future with him, I needed to find out.

He kissed me with more passion and more heat than I had expected, but for me there were no fireworks, no sparks, no melting into him. Nothing that would ever make the loneliness go away.

He was my best friend, and no matter how much I might wish otherwise, that was what he would always be.

"I'm sorry," I said, resting my forehead against his chest. "Really sorry."

I couldn't look at him. Call me a coward but I just couldn't do it.

"I'm not going to give up," he said. "We could make a life together, Chloe, right here in Sugar Maple."

Oh, how I wished I could hand him my heart. There were no secrets between us. We were both part of Sugar Maple. We both wanted the same things. If only that were enough.

He held me close for a second and then pushed me away.

"The cop won't be around forever," he said, "but I will."

15

LUKE

The librarian kicked me out right after Chloe made her abrupt exit.

"I asked you to treat our documents with respect," she said with more heat than you would expect to find in an academic type.

I made the mistake of pointing out that Chloe was the one who had knocked the documents off the table, which earned a snicker from Goober and another severe reprimand from the surprisingly fiery librarian.

I decided to cut my losses and save my

research for another day. Besides I had managed to filch a stack of newspaper clippings and hidden them under my jacket. The Griggs Hardware truck was parked in front of the old pet shop. Wiping monkey spit off the walls sounded pretty damn good to me right about then.

"Johnny went out for pizza," Paul said as I shrugged out of my jacket and grabbed a paint brush. "Pepperoni and mushroom."

"Great."

There were no crazy sparks flying around the room. No golden-boy agenda. We didn't have to talk. Paul had his radio tuned to one of those oldies stations. Hell, if he cranked it up a few decibels higher, we wouldn't even have to think.

I wouldn't miss it. So far thinking hadn't been getting me anywhere. Talking to Janice hadn't yielded anything new beyond a haircut I didn't need and some unsolicited romantic advice about steering clear of Chloe.

I had a few dozen people left to question but I didn't expect any smoking guns. The signs still pointed toward an accidental drowning with no evidence of any complicity on the part of her boyfriend,

Dan Sieverts. He was turning out to be nothing more than your average self-serving politician on the rise.

"Shit."

Paul, who was patching some drywall, shot me a look. "What?"

"Do you have a number for . . ." Goober. Gomer. What the hell was his name? "Gonner?"

"Gunnar," he said, barely suppressing a grin. "No number but I could pass on a message."

"E-mail address?"

"Sorry."

"Chloe probably has his number," I said, stripping off the plastic painting gloves and tossing them in the trash. "Be right back."

I didn't bother with a jacket. That was my first mistake. The temperature had dropped a good ten degrees thanks to a squirrely wind that whipped the snow into minitwisters. The few feet between buildings felt like a trek across frozen tundra.

Second mistake?

I didn't knock.

I'd been sucker-punched a few times in my life, ambushed in a drug raid, clubbed in the gut with a two-by-four that sent me flying.

Good times compared to the sight of Chloe in his arms.

They looked great together. They were both tall. Both blond. Their kids, if they had any, would look like movie stars, just like everyone else in this town.

So much for thinking we had some crazy kind of chemistry going between us. The woman had chemistry with every guy in town. Hell, her knit shop was starting to look like a female version of the Playboy Mansion.

I let myself out the back door.

The sad part was they were so caught up in each other that they never even knew I'd been there.

"Get what you wanted?" Paul asked as I knocked snow off my shoulders.

"More." A monosyllable was the best I could do.

"You left your cell here. It's been beeping its ass off."

The phone was buried under a pile of crap in the anteroom between the bathroom and a store room.

The screen was black. I toggled the switch. Still nothing. The sound Paul heard must have been the low battery warning. Too bad I'd left the charger cord back at the motel. I dug deeper into the pile and found my Blackberry but it was dead. I pulled my laptop out of its case and pressed the ON button. I wasn't surprised when nothing happened there either.

I dragged everything to the front. "Do you have trouble with electronic equipment up here?"

Paul shrugged. "Some. A big storm will knock us out of service."

I gestured toward the snow swirling outside. "Is that big enough?"

He laughed. "Not even close."

I told him about my graveyard of dead electronics.

"The wiring in this place sucks. You probably shorted out when you were recharging the batteries," he said. "You met Lilith, didn't you?"

"Not one of my biggest fans."

"Her husband, Archie, keeps most of our stuff up and running. You should let him take a look."

"Where do I find him?"

I thought I caught a little hesitation but it was gone before I could be sure.

"Archie's is on the town side of the bridge. You can't miss it."

I grabbed for a jacket. "Save me some pizza."

"No guarantees," Paul said with a laugh. "I've got teenagers."

I glanced through the window of Sticks & Strings as I walked past. Chloe was talking to a trio of women who seemed to be hanging on her every word. She looked up and for a second our eyes met but I kept walking.

CHLOE

"Chloe!" The woman's voice was sharp. "You're not listening to me. I still don't understand how you make I-cord stick to the edging."

I was a half step away from telling her to try duct tape when I caught myself. "Let's go over to the worktable, Millie, and I'll show you."

That was when I looked up and saw Luke walk past the window. He glanced in and his eyes settled on me briefly but there was no smile. No wave of the hand. Not even a scowl.

Fine.

Great.

Whatever.

The last thing we needed in this town was another man with an attitude.

No, scratch that. The last thing we needed was a cop with an attitude.

I went on autopilot as I explained the intricacies of applied I-cord to the gaggle of knitters at the table. This whole thing with Luke was my fault. After years of dating selkies and shifters and the occasional troll, the lure of my own kind had been as intense as it was immediate.

And totally irresistible.

I couldn't stay away from him. Put us within ten feet of each other and I flew into his arms like metal to a magnet. The only thing keeping me in my seat right now was the fact that I had three paying customers who would beat me senseless with US15s if I tried to escape before they mastered idiot cord.

It would take more than some wimpy 15s to stop me.

I pushed back my chair and stood up. "Okay, you're doing great. Now we'll need a good twelve inches of cord before we move on."

"You're leaving?" The youngest of the three looked up at me, wide-eyed. "What if we have trouble?"

"I . . . I saw the mail carrier and I have a package that needs to go out right now. I'll be back in a second."

They nodded because, after all, Sticks & Strings was known for top-notch customer service.

I grabbed a poncho from my samples shelf, yanked it over my head, then raced out the door. Where had all of this snow come from? The white stuff swirled all around me, obstructing my vision, making it hard to keep my footing on the slippery sidewalk. I slid past knots of jubilant tourists who were over the moon to be in Vermont on a snowy day in December; I was determined not to let him out of my sight.

He was a football field ahead of me, striding toward Osborne, and I broke into a run. Bad idea. My right foot slid out from under me and the next instant I went airborne.

Visions of broken bones and long recuperations filled my head. The word *No* blossomed inside my chest, growing louder and louder. *No* I wouldn't fall. *No* I refused to give in to the laws of physics and the lure of gravity.

No . . . No . . . No . . .

I was an instant, a heartbeat, away from slamming into the ground when Sorcha, my surrogate mother, moved past my field of vision. I missed her so much I thought my heart was about to break.

This is your future, Chloe . . . Don't be afraid . . .

Time stopped. The street fell quiet. The bustling tourists stopped bustling and stood frozen in space. Down the block Luke paused midstride near the café.

Me? Well, I was suspended in midair like one of those Cirque du Soleil performers who defy gravity and anatomy on a daily basis. I twisted a little to the left, reorienting myself with the ground, and the next thing I knew I was sitting on the snowy sidewalk while a very puzzled Luke looked down at me as the street came back to life.

He wasn't the only one who was puz-

zled. I had just performed acrobatic ma-
neuvers in midair and watched a grown
man levitate the length of a football field
during a snowstorm while forty or fifty people didn't notice anything at all.

"Chloe?"

"Hi." It was the best I could do.

"Are you okay?"

"I think so."

I waited for him to ask how he had managed to fly backward up the street but he
didn't. He looked a little woozy, a tiny bit
off-bubble, but the fact that he had been
yanked one hundred yards by forces beyond imagination just plain refused to register on his wonderfully human brain.

I realized that basically he hadn't a clue.

He looked down at me. I looked up at
him. Neither one of us seemed to know
what to do next until his latent chivalric in-
stinct surfaced through the fog of confu-
sion around us.

"Need a hand?"

I waved him off. I scrambled to my knees
and pushed up, but my hands slipped and I
went splat. I maneuvered myself into position again, slipped again, went splat again.

"Chloe," he said, "take my hand."

Oh, I wanted to. I wanted to touch him again. I wanted to feel his warmth against me. I wanted . . . everything. The whole big fat dream life every thirty-year-old single girl with cats wanted: the husband, the kids, the Golden Retriever, the house with the white picket fence.

The normal.

The regular.

The impossible.

I pictured myself upright, focused myself on the image, and suddenly there I was, standing next to Luke.

"What the hell was that?"

I never played the blond card but there was always a first time. "What was what?"

"What you just did." He made a swirling motion with his hand. "How did you do that?"

I shrugged as the wind blew snow all around us. "You mean, stand up? It's a great skill. I've had it for a long time."

"I've seen people stand up before. That's not what you did."

"I was sitting and now I'm vertical. Somewhere in there I must have stood up."

Too bad I went one step too far. I improvised a little dance step, my feet went out from under me, and I was halfway to being on my butt when he caught me.

You know the falling dream, the one where you're tumbling through space faster and faster and you start yelling to your sleeping self, "Wake up! Wake up!" even though you know it's only a dream and nothing bad can happen to you?

Well, it was like that except it was real. I *was* falling. Faster and harder than I had ever dreamed, faster and harder than anything I'd ever read about in a book or cried over in a movie.

And he caught me before I hit the ground. Sparks shot out from our fingertips, our eyelashes, the ends of our hair. Snow melted at our feet.

Or did it? We moved apart and everything was the way it had been. No sparks. No fireworks. No melted snow. Just Luke and I looking at each other across a divide wider than he could possibly imagine.

"I—I have to get back to the shop."

"I saw you with him."

My breath caught. "I didn't see you."

"You were kissing him. Is that how you treat all your friends?"

"I needed to be sure about something and now I am."

"Good," he said. "Glad you two worked it out."

Now was the time to tell him that I had kissed Gunnar only because I wanted to be sure he wasn't the one, but the words wouldn't come. For weeks I had sensed change was in the air, but I never thought I would be the one to do the changing.

"I'd better go. I left my customers struggling with some I-cord."

"Yeah," he said. "I'd better get going too."

"I'm closing early," I rambled on. "If you need to work or anything, I'll leave a key on the ledge near the back door."

"Sounds good," he said.

And that was that.

LUKE

What the hell had just happened?

One second I was about to turn right onto Osborne and the next I was a hundred yards away picking Chloe up from the ground and there was nothing in between, no memory of getting myself from Point A to Point B.

I mean, I walked it. I knew I walked it. This wasn't the *Starship Enterprise*. Nobody had beamed me aboard. So why the hell couldn't I remember doing it?

It was either love or insanity, and I was coming down hard on the side of insanity. I already knew I didn't do love and I had the divorce to prove it.

I slogged up Osborne through the snow until I reached the foot of the bridge. I saw a dry cleaners and a post office substation but no repair shop. Maybe there was another bridge on the other side of town that I hadn't seen. I spotted a memorial plaque screwed to the side. Toothaker Bridge. Weird name but familiar. I had probably seen it on one of the maps I'd briefly looked at earlier that afternoon in the library.

The snowfall was moving swiftly from moderate to heavy. Visibility was disappearing almost as fast. If I wanted to get back to the motel tonight, I'd better close up the shop, then head out before I ended up spending the night there.

I muttered a few inventive curses as I pushed into the wind. I also gained a new appreciation for those Big Foot down coats and the art of layering. Hell, a pair of gloves and snow boots would have been a good start.

I cut across Bishop Drive and was half-way to the corner of Goode when a big blue minivan angled to a stop in front of me. The driver side window whirred down and Lynette, the Catherine Zeta-Jones look-alike, gave me a big smile.

"I thought that was you. Hop in before you turn into a popsicle."

She had the heat in the minivan cranked up so it felt like the inside of a pizza oven.

"Thanks," I said, unzipping my jacket. "It's intense out there."

"What on earth were you doing down here dressed like that?"

I told her about the dead electronics. "Paul said there was a shop near the foot of the bridge but I couldn't find it."

"Archie's," she said, nodding. "It's tucked away so far even the townies can't find it." She flashed me a wide smile. "We always have trouble with storms. I'll bet if you tried your phone again, it would be working."

"Not a chance. I got the cell equivalent of the Blue Screen of Death."

"Go on," she urged. "Give it a try. You might be surprised."

Surprised was an understatement. The cell, the Blackberry, and the laptop all worked fine.

"Thanks," I said, shaking my head in amazement.

"For what? I didn't do anything."

Unless she had magic powers, she was right. "Okay, then thanks for the lift."

"See that envelope hanging out of the glove box? Reach in and take two tickets for tomorrow's opening night performance and then you can thank me."

I pulled out two theater tickets emblazoned with drawings of Christmas trees and mistletoe.

"You're Mrs. Fezziwig, right?"

"You remembered!" She beamed at me. "I'll make sure you're seated right up front."

The last place I wanted to be tomorrow night was front row center at a community theater for another version of Dickens's Christmas classic. Unless I ended up snowed in and unable to escape Sugar Maple's gravity field, I would need to find a good excuse for not showing up.

"Chloe will be there too."

Another reason to stay away.

"She's going with Janice's cousin Haydon." She offered a radiant smile. "It's a blind date."

On second thought, maybe I'd give the theater another try.

16

CHLOE—LATER THAT EVENING

I'm not sure if denial is a skill or an unfortunate personality quirk, but I was pretty good at it. I mean, what else could explain my uncanny ability to pretend I hadn't just made a man sail backward up the block or caused my own self to perform circus tricks in midair during a miniblizzard?

So this was really happening. It wasn't a dream. It just felt so . . . ordinary. Shouldn't a woman feel at least a little bit different, a little bit more magickal, when she became a sorceress-in-training?

Instead I just felt like me, a skinny blonde with small boobs, big feet, and a whole lot of questions that needed answers.

If you saw me at Sticks & Strings later that afternoon, you would never know that, after thirty years, my powers were starting to kick in. I finished the impromptu I-cord class and sold an insane amount of twelve-ply cashmere to a woman from Toronto. I washed cups and cookie platters, settled receipts, packed three sock-of-the-month kits for mailing in the morning. I cleaned Penny's box, fed her, then checked the basket of roving. It still looked a tad depleted and an uneasy feeling settled itself across my shoulders, but I pushed it aside and closed for the day.

For once I refused to feel guilty about it. Only a Yeti would venture out in this weather, and last I heard they weren't big knitters.

The thought of walking home through the storm made me want to crawl into the nearest igloo and sleep away the rest of the winter but the strangest thing happened: instead of sinking into the snow with every step, I floated above it.

Okay, maybe every third or fourth step I

sank down in a half foot of powder, but for the most part I pretty much glided home until I was about two hundred feet from my front door and my budding powers quit on me without warning. I slogged the rest of my way through the drifts under my own (very human) power and collapsed in a heap inside the front door.

The cats were less interested in my semifrozen state than they were in prodding me toward the kitchen, and I obliged.

Outside the winds howled. Snow splattered against the windows. I changed into my oldest, warmest robe, lit a fire in the hearth, and then curled up in my favorite chair, where I devoured an entire bag of Chips Ahoy then upped my daily calcium intake with a Ben & Jerry's chaser.

The sugar and fat high helped me ignore the fact that the contents of my utensil drawer were working a conga line across the floor and that a dozen watch caps in varying stages of completion were knitting themselves in my work basket.

I stepped over the dancing whisks and ladles and waddled into the kitchen to break a few legs off the gingerbread men Lilith gave me the night of the Town Hall meeting. The gingerbread legs led to a few arms, which led to biting their heads off, and let's face it, what was the point of saving gingerbread torsos? I ate them too, mainly to subdue the freak-out factor that kicked in when the fire crackling in the fireplace started singing "White Christmas" in Bing Crosby's voice.

I needed a drink.

Scratch that. I needed ten drinks.

The thought had barely formed in my mind when the door to the fridge blew open and my box of white zin somersaulted onto the counter and poured itself into a conveniently waiting glass.

I scrambled back to the living room, followed by a flying phalanx of dish towels and oven mitts.

"Stop!" I yelled in the crazy voice that made the cats run for cover. "Quit following me!"

The dish towels flung themselves into the fire like a sacrifice to the gods of kitchen fibers.

I tried telling myself this was normal for women like me. That it was my heritage finally kicking in. Everyone else in town dealt with magick on a daily basis and you didn't see them freaking out about it.

But I was pretty sure their silverware wasn't about to mate with the contents of the utensil drawer right under the watchful eyes of a quartet of cats, who were beginning to look an awful lot like the Beatles on the cover of *Abbey Road.*

Okay, I was now officially freaking out.

Every random thought that passed through my sugar-and-fat-addled brain came to life in front of my eyes, flashing by like outtakes from a twisted Disney movie. When my favorite fantasy, the one about the pirate king and the lost princess, started to play itself out on top of the coffee table, I let out a yell they probably heard all the way in Montpelier.

I heard something slam against the front door. The sound was followed by a string of inventive Anglo-Saxon expressions uttered in a very familiar voice. I swung open the door in time to see Lynette shaking off a few singed feathers.

"You could have warned me you had a fire going," she said as she hurried into the warm house. "I was almost Christmas dinner."

At least I thought it was Lynette. The woman standing in front of me was older, heavier, and a lot grayer.

Before I could say a word, Janice materialized in a spearmint-scented cloud. She was wearing red flannel pajamas and her ever-present Uggs. She was also shorter, older, and not a natural redhead.

"Oh God," I said as a wave of dizziness came over me. "I think I'm going to throw up."

Had the protective charm collapsed or was I seeing the town the way it really was because for the first time in my life I was finally one of them?

They led me back into the living room and I collapsed onto the sofa.

"You look like shit," Janice said. "What's wrong?"

I laughed out loud. "Hello. Have you taken a look around?"

They both glanced at the cutlery conga line, the rock star cats, and the oven mitts warming themselves near the fireplace and shrugged.

"We've seen it coming for a few days, honey." Lynette patted my hand.

"The signs were all there," Janice agreed.

"Your date with Haydon isn't a minute too soon."

"Haydon?" I was afraid to think too hard about anything because it just might cartwheel across my living room.

"My cousin," Janice said. "Your blind date for tomorrow."

I groaned and buried my face in my hands. "I'm too sick to go out with anyone. I think I'm coming down with something."

"You're not sick," Lynette said with a smile. "You're in love."

"Trust me," I said. "This can't be love. This is the flu." I know they said love hurts but this was ridiculous. My head throbbed. My stomach ached. My ears burned. I felt like I had been sacked by the Patriots defensive line and left for dead. If this was really the way love felt, why weren't they selling a cure for it on television along with the headache tablets and antacids.

"Lynette's right," Janice said. "That's why your powers are finally kicking in."

"You're your mother's daughter," Lynette said with weepy eyes. "This is exactly how it happened to her."

"He's the wrong guy, of course," Janice said, and Lynette nodded.

"That goes without saying," Lynette said. "Totally the wrong guy."

"How do you know he's the wrong guy?" I asked through a haze of nausea. "You don't even know who the guy is."

"Please," Janice said. "Give us a little credit."

"We all know it's the cop, Chloe. We've known it from the beginning."

"Which was three days ago," I said. "That's hardly a romantic epic."

"He's all wrong for you," Janice said.

"You already said that."

"You couldn't possibly build a future with him," Lynette said. "Especially not now."

I could hear doors slamming shut all around me. All those dreams of a normal family, of a real future, were disappearing. Love had opened the door to my powers and those same powers made loving Luke impossible.

"I'm not looking to make a future with anyone." I pointed toward the knives and forks square-dancing in the hallway. "I'd be happy if I could figure out how to keep the cutlery from kicking my ass."

They were my friends and they loved me but they couldn't help me. Only the

Book of Spells could do that, and until we figured out where Sorcha had hidden it, I was flying blind.

Literally, as it turned out.

I sneezed and did a revolution around the living room. The ceiling didn't look half as good from up there as it did from ground level. At least from ground level you couldn't see all those nasty cobwebs in the corners.

"You really do need help," Janice said after she and Lynette grabbed me by the ankles and pulled me back down from the ceiling. "What are we going to do?"

Lynette suggested tethering me to a table leg. I suggested we drink our weight in margaritas. Janice suggested I go through Sorcha's notebooks to see if there might be a clue hidden in one of them that might lead me to the Book of Spells.

I went to pull down the attic ladder so I could get the notebooks when it occurred to me there might be an easier way. Stilling my mind, I concentrated on the box of notebooks. Across the room, twelve back issues of *People* magazine stood up, straightened themselves out, then marched over to me single file while my friends applauded.

I tried again, concentrating more deeply, but this time *TV Guide* and the latest *Interweave Knit* flung themselves into the fireplace. I gave it one more shot, visualizing the fabric-covered box, picturing where I had stowed it under the eaves, imagining it inching its way toward the ladder then bumping its way down to me.

Unfortunately what I got was a dusty old box of newspaper clippings that dated back to FDR.

"You two might as well go home," I said. "This might take a while."

"Why don't you just go up to the attic and get the damn thing?" Janice said.

It sounded like a plan.

LUKE

I made it halfway down Osborne Avenue before giving up the ghost and turning back. Staying in town for the night was the only option.

Chloe had told me where she hid the key to Sticks & Strings. She had a TV in there, a big sofa, a working fireplace, a cat. I'd already picked up sandwiches and a bag of chips from the sub shop on the corner so I wouldn't starve.

And it wasn't like I had anyone waiting for me back at the motel.

I didn't go in there planning to snoop around, but I've got to tell you there isn't a hell of a lot to do in a knit shop if you're not a knitter. It took me maybe five seconds to register the fact that there was a lot of yarn in the place and some of that yarn cost more than a car payment. Add another ten seconds to stare at the assortment of pointy sticks, hooks, weird gadgets, and maybe a full fifteen to check out the sweaters and scarves on display, and you could kill half a minute without even trying.

The TV didn't work. I couldn't find a radio. Thanks to the storm, my laptop wasn't able to hold an Internet connection for more than a few seconds.

By seven o'clock I was ready to teach myself to knit. I thumbed through a few of the how-to books but stuff like *picot cast on* and *s1 k2Tog psso* made my brain hurt. A neat stack of shiny white binders marked CHLOE'S DESIGNS caught my eye. What the hell. It wasn't like I was reading her diary.

I'd be lying if I said I knew what I was

looking at. Page after page of graphs with hieroglyphic symbols and arcane text that was tougher to decipher than the Dead Sea Scrolls. I liked her trademark, though: a simple drawing of a beautiful woman holding a glowing sun aloft. It was Chloe and it wasn't, and it pulled me in the same way the real woman did every time I saw her.

There was something about being in her space. Her scent lingered in unexpected places. Handwritten notes were scattered across the top of her desk. At least a dozen sketches of a dozen different pairs of socks. Some were lacy. Some were striped or braided or had colorful designs of boats and hearts and kittens. Little squares of knitted fabrics in all the colors of the rainbow were pinned to the wall. A list of incoming orders rested near the printer along with a store inventory.

I suppose I could have stopped there but I didn't. I did what cops weren't supposed to do without a warrant. I opened cabinets, drawers, closets. I don't know what I was expecting to find but no dead bodies tumbled out, no smoking guns hidden behind a few hundred skeins of soft

purple stuff with a name I couldn't pro-
nounce.

I found a stash of Chamber of
Commerce–style promo materials behind
a nest of hairy pink balls of yarn. Restaurant info. A glossy brochure about the Inn
that never had a room available. Lots of
stuff about the various shops and busi-
nesses. They even had a foldout map, one
of those simple ones that spelled out all
the tourist sites in big block letters.

I spread it out on the counter in the small
galley kitchen. There was Sticks & Strings,
marked with a big red dot. Fully Caffeinated.
The parking lot over there at the north edge
of town. The Town Hall/old church. Janice
Meany's Cut & Curl. The library. I even found
a smallish red dot marked Archie's Electronics at the foot of Toothaker Bridge exactly where Paul Griggs said it would be but
wasn't. If I was still there during spring melt,
I'd have to take another look.

Toothaker.

The damn name still sounded familiar. I
took another look at the map in front of
me. Carrier and Nurse, Osborne and
Good, Wilber and Parris and Hubbard.
The been here/seen that feeling that

started when I drove into town for the first time returned full force and it pulled me back through my years in Boston to Bradford, the town where I grew up.

That wasn't it—our streets had been named for the children of the first wave of 1950s tract house owners—but I was on the right track. It wouldn't help me wrap up the loose ends of Suzanne's death, but it was something to think about when life got too close for comfort.

Penny leaped out of that basket of fluff and meowed her way over. She twined herself around my ankles, letting me know she wouldn't mind something to eat.

"I'm with you, cat." I followed her into the makeshift kitchen and split a turkey club and some chips. I was more of a dog person but Penny had an old soul feeling to her. If you had to spend the night in a knit shop, it was good to have some company.

Dinner took about ten minutes, which brought me all the way to nine o'clock. I fell into one of those catatonic sleeps brought on by unremitting boredom then started awake a little after eleven.

Which meant there were another seven or eight hours until daylight.

With a little luck they would feel like only twenty or thirty.

CHLOE

By midnight I had learned how to keep small appliances, cutlery, and myself from launching unexpected aerial reconnaissance missions around the house. The cats finally decided it was safe to crawl out from their various hiding places and grab something to eat before the next surprise.

I was, however, having trouble keeping random thoughts from turning into random visits from my poor, unsuspecting friends.

Janice threatened me with permanent split ends if I transported her out of bed one more time. Lynette made me promise I would never tell anyone what she looked like without her eye makeup on. And I'm not sure I'll ever recover from the sight of Frank and Manny from the retirement home without their vampire dentures in place and their hairpieces on. Of course, the bigger issue was why I was thinking about Frank and Manny in the first place but I refused to go there.

And then there was Luke.

He was sound asleep when he landed on top of the washing machine. He hit with a thud, grunted, then slid onto the floor with another, softer thud. The stack of knitted blankets awaiting felting cushioned his fall. Stubble dotted his jawline. His thick dark hair stood up in spiky tufts. And did I mention he was warm? I could feel his warmth all the way across the room and I couldn't resist. I crossed the room and knelt down next to him.

He looked up at me with unfocused eyes. "What the hell—?"

"You slid off the washing machine."

"What was I doing on the washing machine?"

"It's a long story." Transport was brutal on mortals. We're not built for astral travel. Our brains have trouble convincing our bodies that the laws of physics don't always apply, and the war wreaks havoc on our systems. Right now Luke was disoriented, unable to process what had just happened to him. In effect, his brain was short-circuiting.

The human body didn't fare much better. Transport was more physical than *Star*

Trek would lead you to believe. Tomorrow morning he would feel like he'd gone fifteen rounds with the current heavyweight champion and lost.

He gave me a loopy grin. "I'm still asleep, right?"

"You're not asleep."

"Sure I am."

I decided not to argue the point.

"Come on," I said. "You can't stay here."

I slipped my hands under his arms and tried to help him to his feet but no luck. Moving a grounded 747 would have been easier. His brain still wasn't communicating properly with his body and wouldn't for at least another six or seven hours if my own past experience was any indication.

He fell back into a deep sleep and I used the opportunity to grab some pillows and blankets from my bedroom.

"You're going to wish I'd left you at Motel Six," I murmured as I tried to make him comfortable. "These aren't exactly first-class accommodations."

He didn't understand a single word I said but it didn't matter. Even if he did, he wouldn't remember it in the morning.

He groaned as he turned on his side and my heart seemed to shift inside my chest. The cats peered in at us from the doorway then, curiosity satisfied, they turned and went back to their respective beds.

He held out his hand for me and time stopped. The past didn't matter. The future didn't exist. There was only now.

The explosion of sparks when our hands met took my breath away. Or maybe it was the warmth of his touch that did it. We interlocked fingers and it was the most intimate thing I had ever done with a man, more intimate than kissing or making love. The sense of rightness, of connectedness, made me feel something I had never felt before.

Was this love? Janice and Lynette thought so but I had only books and movies to guide me. I felt sick to my stomach, headachy, dizzy—I'd never seen those symptoms mentioned in love poems or Valentine's Day cards. But my heart felt suddenly too big for my chest, and I had the beginnings of powers I never thought would be mine. That had to mean something.

Maybe I was my mother's daughter in

ways that went beyond a talent for knitting. Love had brought her budding gifts to full life. If she had chosen life, to stay here in Sugar Maple, most villagers believed she would have been the most powerful of Aerynn's descendents.

But the power of love had been stronger.

I would never forgive her for leaving me, but maybe I was finally starting to understand.

Just a few nights ago I had walked up Osborne with Gunnar and shivered at the thought that change was coming, but I never guessed that the change would be happening inside me.

That night I didn't care about protective charms or the Book of Spells. Not even the possibility that Isadora might win and drag Sugar Maple through the mist and into the world of the Fae was enough to dim my sense of wonder. My life was changing faster than I could comprehend. Magick had already started to bubble through my veins. My heart beat to a new, strange rhythm that left me breathless. By this time tomorrow my chance for something real would be gone forever. I would have to accept the fact that I had changed and that my dreams would have to change along with me.

Luke drew me close and I lay down beside him on the soft bed of blankets. He wouldn't remember any of this in the morning. The rigors of transport would wipe away his memory of these hours. They would exist only in my heart.

So I did something I swore I would never do.

I told him everything.

17

~

CHLOE—JUST BEFORE DAWN

"Don't worry," Janice said, looking down at a sleeping Luke MacKenzie. "Remember how long it took you to snap back the summer Gunnar accidentally called you to the lake? Humans just aren't built for astral transport."

"I didn't do it on purpose," I said. "You know what it was like around here last night. Every thought I had—" I stopped.

The look she gave me could have curdled cream. "Don't tell me you slept with him. Please don't tell me that!"

"He slept," I corrected her. "I watched."

"What the *hell* does that mean?"

"He slept on the floor of the laundry room while I watched."

"You watched?"

Now I was really starting to feel uncomfortable. "Stop repeating everything I say. Transport hit him hard. I watched to make sure he was okay."

It wasn't exactly a lie but it wasn't the truth either. If I told Janice that I had spent the night in his arms, spilling the truth about my family, myself, and Sugar Maple, she would spontaneously combust.

"He doesn't look okay," Janice observed. "He looks like he's in a coma."

I took a deep breath. "He won't remember any of this, will he?"

She shook her head. "From the looks of him, he'll be lucky if he remembers his name."

She was being her usual funny, sarcastic self, but I couldn't manage a smile, much less laughter.

"You have to help me get him out of here before he wakes up."

"Your powers got him here, honey. Let's

see what you can do about getting him back again."

"I tried but he ended up wedged upside down in the doorway."

She could have laughed but she didn't. Sometimes good friends were worth their weight in cashmere.

"Poor guy," she said, shaking her head. "He'll need therapy after this."

"We'd better hurry," I said. "The sun's coming up. The day-trippers and everybody else will be out and about before we know it."

"We could wrap him up in a blanket and carry him to your car."

"He's six-three and two hundred pounds!"

"We could call Gunnar to come help."

"Don't even think about it." Explaining this to Gunnar was not high on my list of things to do today. "There must be a foot of snow out there. I hope the highway's been cleared."

"Why do you care about the highway?" Janice asked.

"We have to get him back to his motel."

"He didn't make it to the motel last

night. I saw his truck in front of Sticks &
Strings."

"He was at my shop?"

"I know," Janice said. "It freaked me out
too."

I glanced at Luke then back at Janice.
"Do you think he'd snoop?"

"He's a cop. That's what they do. They
can't help themselves."

"Don't they need warrants or something
before they start poking around?"

"I never thought I'd say this to you,
Hobbs, but you need to watch more television. Some cops do what they need to do
and worry about the details later."

My shop was all about the knitting. Except for the basket of roving from my
mother, there wasn't a drop of magick anywhere.

We couldn't use any of Janice's magick
because he was still zonked from transport so we ended up wrapping him in a
blanket and dragging him through the
snow to my Buick. We just about had him
folded into the backseat when one of those
spine-chilling wails rolled toward us from
the direction of Procter Park.

Our eyes locked over Luke's blanket-clad body.

"I didn't hear that," I said. "Did you?"

Janice shook her head. "Hear what?"

We both shivered as the sound faded away.

After much manipulation, we got Luke into my car and headed toward the shop.

It had been a night for the strange and the new. My quiet, bucolic village was as crowded as Times Square on New Year's Eve. Spirits were everywhere. In the trees. On rooftops. Walking arm in arm down the streets. Drifting overhead. Africans who had escaped the slave trade. English men and women who sought religious freedom. Dutch. Irish. Abenaki Algonquins who had welcomed the newcomers and taught them the ways of the land.

Spirits from our earliest days mingled with spirits who fought in the War of Independence and the War Between the States. A flyboy shot down during World War II saluted me as he sailed overhead. The energies I had sensed all around me for my entire life were suddenly visible, and I alternated between wonder and fear as I steered the car down Osborne toward the shop.

It was too much. My head throbbed from the assault on my senses. Was this the way Sugar Maple looked to Lynette and Janice and Lilith and everyone else? How did they stand this on a daily basis? It was like living in the middle of a teeming city filled with colors and sounds and people everywhere. There had to be a way to turn it off or I would go crazy.

Thirty minutes later we managed to get Luke installed on the sofa in the shop. Janice, in an uncharacteristically indulgent mood, covered him with one of the throws I'd knitted during my 2004 *Ab Fab* frenzy. I smiled as Penny abandoned her roving basket and curled herself around his feet and started purring.

Me too, I thought as I followed Janice out the back door. *Me too.*

LUKE

I woke up at seven thirty the next morning feeling like I'd spent the night inside a cement mixer instead of a yarn shop. Everything that could hurt did. Four years as goalie on a losing college team had taken less of a toll on my body than one night on Chloe's couch. I would have been better off sleeping on a bed of nails.

Penny the cat was curled up at one end of the sofa from hell. She opened one yellow eye and looked at me then went back to sleep. Easy for her to do. She had more padding.

And what was with the headache? I felt like there was something inside my brain trying to gnaw its way out.

Was there such a thing as wool poisoning? I'd spent most of the night surrounded by sheep by-products. Maybe the fibers had somehow worked their way into my brain. I usually didn't remember my dreams but the ones I had last night were clear as the Super Bowl on a big HD screen. Like the one where I flew across Sugar Maple. Literally flew. I sailed over the tops of the trees, swooped down over the lake, maneuvered around entire families who needed to learn the rules of the aerial road. Finally I landed on one of the Inn's peaked gables, right next to a World War II ace who offered me a Lucky Strike.

But it was the dream just before I woke up that I didn't want to forget. In it Chloe was lying next to me, curled against my body like she had always been there.

Like she would be there forever.

We were on the floor of a small, windowless laundry room, lying on a stack of quilts or blankets. Something soft and fluffy. A washer and dryer were pushed up against the long wall. Bottles of bleach and detergent and fabric softener lined the shelf overhead. I curved myself around her, one leg slung over hers, arm resting just beneath the swell of her breasts, my face buried in her hair.

It was so real I could still feel her warmth against me.

I could also hear the sound of her voice. She had talked a lot in my dream. I could feel the rhythm of her words, but except for some seriously weird stuff about vampires and retirement homes, the content remained out of reach.

I fumbled around the makeshift kitchen, starting coffee and digging up something for Penny to eat that didn't include fish. She'd have to settle for leftover turkey from yesterday's club sandwiches.

I poured myself a mug of coffee then walked over to the front window to survey the damage. That had been serious snow last night, ten inches and counting by the time I fell asleep. The kind of snow that taxed Boston's snow removal budget to the max and had its citizens digging out for days afterward.

I opened the shop door and stepped outside.

The sidewalks were clear and dry. So was the street. Fluffy white snow was piled neatly at the curbs and the corners. No slush. No ice. Even my truck, the only vehicle parked on Good as far as I could see, was dug out and snow-free.

Either the sanitation crews had nothing else to do or they were paid like rock stars because not even the White House saw snow removal like this.

I ducked back in the shop and gathered up sandwich wrappers and empty soda cans. I swept up some silvery-blue glitter from the floor near the sofa, the kind of stuff that spilled from greeting cards sent by sadistic friends with a bad sense of humor. Penny was curled up on the sofa, almost hidden by the fuzzy multicolored throw. The fire was out. I was about to grab my jacket and leave when I took another look.

Good thing I wasn't planning a life of crime. I'd left enough clues behind to fry my ass. Binders and booklets and maps were scattered from one end of her worktable to the other. I shoved the binders back onto the shelves where I'd found them and stacked the town promo brochures.

The one featuring the Sugar Maple Inn was on top and the photo caught my eye. The main house dated back to the early nineteenth century, all dark wood and gables like the house in the Hawthorne novel. It beat the hell out of the Motel 6 where I was staying. Maybe I would walk over there and see if I could get on some kind of wait list for a room. Total occupancy all year long was just damn hard to believe.

Clearly Hawthorne's House of the Seven Gables had been the prototype for the Sugar Maple Inn and the prototype for Hawthorne's house could be found in Salem, Massachusetts, a town I had known well as a kid.

Was that the reason for the déjà vu sensation I had been feeling since I first drove into town?

I hadn't thought about Salem in years. When I was in high school, Salem had been our arch rival. Hockey. Basketball. Football. It always came down to Bradford versus Salem in a do-or-die battle.

We didn't pay much attention to our rival's history but enough of it had filtered into my consciousness and stuck. Salem: scene of the infamous Witch Trials that resonated down through the centuries. Names like Good and Nurse and Carrier and Proctor and Osborne, even Hobbs and Griggs, still echoed in memory.

"Holy shit," I said out loud to the empty room as it all came together.

That was it. Sugar Maple seemed familiar to me because it *was* familiar to me. The town had been laid out to replicate Salem. The names of its streets were names that were important to the small seafaring town. The lighthouse on the village green finally made sense to me. It was a model of Salem's lighthouse.

Cities sometimes had sister cities. Towns had sister towns. The founders of Sugar Maple had designed their village as a tribute to the town that had defined intolerance in the late seventeenth century.

Freaking weird choice if you asked me.

CHLOE

By 7 A.M. the street had returned to normal. Or at least what I had always thought was normal before last night. No spirit families flying overhead. No spirit kids tobogganing up Osborne. We were back to the basics of people, buildings, trees, and sky.

I was still having a little trouble adjusting to the differences in my friends' appearances, but compared to the traffic jam in the air space last night, it was nothing more than a curiosity.

Janice transported herself back home. I left the Buick in the driveway between Sticks & Strings and the pet shop and walked home to shower and eat breakfast.

Two hours later when I returned to the shop, Luke was gone. Sandwich wrappers peeked out from the trash and I noted an empty can of Pepsi in the recycling bin. I had a bad moment when I saw a sprinkling of Gunnar's silver-blue glitter on top of the sandwich wrappers, but there was no way Luke would have been able to make the connection between glitter and the Fae. Nobody outside Sugar Maple could have.

But the rearranged binders and folders were something else again.

Janice was right. He'd snooped. I wasn't one of those obsessive-compulsive neat freaks who alphabetized spices and color-coded their underwear according to the days of the week, but I usually knew when somebody had been messing with my stuff.

I probably should have been annoyed, but mostly I was disappointed that he hadn't stumbled across the Book of Spells while he was poking around. I needed all the help I could get right now to handle these random bursts of energy. The most recent surge sent the hands of my watch spinning counterclockwise and a pair of clogs sailing across the room.

The store would be open for business in another hour, and for the first time I found myself hoping the snow would keep customers away. I'm not sure I would know how to explain a cardi that seamed itself then sewed on its own buttons.

Then again Sticks & Strings already had a reputation as a magical kind of shop. It might just add to the mystique.

The coffeepot was plugged in and I gratefully poured myself a mug then broke with tradition and added both sugar and cream. All that flying around the living room that I did last night was even better cardio training than blocking lace.

Which, of course, made me think of Suzanne Marsden.

Suzanne and Luke had a history. Not a romantic history but their lives had been intertwined since childhood. I hadn't given a lot of thought to his loss but now, suddenly, I got it. I tried to imagine the two of them as children, but the image of Suzanne in her glittering naked dress overshadowed everything else.

I didn't want to think about that night, but I couldn't seem to shake the image of her gliding across the ice with the Orenburg shawl trailing behind her in the night breeze while a man watched from the shore. He was tall and broad-shouldered but the shadows obscured his face. I knew it was only my imagination at work, but it seemed so real that for a moment I felt the chill bouncing off the ice, the heat of the attraction between them.

I poured myself another mug of coffee then wandered back into the front of the shop. Gunnar, still wearing his coat, was slumped in one of the easy chairs. He seemed lost in thought. I quickly glanced at the floor. No glitter. I could have kissed him for using the front door.

Like Lynette and Janice, he looked older than he had before my powers began to blossom, but it was more than lines and wrinkles. Over the last few months I had noticed signs of physical vulnerability, but nothing had prepared me for what I saw that morning. It wasn't just the bruises and cuts he'd sustained in his brawl with his brother. The spark inside him was dimming and it scared me.

"You look terrible," I said. "What's wrong?"

"Try spending the night with my family and see how good you look."

"I'm serious. You have to stop letting Dane drain your powers this way. I can almost see right through you." And I meant that literally.

"We had a family council," he said,

grabbing for my mug of coffee. "Isadora wants me to help bring Sugar Maple through the mist."

"You told her no, didn't you?"

"She doesn't recognize the word *no.*" Isadora needed a full-powered Fae to partner her in order to effect the change. Dane and Gunnar together would fill the bill, but Gunnar refused to join forces with them. He told me that she had even approached the Weavers about helping her transition Sugar Maple beyond the mist.

"Renate wasn't interested, but Colm . . ."

I had no trouble filling in the blanks.

"What would happen if he joined forces with her?" I asked.

"She'd have the muscle, but without the Book of Spells, she still wouldn't have the formula."

"She trashed my place looking for it the other night." I told him about finding purple glitter and Dane's telltale steel blue everywhere.

"It's only going to get worse," he said. "She knows your powers are kicking in."

"Nothing like starting the morning with a DEFCON 3 warning," I said lightly.

"Hey, we're in this together," he said.

"Sugar Maple belongs here, not under my mother's control. I'm not going to let her win this fight."

He went into the kitchen to pour himself some coffee then reclaimed the chair. "By the way, your friend the cop is at the Inn trying to snag a room."

"What?" My stomach went instantly into a knot.

"You sound surprised."

"I *am* surprised."

"After last night I figured you knew his plans."

"What's that supposed to mean?"

He took a long sip of coffee. "He spent the night with you."

"Have you been spying on me?"

"There aren't many secrets in Sugar Maple, Chloe. Half the town saw him sitting on top of the Inn last night with Captain Wilcox."

"Nothing happened," I said. "I didn't summon him but he showed up and I couldn't send him back."

"So he's the one." The look in his eyes almost brought me to tears.

"I didn't say that."

He forced a smile. "You didn't have to."

Our shared history was contained in those words.

"We both know it can't go anywhere," I said, as much to myself as to him, "but at least I might get my powers out of the deal."

"You never did do irony very well," he said.

He was right. I didn't do irony well at all.

Or love, for that matter. It was a family tradition.

Hobbs women loved only once and so far none of us had managed the happily-ever-after ending we all dream about.

Gunnar reached for my hand and held it tightly in his. We might not be lucky in love, but when it came to friendship, we were jackpot winners.

18

LUKE

When they said "No Occupancy" at the Sugar Maple Inn, they meant it. I had tried everything short of bribery or pulling a gun, but Renate Weaver wouldn't budge.

"I'm sorry," she said firmly, "but we just don't have a room for you."

"The place is empty," I said. "The only time I've seen people in here is when the restaurant's open."

Renate gave me a big smile. "And your point is?"

"I don't care if all you have is a broom closet. I need a room."

"And we don't have one to give you." She patted my hand. "I'm truly sorry, Detective, but our rooms are booked years in advance."

I could have pursued the booked-but-still-unoccupied argument, but I had the feeling it wouldn't get me anywhere.

She offered me a cup of coffee and a freshly baked pumpkin donut. I hated playing into the whole cop/donut stereotype, but what the hell. I really do have a jones for donuts. I asked Renate a few questions about the night Suzanne died, but she didn't offer anything new. Suzanne waited. She drank. She waited some more. She paid her check. She left. Nothing much there to go on.

I polished off the coffee and donut and thanked her for her time.

"If you have any more questions, you know where to find me," she said with a sunny smile.

The storm had blown itself out overnight, leaving behind bright sunshine and a winter blue sky. I walked the perimeter of the Inn, taking in the familiar architectural details. The structure was a perfect replica of Salem's House of Seven Gables, right down to the weathered shingles and slightly crooked first-floor windows.

It was always good to get confirmation that you weren't crazy.

One of the businessmen who had been dining at the Inn the night Suzanne died returned my call while I was trying to charm Renate Weaver into letting me have a room. No surprise when he said he remembered Suzanne clearly. Most men, straight or gay, would. It was what he said next that surprised me.

"We were driving from the parking lot to that little bridge that leads to the highway and I saw her—Suzanne, you said her name was?—walking along with a guy."

"Could you see his face?"

"It's winter in Vermont," he said with a short laugh. "He could've been Sasquatch for all I could see of him." The man in question wore a long black coat and a few yards of scarf wrapped around him.

"Hair color?" I asked.

"Silver, I think. Or maybe one of those

white blonds. Sorry. That's the best I can do."

Suzanne had been looking up at the guy and laughing. That much the businessman was sure of.

I liked knowing there had been laughter near the end.

Sieverts was a short, stocky guy with a wrestler's body. Suzanne was easily six feet in heels. The guy she had been walking with couldn't have been the politician.

So who the hell was he? Goober and his cross-country brother both had that kind of silvery-gold hair, and Goober had been working at the Inn that night. I was still waiting for return calls from four other men who had been in the dining room that night. It could be any one of them.

Life was messy. Accidents left loose ends that took a long time to tie up. Suzanne's trajectory from the moment she walked into Sticks & Strings until Paul Griggs and his sons pulled her from the frozen lake had been arrow-straight.

Almost too straight.

I caught myself midthought. There was nothing wrong with a straight line investigation. I was applying a big-city mind-set to a small-town way of life. This was the town without crime, right? The odds of suddenly finding one were maybe ten million to one.

"Morning!" A group of day-trippers breezed by me, faces bright with that special Christmas consumer glow.

The streets bustled with activity. Cars, pedestrians, a horse-drawn carriage driven by the Santa Claus clone I'd met at the parking lot my first day in town. The place looked like the mall on Christmas Eve.

The pet shop was out. The Griggs boys were busy painting the newly washed and primed walls while rap music pounded at a decibel level that was probably illegal in some states. No wonder Paul was staying away until afternoon. I could always go back to Sticks & Strings and set up my laptop in the storeroom but I wasn't ready to be that close to Chloe. Last night's dream was still too real for comfort.

I knew the softness of her skin. The sweet smell of her hair. The way her breasts felt against my chest.

Hell, why didn't I admit it? It might have been a dream, but for a little while I had been happy. I had been given a glimpse into the kind of future I didn't believe existed for me. A future where a man woke up in the morning happier than when he went to bed the night before.

I had stopped believing in soul mates a long time ago. Things didn't always work out the way you hoped they would when you took those vows. Shit happened. Life happened. And sometimes the only thing you could do was keep moving.

The dream would fade. By the end of the day I wouldn't remember how she had felt in my arms.

But that didn't change the fact that if I saw her in Goober's arms again, I would probably knock his perfect teeth down his throat and singlehandedly bring crime back to Sugar Maple.

Okay. So maybe I wasn't ready to go back to the store yet. The morning was sunny and bright. The streets and sidewalks were dry and clear. The cemetery was just up the road. Nothing like a walk among crumbling tombstones and grave markers to take a man's mind off a woman.

The road crew was gone and the gates were wide open.

The cemetery was as perfect as everything else in Sugar Maple. The pathways were shoveled free of snow. No patches of ice to send an unsuspecting visitor sprawling. The graves were all well kept and decorated with sprigs of holly and frozen poinsettia plants. I was almost surprised they didn't have a tour guide with a thermos of hot chocolate.

There were a few stones from the early days, the inscriptions worn almost unreadable by time and the elements. There might have been some unmarked graves beneath the snow cover but I doubted it. Someone had taken care to make sure each grave was marked and that the markers were visible.

The two flat markers that rested beneath a gnarled elm at the southwest corner were a perfect example. The snow had been carefully cleared away and only a thin layer of ice remained. I bent down and brushed it away. There were no names on the markers, only symbols: a sun and a crescent moon.

"Chloe's parents."

The woman's voice seemed to come from nowhere. Low, musical, the kind of voice that got a woman noticed.

She was standing behind me, backlit by the sun, one of those women who could have been anywhere from twenty-five to fifty. Medium height. Fair skin. Eyes the color of turquoise. She was probably slim but I couldn't be sure because most of her was hidden inside a huge furry coat that had cost three or four animals their lives.

She was also drop-dead gorgeous, but hey, this was Sugar Maple. That seemed to come with the territory.

"Excuse me?" I asked.

She gestured toward the markers. "Chloe's parents are buried there."

"You knew them?"

"Very well." She moved closer. She wore dark green leather boots with wicked high heels. "You're our new police chief."

"Luke MacKenzie." I stuck out my right hand.

"Isadora."

I didn't catch her last name but at the moment that didn't matter. I was too busy wondering why she didn't shake my hand.

"I have a cold," she said, reading my mind. "Hand-to-hand contact is the easiest way to spread disease. Unless you carry around a bottle of Purell . . ."

I didn't. I thanked her for keeping her cold germs to herself and she laughed.

I don't want to say it was a weird laugh but there was definitely something off. I couldn't say if it was the pitch or the volume or maybe the duration. All I knew was that it lifted the hairs on the back of my neck the same way the sound of the not-really-a-banshee had the other night.

"Our little village must seem dull to you after Boston."

"I'm a small-town kid," I said. "I'm comfortable here."

"In the cemetery or our little village?"

The bright sun had rendered me snow blind and I couldn't make out the expression in her eyes. I was searching for a suitably witty and evasive answer when my cell rang.

"Go ahead," the woman said. "You're working. Take your call."

I was surprised to see my former brother-in-law Jack's name on the display screen. I turned and stepped a few feet away. He and Suzanne had married straight out of high school and divorced not long after, but they had also managed to stay close. Jack and some of the old crowd were throwing a mass and a memorial service for Suzanne tomorrow and wanted me to attend.

I wasn't big on wakes, funerals, or memorial services, but the old crowd had been there for us when we needed them and I was going to return the favor. It would mean leaving this afternoon but this was Suzanne we were talking about. I told him I would be there.

"Sorry I took so long," I said, turning around, "but—"

The woman was gone.

Some ominous clouds moved across the sun. I glanced around the small cemetery but it was as empty of visitors now as it had been when I first arrived. I had been on the phone less than three minutes. How far could a woman in high-heeled boots get in less than one hundred eighty seconds?

Still there was no sign that she had ever been there.

I walked the perimeter of the cemetery, moving systematically from stone to stone: 1654, 1682, 1701, 1703, 1753, and then nothing until Chloe's parents had been laid to rest here approximately twenty-five years ago. A gap of almost two hundred fifty years would catch anybody's interest.

Like many things in Sugar Maple, it was weird but not criminally weird. There was probably another cemetery somewhere on the outskirts of town that I hadn't seen. Or maybe they outsourced their dead, and all of their death records were on file in another town.

There was no hospital in Sugar Maple. No wellness clinic or emergency care center. Unless a woman chose to have her baby at home, the record of birth would be filed with the hospital in whatever town the hospital was incorporated.

That didn't answer the question about death certificates since death didn't always come with a warning, but it was reasonable to assume that many of Sugar Maple's citizens had died in a hospital or away from home. Which meant outside the village's jurisdiction and therefore not documented in the records.

Either way it wasn't my problem. Let Chloe and Joe Randazzo work it out. The Sugar Maple Graveyard Tour was now officially over.

The clouds were growing thicker, and it looked like we were in for more snow. When you had a three-hour drive ahead of you, snow wasn't exactly something you looked forward to. I had figured on leaving around six in the morning and hitting Bradford in time for breakfast before the services began, but I hadn't factored in another storm. I decided to leave early that evening, crash with Jack and his family, then drive back tomorrow after it was over.

A low rumble sounded close by. Thundersnow didn't happen often, but when it did, it grabbed your full attention. It ran counter to the natural order of things, crawled under your skin, and moved along your nerve endings like the electricity it was looking to discharge.

I was a few feet away from the gate when I stumbled over an uneven paver and hit the dirt as lightning struck the tree not two feet away from me.

The crack as the bolt hit the dense wood was deafening. The air was filled with the smell of ozone and charred wood. I was about to lift my head to make sure things were all clear when another bolt of lightning zoomed past the other way and hit a different tree.

I heard another sharp crack and looked up in time to see the top part of the second tree separate from the trunk. I barely managed to roll out of the way a split second before it crashed to the ground right where I had fallen.

I could have powered three cities on the adrenaline rush surging through my veins.

Live wires.

Bolts of lightning.

Falling trees.

I hadn't had this many near misses when I walked a beat in the worst part of Boston.

If I didn't know better, I would think the town was trying to tell me something.

19

CHLOE

I looked out the front window at the dark-ening sky. There was something freakish about thundersnow, like Mother Nature had a little surprise up her sleeve that she couldn't wait to share.

Penny had abandoned the basket of roving at the first clap of thunder, and from the looks of the basket, I didn't blame her one bit. The roving was looking sadly de-pleted today. She cautiously peered out at me from her hiding spot beneath the sofa, and I dropped a few discarded mohair swatches into the basket and a sample shawl I was planning to frog any day now in an attempt to plump things up a bit for her aged bones. It still didn't look particularly inviting but Penny circled the basket, looked up at me with her amazing yellow eyes, then leaped in.

Two and a half hours later I was ready to reconsider my opinion of thundersnow. Apparently it brought out every knitter, spinner, and crocheter in New England, all of whom had money to burn. My stock of Kureyon sock yarn was sold out, half my inventory of Lorna's Laces, and six bags of hand-dyed alpaca that I was almost sorry to see go.

"Not a bad day," I said to Penny, who ignored me.

I flipped the OPEN sign to CLOSED and sat down with a cup of yogurt and some knitting, determined to spend an hour not thinking about Luke or the Book of Spells or the fact that life as I knew it was spinning out of control.

Normally I could lose myself in a complicated lace pattern or drown my sorrows in the comforting repetition of a familiar sock, but today nothing worked. I dropped stitches, screwed up repeats, generally made an utter and complete hash of things until I was this close to bursting into tears of frustration. And believe me, it had been years since a sock made me cry.

A sudden memory flashed to life in front of me. I saw my mother at the wheel, sunlight spilling over her shoulders, as she spun roving into yarn finer than spider's silk. She was young and beautiful. She was in love with a man who loved her. She had the world of magick at her fingertips.

And there in a Moses basket at her feet was the baby daughter she would abandon a few years later to follow the man she loved into the earth.

My anger was dark and hot and twisted and it scared me. Anger like this had a power all its own. I tried to push it down to some safer, quieter place deep inside, but it bubbled up again like lava from a long-dormant volcano.

Some bonds were inviolable. They transcended the divide between human and magick. The bond between a mother and child was one of them. No matter how hard I tried to romanticize my mother's decision, I would never understand how she could have left me behind.

And I would never forgive her.

I tried to conjure up the memory of my father instead, but all I could find were shadows and whispers. He had lived here in Sugar Maple for almost six years and not once had anyone offered up so much as an anecdote for me to hold on to. It was as if he had passed through the town and not left so much as a footprint behind.

Everyone acknowledged the fact that I was half-human, but nobody ever talked about my father, the man my mother married. I remembered that he was tall and strong and that he smelled like freshly cut grass after a long rain, but his smile and the sound of his voice were lost to me. My mother's memory overpowered all else.

When I looked in the mirror, I saw a blurry version of her face. When I spoke, I heard her voice. When I sat down at the wheel or picked up my needles, it was her hands that I saw at work.

Oh, I was definitely my mother's daughter, right down to falling in love with a human. I had spent my entire life yearning for what my mother had found with my father, but I had never taken a minute to think it through. To understand what it meant to love someone who belonged to the world beyond Sugar Maple.

I guess the joke was on me.

I picked up my sock and started knitting again, willing myself to disappear into the stitches and be all about color and texture and shape. No words. I didn't want any more words. I didn't want to think, because if I did, I would have to admit that even the loneliness was better than this . . . this empty, hollow feeling of loss.

So far I wasn't all that impressed with love.

Penny meowed softly and changed position for what must have been the twentieth time.

"You're the lucky one," I said, putting down my sock to see if I could help her get comfortable. "No more chasing around after the boys. You'd just as soon take a nap."

The roving had decreased noticeably from where it had been less than an hour ago. I plunged my hands into the softness and tried to fluff it up around Penny. For as long as I could remember, that basket had been full to overflowing with the most gloriously soft and workable roving you could ever imagine. It took dye like silk, was soft and warm as quiviut, had the elasticity and durability of wool. And best of all, it was always there waiting for me in whatever amount I needed.

At least it had been up until now. I wiggled my fingers deeper then muttered something mildly unprintable when my mother's Welsh gold wedding ring snagged on the edge of the basket. Penny gave me one of those "we are not amused" looks.

"Sorry," I said. "If I can just get unsnagged, I'll—"

A jolt of electricity sizzled up my arms, through my chest, and out the top of my head.

And then everything faded to black.

LUKE

I tried to tell the Griggs boys about the lightning bolt with my name on it, but all they wanted to know was if they could take the rest of the day off and go snowboarding.

"What about school?" I asked.

"Snow day," Jeremy said.

I glanced around the shop. They had done a day's work in record time. What the hell, I figured. Snow days didn't come along often enough in life. "Go," I said, tossing a few twenty-dollar bills their way. "An advance on your check."

You would have thought I had handed them the keys to a new Porsche.

"Mrs. Stallworth called," Johnny said just before they took off. "She said she has something for you. She'll give it to you tonight at the show."

I had stopped by the knit shop earlier to tell Chloe about my near miss, but the CLOSED sign was up and the blinds were drawn. Closing the shop in the middle of what looked to be a high tourist traffic day struck me as odd, but then again so did just about everything today.

We weren't friends. We weren't lovers. We weren't even dating. I didn't know what we were to each other. I had held her in my arms, kissed her until neither one of us could breathe. Sparks flew when we touched.

And I still didn't know what the hell any of it meant.

If it meant anything at all.

I closed the pet shop and walked across town to the Stallworth Funeral Home. I wouldn't be at the show tonight. I would be on my way down to Bradford for Suzanne's memorial.

The parking lot was empty except for a dark blue Chevy that I recognized as the one Midge had been driving the other night.

I don't know why funeral homes always set up shop in the warmest, most welcoming house in town. The house with the most kids, the biggest Christmas tree, the loudest music.

It was almost enough to make you forget the dead people in the basement.

Some people took comfort from sitting with the dead, but death made me want to punch a wall.

I cut across the courtyard and walked up to the front door.

The locked front door.

I thought they didn't believe in locks here in Sugar Maple.

I tried the door again. Definitely locked.

I searched around for a bell but couldn't find one.

I knocked, waited, then knocked again but nobody answered.

Okay, this wasn't going to be the day I interviewed the Stallworths.

I was halfway to the sidewalk when I heard a voice call out my name.

"Detective MacKenzie! Yoo-hoo! Here I am!"

Don't get me wrong. I liked Midge Stallworth. But over the years I had visited enough funeral homes to last me the rest of my life.

The front door was partway open, but the only thing I saw of Midge was a hand waving at me.

"Come in! Come in!" she called out in her cheerful helium-balloon voice. "You'll freeze your donuts off out there!"

I didn't know how to break it to her, but it was even colder in the lobby. I was surprised there weren't icicles hanging from the curtain rods.

It was also dark. Considering the clientele, I guess it made sense.

"I'm embarrassed!" Midge patted her

hair curlers and giggled. "I wasn't expecting anyone." Her face was free of makeup and she wore a hot pink zip-front velour bathrobe, the type my grandmother wore thirty years ago. Basically she looked like she was getting ready for bed at eleven in the morning.

"The Griggs boys told me you called and I figured I'd walk over and save you the trouble." I told her that I wouldn't be at the Playhouse that night but I didn't tell her why.

"No apologies!" Even her gestures were cheerful. "Business is bad right now, which means life is good. I have time to putter around catching up on my beauty routines."

We were verging on TMI.

"So you found something that belonged to Suzanne Marsden."

"Yes, I did," she said as she motioned for me to follow her down the hall. "I'm not usually this forgetful. I think Christmas does something to the brain cells."

She made pleasant chitchat, and I tried not to think about what went on in the basement of the old house on the hill.

She led me into the dimly lit office. The blinds were down, curtains drawn, heat turned off. The only source of light was a small battery-operated candle on a book-shelf.

"Saving energy," she explained as she rummaged in the top drawer of an old ma-hogany desk. "Every little bit helps these days."

I couldn't argue against that, but the place was so cold a polar bear would be begging for a sweater.

I walked over to the bookshelf. Maybe the battery-operated candle was throwing off a little heat. Family photos lined the shelf, tucked in between hardbound edi-tions of *People* Magazine yearbooks and the complete works of Jackie Collins.

"Your kids?" I asked, pointing toward photos of a smiling bunch on ice skates.

"Aren't you nice! Grandkids," she cor-rected me. "Eleven of them and counting. We took that the night of the Moonlight Festival last year."

Goober's brother went cross-country skiing through a forest at night. Kids skated after dark. Life in a town without crime could be pretty damn good.

"Is the Moonlight Festival a big deal around here?"

"Oh yes, indeed, it is. It's our Winter Solstice celebration. You'll just love it."

I scanned the photos, grinning at the wide-open enthusiasm on the kids' faces. There was even one of Midge and a man I assumed was her husband, posed near the tree that had caught my eye the first night. Inside the perfect circle burned into the bark were other markings (initials? symbols?), but the image was too small for me to make them out.

"I know I put it in here," Midge was saying. "Wait . . . I think . . . here it is!" She handed me an envelope. "I'd lose my head if it wasn't attached."

I opened the envelope and pulled out a small gold pin in the shape of a star.

"We found it on the floor after the boys from Montpelier came for her. I guess it had been attached to her coat."

I knew that star. Suzanne had worn it all through high school, pinned to the collar of her uniform blouse. Later on, as her tastes grew more sophisticated, she wore it pinned to the inside of her purse or to a pocket. She called it her lucky charm. In the end it had been anything but.

"You don't look so good," Midge remarked, peering up at my face. "You want some juice or something? I think your blood sugar's low."

"I'm fine," I said, slipping the pin back into the envelope then into my pocket. "But thanks."

"You know," she said as she led me back down the endless hallway, "my feelings are hurt. You questioned Janice. You have an appointment with Lynette. But you never questioned me."

"No offense meant, Mrs. Stallworth."

"Midge, dear. Call me Midge."

The Stallworths had provided a detailed description of the condition of Suzanne's body to county authorities, including the standard photos.

It would be a long time before that faded from my memory.

I started to explain that I definitely wanted her observations, but first I needed to interview people who had seen or spoken with Suzanne *before* she died. However, I was there. She was there. Why not get it over with?

"We could do it now," I said, and she laughed.

"Oh, honey, now isn't such a good time. I'm not much of a morning person. You come over one night next week for dessert and you can ask all the questions you want." She smiled and I had a close-up look at big white teeth that could light up a room. (But what was with those incisors?) "How does that sound?"

We set it up for Wednesday evening. I hoped everyone in Sugar Maple stayed healthy between now and then.

Midge stifled a yawn, and I used that as an excuse to thank her for passing along Suzanne's star pin and said good-bye before she roped me into a guided tour of the premises.

20

CHLOE

I was pretty sure I was dead. I mean, if you opened your eyes and found yourself lying flat on a cold hard surface while your dead surrogate mother smiled down at you, what would you think?

The face was Sorcha's. The bright smile. The dark brown eyes that saw everything, even your secrets.

"It's about time!" said Sorcha in the same tone of voice she'd used when I was running late for school. "I don't have all day, honey. I was afraid you'd sleep through my visit."

"You mean I'm not dead?"

"Of course you're not dead! Why would you even think such a thing?"

I jumped up and threw my arms around her, and the years fell away.

"There, there," Sorcha murmured as she stroked my hair. "We don't have time for tears. I petitioned The Council to grant me this visit, and we must make good use of every second."

I laughed nervously. "The Council?" I asked, trying to make a joke. "Are they the ones who gave you that robe?"

She looked down at the heavily embroidered garment. "A bit much, isn't it? But it's all the rage where I am now."

"It's a big change from your tracksuit and Birkies but I'll adjust." I hugged her again. "Are you hungry? I have some leftover mac and cheese in the fridge. And cookies! There are plenty of cookies. I think I have some Ben & Jerry's too. Maybe we could—"

"Sit down."

I blinked. "What?"

"My time is short and I have much to tell you."

"Thank God!" I beamed a happy smile at her. "Isadora's been tearing up my house trying to find the Book of Spells." My smile faded a fraction. "You are going to tell me where you hid it?"

"No, daughter," she said with a gentle sigh. "I'm going to tell you the truth about your parents before it's too late."

My stomach twisted into a tight knot. "I know their story, Sorcha. Everyone in town knows their story." Love at first sight followed by a few years of bliss and a tragic ending. The kind of thing Hollywood turned into gold on a regular basis.

She reached for my hand and held it tightly. Her bones were so fine, so fragile, that I felt like I had been captured by a bird. "That isn't how it was."

I tried to pull my hand away, but she wouldn't allow it. For a woman who had probably seen three centuries on this side of the veil, she had one hell of a grip.

"My father was working as a carpenter at one of the summer camps. My mother was teaching the kids how to card and spin their own yarn." I waved my hand in the air. "Sparks flew. They fell in love. He gave up everything to stay in Sugar Maple with her."

"Except that isn't the entire story. Your mother fell deeply in love with Ted Barrow the moment she saw him, and she vowed that he was the man she would spend the rest of her life with."

"She got her wish," I said.

"Yes, but not without magick."

I stared at her. "What did you say?"

"Ted fell hard for Guinevere but not hard enough that he was ready to give up his life in the real world. He was starting his internship at Mount Sinai, and he wanted her to leave Sugar Maple and go back to New York with him, but your mother refused."

"My father was a doctor?"

"He would have been, yes."

"He gave up a career in medicine for my mother." Even though I knew the ending of this particular story, I had to fight to keep from being swept away again by the romance of it all.

The heavy lines on her beloved face

seemed to grow deeper. "No, daughter, he didn't. He said he had to go back, that he had made a commitment he wouldn't break. He said he loved Guinevere, but she would have to be the one who moved."

"But she couldn't leave," I whispered. "The town depended on her."

"She loved Sugar Maple and she loved your father so she did the only thing she could think of: she cast a spell that bound him to her side forever."

A ribbon of memories unfurled before me. The soft sounds of their laughter floating through their closed bedroom door. The look in my father's eyes every time she walked into the room. The way he used to say he was the luckiest man in the world, that not even a king had more to be thankful for than he did.

"He seemed so happy," I said, choking back tears. "Are you telling me that was all a lie?"

"He *was* happy," Sorcha said. "Every moment of his time with your mother. He was a supremely happy man."

"But none of it was real." All of those happy memories I had clung to over the years. "If she hadn't cast a spell over him, he would have gone back to New York and become a doctor." *He would still be alive today.*

"Your memories are real," Sorcha said. "They belong to you, and you should hold them close. But know that for your mother it was very different."

According to the woman who had raised me, my beautiful, self-confident mother had spent every day of her married life afraid to undo the spell and trust that love would prove stronger than magick.

"When your father was killed in the accident, she was overcome with both terrible grief and an overwhelming sense of guilt."

I could feel my heart hardened against her once again. "So she took the easy way out."

Sorcha's dark brown eyes filled with tears. "She took the only way she saw."

"She shouldn't have left me."

"No," Sorcha said, "she shouldn't have. But that was the path she chose."

"This is really about Luke, isn't it? You think I'm making the same mistake. That's why you needed to talk to me before it was too late."

"Your mother's powers grew slowly over the years. They burst into full bloom when she fell in love with your father. She was very young and helpless against the temptation they presented."

"I'm not my mother," I reminded her. "I grew up human."

"You used your powers to bring him to you last night."

"I didn't mean to."

"Are you certain of that?"

I had never been able to lie to Sorcha. She saw through me every time. "No," I admitted. "I'm not."

"Let him go, daughter," she urged. "I'm too late to keep you from falling in love with him but not too late to keep you from ruining his life."

"Thanks a lot," I said. "I didn't realize loving me could ruin a man's life."

"It would ruin *his* life."

"You're starting to make me wish you weren't here."

Her smile was gentle. "That's a risk I was prepared to take."

"I would never cast a spell to make him love me."

"Your magick is new and untried. It fills your head with dreams, makes your blood thunder through your veins. You live in a town where magick is an everyday occurrence. A few whispered words and he could be yours forever. That's a serious temptation."

I thought about how wonderful it would be to wake up every morning in his arms. To know that I wasn't alone any longer. I could have that and more by whispering the right words. The realization stole my breath away.

"Humans trick other humans into making promises they can't keep," I reminded her, "and they don't need magick to help them do it."

She seemed to grow smaller, older, right before my eyes. "I have said what I came to say, daughter. The rest is in your hands."

I owed everything to Sorcha. When I was a child, her love and wisdom had made my broken heart whole. Now she was here once again to ease my heart and give me guidance when I needed it most and I couldn't find it within myself to embrace her words.

"Please stay, Sorcha. The town is in danger and I'm not sure I can hold Isadora at bay much longer."

"I would give all my memories to be here with you, but only a daughter of Aerynn has the power to keep Sugar Maple safe from harm." She reached for my hand, and for an instant I felt her remembered warmth. "Your fate was determined three hundred years ago, Chloe Hobbs. Now it's time for you to meet it."

And then she was gone.

LUKE

I stopped at the pizza place midafternoon to grab a slice. The place was crowded with day-trippers and townies. My pal Goober was crowded in a booth with some people I didn't recognize. Janice blew in while I was waiting for my soft drink and dragged me over for introductions.

Gunnar raised a bottle of Sam Adams in my direction. His bruises were starting to settle in. The pattern of purples and yellows had shifted since the last time I saw him, and some of the swelling had gone down. It probably didn't say much for my character, but I liked knowing his brother had gotten the better of him.

Janice ruffled his hair in an older-sister kind of gesture, which he pushed away with feigned annoyance. She seemed to like him as much as Chloe did.

"Verna, this is our new policeman." Janice turned to me. "Verna is Paul's wife."

I shook hands with the friendly woman with the dark, curly hair and made the appropriate noises.

"And this is Archie."

The short, round man with the Harry Potter scarf around his neck raised his slice in greeting.

"From the electronics store?" I asked, and he nodded. "You're the man I need to see." I gave him the condensed version of my troubles.

"You're working out of the old pet shop, right?" he asked. "I'll drop by and see what needs doing."

Small-town living at its best. I could get used to this.

"Anyone see Chloe today?" Janice asked the table in general. "I thought we were having lunch but the shop's shut tight."

"Is that unusual?" I tried not to use my cop voice but she tightened up.

She shut down in that way people do whenever a cop asks a question. "Not really," she said with an unconvincing shrug. "Just asking, that's all."

I hung around a few minutes, grabbed a second slice to go, then headed back to the pet shop. Janice was right. The sign at Sticks & Strings was still turned to CLOSED, but it was the moving van idling in front of the pet shop that caught my attention.

"Delivering on a Saturday?" I asked as I unlocked the front door.

"Overtime," the driver said. "Six kids and it's two weeks before Christmas."

"Got it," I said.

The driver took a step back. "Damn! You've got yourself one hell of a flood in there."

It looked like a tributary of the Connecticut River. We made arrangements for a redelivery the following week.

I wasn't a plumber, but I knew a few things about busted water pipes. If I'd had the tools, I would have made a stab at it. I phoned Chloe for the name of a local plumber but she didn't pick up. I crossed the alley and rapped on the back door.

Nothing.

I still had the key. I tried to fit it into the lock, the same lock it had opened last night, but it didn't fit. What the hell? It wasn't like she'd changed the locks. I checked to make sure I'd used the right key and tried again. Still wouldn't fit.

I ran down to the hardware store and borrowed some stuff from Paul, who said he'd be by within the hour to help out.

I liked working with my hands. I didn't mind getting dirty, but there was nothing fun about busted water pipes in the middle of December.

I was up to my ass in duct tape and solder when Paul showed up two hours later.

"That's new pipe," Paul said as he surveyed the damage. "They had everything replaced last year." He looked at me. "What the hell happened?"

"Like I'm supposed to know? I opened the door and there was Lake Ontario."

"Shove over," he said. "Let's see what's going on."

The more I saw of Paul Griggs, the more

I liked him. He reminded me of a hairier version of my older brother. We made a good team. He knew what to do and I did what he told me.

We talked about the Pats' Super Bowl chances, bitched a little about the Red Sox, the state of the economy, taxes, and the snowplows of Sugar Maple.

"So why Salem?" I asked as he held the blowtorch to the soldered joint. "I grew up two towns over from witch central. What made your founding fathers design the town after it?"

He moved the blowtorch a little more to the right. "Never gave it much thought."

"You've got to admit it's a strange choice," I said. "I mean, the town was known for witch hunts."

Paul shrugged. "Don't know what to tell you. It was a few hundred years ago. Why do politicians do anything?"

"Good point."

An hour later there was nothing left to do but wet-vac the floor and call it a weekend.

Paul went back to his own store while I finished. It was after six when I doused the lights and locked up. Once again I cut across the yard to see if Chloe was around. The doors were still locked. The CLOSED sign was still prominent. But this time the lights were off.

I debated driving up to the motel for a toothbrush but decided against it. They had toothbrushes in Massachusetts. I'd pick up what I needed when I got there.

It took two tries before the truck started. I let it warm up then pointed it in the direction of the gas station, which happened to be on Chloe's side of town. And since I was only a few blocks away from her house, I figured I might as well stop by and let her know about the flood and tell her I wouldn't be back until Monday morning.

Nothing personal.

Just as an FYI.

21

CHLOE

I didn't know much about my newfound magick, but one thing I did know was that it was bad for business.

Up until my powers started to kick in, I had never closed Sticks & Strings early and I had definitely never closed down in the middle of the day so I could go home and eat an entire bag of Chips Ahoy with a rocky road chaser while I contemplated my life.

Sorcha's visit had shaken me to my core. Knowing that my parents' love story was built on a foundation of magick and not the deeply human connection I had longed for my entire life made me feel as if someone had cut me free from my familiar moorings and set me adrift in uncharted waters.

The thing was I understood why my mother did it. In the deepest part of my heart I got it. Humans claimed all was fair in love and war and maybe they were right. Guinevere had been blessed with beauty and talent and magick. They were all part of who she was. She fell in love and used magick to tip the balance in her favor. You used what you had. We all did.

It's not the same thing, daughter, and you know it. I could hear Sorcha's voice loud and clear inside my head. What if my father had known the truth about Sugar Maple and realized he couldn't commit to a lifetime in a town where he was the only mortal being? He had deserved the chance to decide for himself. I was old enough to know that in the human world love wasn't always enough to bridge the gap between people.

Maybe Sugar Maple wasn't so different after all.

Remember that future I had spent my life

dreaming about? The one with the home and the kids and the normal everyday life? It wasn't going to happen. I could dream and wish and pray all I wanted, but "normal" and "everyday" weren't in the cards for me.

The last thing I wanted to do was get all dressed up for Lynette's opening night, but a promise was a promise. I dragged myself off to the shower and hoped my mood would improve at least a little by the time the curtain went up.

I was fiddling with my eye makeup when someone knocked on the door.

A smarter woman wouldn't have answered it. My hair was wrapped around bright red Velcro rollers the size of soup cans. My right eye was shadowed and mascaraed. My left one wasn't. I was wearing my favorite pair of toe-up candy-striped knee socks and an old hoodie from my brief time at BU.

Luke MacKenzie was the last person I expected to see on my front porch.

"Luke!" I ducked behind the door. "I'm not dressed!"

"I tried calling but you're not answering your phone."

"I—uh, I had a busy day."

"The shop was closed."

"That doesn't mean I wasn't busy."

"I knocked a few times but you didn't answer."

"That's because I went home early." I hoped I didn't sound as lame to him as I sounded to myself.

"You found time to change the locks."

That pulled me out of hiding. "I didn't change the locks."

"The key you gave me fit yesterday but it didn't fit today. What's up with that?"

"Maybe you used the wrong key." I couldn't tell him that it was probably another random act of magick, courtesy of the good citizens of Sugar Maple, designed to make his life difficult.

His eyes swept over me from the rollers on my head to my freshly polished toes. He lingered on my legs just long enough for me to forget the fact that I was one giant goose bump.

"Why are you here?"

"I wanted to talk to you."

"I mean, really. What made you decide to come over?"

He frowned. "I already told you. I wanted

to talk to you and you weren't answering your phone."

"You're here of your own free will?"

"Yeah," he said, taking a step back. "What's with the weird questions?"

You don't want to know.

"It's ten degrees out here," he said. "Do you think we can talk in the hallway?"

I felt like I was the one under a magic spell. My heart leaped into my throat as he stepped into my tiny foyer. Would he remember that he'd spent the night here last night?

"You look uncomfortable," he said.

"My hair's in rollers, my makeup's lopsided, and I'm half-dressed. You'd be uncomfortable too."

"Half-dressed is good."

I tried to say something but we were in each other's arms before I could form the first word. The room glowed with silvery sparks that made my skin tingle with excitement.

The kisses were long and slow and sweet. They were everything I had ever imagined kisses could be. I wanted to lose myself in them again, dive deep into this sensual ocean and never surface.

I wanted more kisses. Deeper kisses. Longer kisses. The kind of kisses a woman didn't recover from without more kisses.

His hands slid along my rib cage and I shivered with pure pleasure. Last night had been part magick, part fantasy. I had danced close to the edge but somehow I hadn't gone over it. I didn't want him through magick. I wanted what happened between us to be as real and as human as he was.

As human as I once was and would never be again.

He was here because he wanted to be here. He was kissing me because kissing me was what he wanted to do. No spells. No charms. No magick potions.

My Velcro rollers went flying. His heavy coat fell to the floor. He inched my hoodie up. My hands slid under his heavy sweater. I couldn't hear over the pulse beating in my ears. I couldn't think beyond the next kiss, the next touch. I didn't want to. Not tonight.

Desire had a choreography all its own and it never stumbled. The kissing never stopped yet somehow we managed to get naked. Still kissing, we found our way to the sofa.

Did you ever have a moment when you were more yourself than you had ever been before? A moment when everything you were and everything you would ever be rushed together in a radiant burst of heat and light and you realized you were happy. The kind of happy you knew could never last but the memory of it would be enough to get you through the next thirty or forty years.

That's how it was for me.

Who knew that twenty minutes could change a woman's life.

I remember every second of our time together. I remember how he sounded, how his body felt poised over mine, the way his skin tasted. I took those details into my heart and embedded them deeply into my memory where nobody else could ever reach them.

I don't know how long we lay together while the world reassembled itself around us. I only know it wasn't long enough.

"I'm driving down to Massachusetts to-night," he said into my hair.

A sense of foreboding edged out some of the afterglow. "Leaving us so soon?"

He explained about the call from his former brother-in-law and the memorial service some friends were holding for Suzanne Marsden. "I'll stay at Jack's and be back here Monday morning."

I did what I always did when faced with real emotion: I hid behind a cheap joke. "Can't face Lynette's *Christmas Carol*?"

He held me closer. "Can't face seeing you with a blind date."

I started to laugh. "Janice's cousin! I totally forgot about him."

"Don't go."

I leaned back and met his eyes. "What?"

"Ditch the play and come to Massachusetts with me."

I pressed my face against his chest. "I can't."

"Sure you can."

"I have a store to run."

"Play hooky."

I wanted to throw responsibility to the wind and say yes, but I knew that if I walked away from Sugar Maple now, even for a night, I might as well hand it over to Isadora.

"It's my busiest season. I can't."

He held me closer. The warmth from his body flooded mine.

"I don't want to leave," he said.

But we both knew he would. Suzanne had been his friend, and friends were rare in this world. When you lost one, that loss had to be acknowledged.

I heard the sound of a familiar car crunching its way through the snow.

"Are you expecting someone?" he asked.

"Oh no," I murmured against his neck. "It's Janice."

He groaned. "And you didn't lock the front door."

"That's a fact, Detective."

I didn't tell him that it would take more than a lock to keep Janice out once she realized the truck in the driveway belonged to Luke.

I grabbed his clothes and threw them in the general direction of the sofa. My hoodie was inside out. I fumbled around with it then yanked it over my head the way it was. It beat being caught naked by Janice, the most judgmental woman in Sugar Maple. I loved her, but when it came to my romantic future, the woman had issues.

I glanced over at Luke, who was sitting on the edge of the sofa. "Put your pants on! She'll be here any second."

We probably looked like cartoon characters scurrying around the living room in search of runaway clothing, but we managed to get ourselves decently covered with not a moment to spare.

Janice knocked once and swung open the front door. "Hi," she called out in a fake cheerful tone of voice. "Hope I'm not interrupting anything."

Which meant she knew she was.

There was something to be said for police training. Luke's expression gave away nothing. I looked for a glimmer of connection between us, but it had disappeared beneath some kind of emotional armor.

Janice, who had been expecting fireworks, looked disappointed as he said hello and shrugged into his coat.

"You have my cell number, Chloe." He didn't sound like a man who had been naked less than three minutes ago. "Call me if the shop floods again."

"I will." Unfortunately I did sound like I had been naked less than three minutes ago. And the whisker burn probably didn't help matters. "Drive safely."

We locked eyes. We probably shouldn't have but we did, and the air between us shimmered with heat.

Janice waited until he was in his truck before she let me have it.

"No." I raised my hand to stop her. For once in my life I didn't want advice, no matter how well-meaning or on target.

Her eyebrows lifted. *"No?"*

"Really, Jan." I looked straight at her. "No questions. No explanations."

"I think I liked you better before you got your powers."

"Janice—"

"Honey, the guy's hot. I don't blame you. But don't turn it into something it isn't."

"I'm not having this conversation."

"Enjoy it for what it is, but don't expect more."

"I don't expect anything."

"Of course you do. You're your mother's daughter. But you can't have it with your human, Chloe."

"You don't know that." There was nothing she could throw at me that logic and passion couldn't refute.

"I know that he won't stay here forever and I know you'll never leave."

Except for that.

LUKE

I hung around at the end of Chloe's driveway for a few minutes before I pulled away. I wasn't sure what I thought was going to happen, but I couldn't make myself leave until I saw her through the window as she pulled on her coat and wrapped her scarf around her neck.

I could still feel her against me, smell her on my skin, hear the sounds she made low in her throat. My body was still warm from hers. In a perfect world we would be lying naked in her bed right now and we wouldn't leave it until Monday morning.

And that was only half of the story. Something more than sex had happened back there. The connection between us was more than physical. For a little while, in that small cottage, on her narrow couch, I had been happy, and unless I missed my guess, she had been happy too.

About an hour later I pulled off the highway at a rest stop for gas. The full moon was moving higher in the sky. I was thinking about grabbing a couple bags of chips and some coffee when I remembered my former brother-in-law had moved since I'd last been down in Bradford and I didn't have the new address.

The old phone number was still good and one of his sisters picked up on the second ring.

"Jackie's not here," Sherry said. "He and Lisa went down to Florida for their anniversary weekend." Sherry was watching the kids, the dogs, and the house for them.

There was no memorial service for Suzanne that weekend. No gathering of old friends and ex-family. Nothing.

"I don't know what to tell you, Luke," Sherry said, "but it's great to hear your voice."

I paid for the gas, grabbed a coffee and two bags of chips, then climbed back behind the wheel. I knew Lisa had problems with Suzanne. Knowing your husband was still friends with his ex would be tough enough for a woman to swallow, but when the ex looked like the ultimate trophy wife, trouble was inevitable.

And then there was the fact that Jack had never really gotten over Suzanne.

It wasn't hard to picture him drunk dialing old friends to set up a memorial service for his first love, only to be reminded by his present love that they had anniversary plans for a weekend in Orlando.

With a little luck I'd be back in Sugar Maple before Scrooge took his final curtain call.

CHLOE

The Pendragons really knew how to throw a pretheater cocktail party. The lobby was packed with townies and tourists toasting the season with hot buttered rum and mulled wine. Vivid scarlet poinsettias decorated every available surface. Glossy dark green holly, punctuated with plump red berries, framed windows and entryways. Old-fashioned Christmas carols, the kind that made you cry because you knew not even Bing Crosby had perfect holidays, filled the air. A full winter moon hung in the sky like polished silver.

And to make it even better, my blind date had stood me up. Apparently Janice's cousin Haydon didn't date women with less than full powers and had decided to drive on through to Canada. Janice said she had tried to convince him that my human side was only a technicality, but he wasn't interested.

"Where's Gunnar?" I asked Janice as the lobby lights flickered. "I haven't seen him."

"Lynette had a minor emergency. He's backstage helping out."

"Where are you sitting?"

"Row G on the left." She rolled her eyes. "The Meany clan takes up the entire row. Where are you?"

"C1 and C2 center." We made plans to meet during intermission to compare notes on this year's Scrooge, a selkie named James who was scheduled to return to the sea sometime this coming spring.

I made my way to Row C and claimed the aisle seat as the music rose and the lights went down and I got ready to be swept back to Dickens's London and a different kind of magic.

At least that was what usually happened when I watched a show at the Playhouse. This time, however, I had brought my own magick with me and saw sights I had never seen before. I gasped at the sheer volume of theatergoers who didn't need numbered seats. The Harris family hovered above the orchestra. The Souderbushes were perched on the chandeliers. Benjamin, his wife, and extended family had claimed front row center, sharing the seats with tourists from Quebec who hadn't a clue.

Ordinary-looking people I had believed were pure human exhibited nonhuman characteristics when seen through my newly magicked eyes while suspects I would have bet my roving had special powers were totally earthbound.

"I hear you were stood up."

I jumped as Gunnar popped up next to me in the aisle.

"Your lucky day," I said, gesturing toward the empty seat next to me.

"Clarence drank too much rum. I'm

taking over the lighting." He glanced around. "Where's the cop?"

"On his way back to Massachusetts."

He arched a brow. "Permanently?"

"For the weekend."

He studied me carefully but didn't pursue the topic. "You'll be at the after-party?"

"Pigs-in-a-blanket and sangria. Try to keep me away."

He touched my shoulder and the next instant he was gone.

22

LUKE

I was exiting the highway when the truck climbed up the outer edge of the curve and came close to tipping over the embankment before I was able to regain control and ease it back down again.

"Shit." I pulled over onto the local road and waited for the adrenaline surge to fade. Twice in a few days? If things kept going this way, I wouldn't make it to the end of the winter in one piece.

The twenty miles of local road between

the highway and Sugar Maple were un-lighted so I kept my speed relatively slow even though the full moon cast a brilliant glow over the snowy fields. Deer crossing signs appeared every hundred yards or so. I passed a buck standing in the shad-ows and saw a doe a few feet behind him, a pair of fawns by her side.

You knew you were in trouble when a family of deer had a better chance of living happily ever after than you did.

Not that I believed in the fairy tale end-ing. I had spent my adult life cleaning up the mess left behind when the ending didn't match the dream.

Chloe knew I was a cop. She knew I'd been on the force in Boston. She knew I was divorced and that I believed in locked doors, hot sex, and not much else.

Up until tonight I would have figured that was enough.

Now I wasn't sure about anything.

A giant fir tree lay across the foot of the Hollandsworth Bridge, which linked the secondary roads to Sugar Maple.

"Now what," I muttered out loud. Three hours ago the road had been passable.

I was still a stranger in the area. I didn't know the side streets or the shortcuts locals used. I was tempted to aim the truck toward town and off-road it through the woods, but I'd probably end up in Cincinnati.

Nothing wrong with utilizing a little twenty-first-century technology. I flicked on the GPS and the NO SIGNAL message blinked back.

I should have taken that class in celestial navigation back in high school.

At this rate I'd be lucky if I made it back to Sugar Maple in time for Christmas.

CHLOE

I started feeling not so great around the time the Ghost of Christmas Past took Scrooge by the hand and led him down the avenue of lost dreams.

Normally I'm a pushover for the story. A sick kid. A cranky old man. Redemption on a grand scale. It didn't get much better than that.

Tonight, however, it wasn't working for

me. When I looked at the stage, I didn't see nineteenth-century London: I saw a family of Vermont shapeshifters and one immigrant selkie playing pretend.

I wasn't an expert on energy fields but the room felt off balance and so did I. I told myself it was probably my burgeoning powers creating a disturbance around me but that wouldn't explain the sweaty palms, the nausea, or the throbbing pain behind my eyes.

Oh wait. I forgot. This was how it felt when a Hobbs woman fell in love.

I tried to concentrate on what was happening on stage, but I couldn't take my eyes off the spirit cats clawing their way up the heavy velvet curtains. Tabbys, calicos, Abyssinians, tuxedos, and a very familiar black cat with golden yellow eyes, who stared down at me from the top of the curtain.

Penelope?

I watched in astonishment as she grabbed one of the tattered shreds between her front paws and swung across the stage like a feline Tarzan, landing atop a huge basket of brightly colored yarn that belonged to Mrs. Fezziwig.

"Sit down, Chloe!" Verna Griggs whispered from the seat right behind me. "You're blocking the view!"

"Did you see that?" I asked, pointing toward the stage. "Penny—"

"Down in front!" an angry voice shouted.

I looked back at the stage. The curtain-clawing cats were gone, but Penny had grown to three times her size and was standing at the foot of the stage hissing red and orange flames straight at my head.

And that wasn't even the weird part. The weird part was the fact that nobody in the entire theater seemed to notice what was going on.

Penny expanded from bobcat size to full-grown lioness. She howled and flames shot from her mouth, over the heads of the audience, then wrapped themselves around me. I could feel the heat but not the pain. The flames clung to me like a second skin but they didn't burn.

And still nobody noticed.

I had to get out of there before I went crazy.

I raced up the aisle past the curious faces of friends and strangers then burst through the double doors into the brightly lit lobby. A gathering of spirit women in nineteenth-century clothing looked up from their quilting bee set up near the refreshment counter.

"Join us, Chloe," the oldest one said with a smile. "We've been waiting."

Oh god.

I ricocheted past a Colonial-era serving wench, barely missed a World War I nurse, and then exploded out the door to freedom.

I wanted it to stop. I wanted the magick to go away. Giving me magick was like handing a toddler a loaded gun and expecting her to shoot straight every time. The odds were definitely against it. I couldn't even attend Lynette's opening night performance without freaking out because my cat was trying to muscle in on Tiny Tim's territory.

I mean, if I couldn't handle some feline histrionics, what hope was there? I had lived in Sugar Maple long enough to know that magick wasn't always neat and predictable and neither were the men and women who practiced it. If I flipped out every time a cat talked to me, I wouldn't make it to next Thursday with my sanity intact.

I leaned against a tree and struggled to

catch my breath. All sorts of crazy images spun past me. Luke behind the wheel of his truck, his face illuminated by the light from the full moon. My mother at her spinning wheel. Sorcha, her dear face creased and lined with worry. Isadora, bathed in a shimmering mist, as she ripped through Sticks & Strings—

"No!" The word exploded from my throat like gunshot. If Isadora managed to claim the Book, Sugar Maple was doomed.

A thick purple cloud had settled itself over the town like shrink wrap. The air grew syrupy and sickeningly sweet, like roses past their prime. My stomach lurched sideways. I thought I was about to be sick until the tree I was leaning against suddenly threw its limbs around me and tried to squeeze me like a tube of Colgate, effectively taking my mind off my nausea.

I don't know if it was magick or good old human adrenaline but power surged through me like an electric current. I wasn't going to give up without a fight. I leaned back into the tree and closed my eyes, gathering together every ounce of strength I had at my command.

When a sugar maple grabbed hold of

you, it meant business. Sharp branches dug into my rib cage. Rough bark sliced through my down parka and tore skin from my face as I fought against it. I might as well have been a flea fighting an elephant.

With a yell, I threw myself forward one more time and heard a loud crack as the branches snapped in two and I fell free. My left knee hit the ground. I think my hip did too but I didn't have time to care. I scrambled to my feet and propelled myself toward Sticks & Strings and I didn't look back.

LUKE

After five minutes of dead ends, the light dawned. I remembered reading about abandoned logging routes in some of the research materials I'd snagged from the library. Supposedly they had run from the base of what became the highway to the southwest boundary of Sugar Maple, right near Snow Lake. With a little luck, maybe there was a map tucked in with the newspaper clippings and magazine tear sheets.

I pulled over and clicked on my hazard lights. I reached into the back and grabbed

for the huge stack of stuff I'd rubber-
banded together. Menus. Promo materials. Where to ski. Where to fish. Where to
shop. Where to skate.

I stopped flipping through the stack and
pulled out a clipping from the *Sugar Maple
Gazette.*

CHLOE HOBBS CROWNED WINTER
FESTIVAL QUEEN
**Sixteen-year-old Chloe Hobbs of Maple
Drive greets
her loyal subjects on Day One of the
Winter Festival.
The Queen's Loyal Court performed a ballet
on ice to tunes
provided by the Sugar Maple High School
Marching
Band while the Queen watched from her
throne.**

She looked very young and very self-
conscious standing there next to a big
maple tree while a dozen little girls in old-
fashioned skating costumes knelt in front
of their queen. She hadn't changed much
in the last dozen years. She was still tall,
still skinny, still blond. And she still had

that oddly appealing blend of confidence and uncertainty that made me want to get closer.

She'd be hearing about the big hair . . .

I tossed the clipping on the passenger seat and continued the map search when something clicked. I looked past Chloe, past the little girls, and zeroed in on the huge maple tree next to them.

I knew that tree. I had noticed it on my drive-through the first night in town, the tree with the big circle gouged into the bark. I remembered feeling relieved that there was at least a spark of rebellion alive there in Stepford. But I hadn't realized there were other symbols carved or burned within the circle itself.

A crescent moon. A full sun. Symbols so common they barely registered when you saw them. Hell, half the kids under twenty-one probably sported tats of the sun and the moon or one of their variants.

Chloe's store logo was a line drawing of a beautiful woman holding the sun aloft in the palm of her hand.

That wasn't it either. There was something else, something darker and more recent.

The cemetery.

Carved into one of the flat, white marble stones that marked the resting place of Chloe's parents was a big round sun with dozens of rays extending outward. Carved into the other was a crescent moon.

I pictured moonlight sweeping across the frozen pond. Starlight shining down. I imagined Chloe's parents carving symbols instead of initials in the tree, crazy/drunk with young love. Thinking it would never end.

But it did. Everything did sooner or later.

Bad things happened every day to good people, and they'd been happening since man stood upright and took his first step. Thinking about things you couldn't change was a waste of time.

But something wasn't right back there in Sugar Maple. I could find a way to explain the lack of crime, the missing birth and death records, the general sense that I was the only one not in on the joke. But when you added them up, what you got was way outside my comfort zone.

Take the woman at the cemetery. People didn't disappear like that. Not in a relatively open space with no place to hide. But it happened and I still didn't know how.

And the Salem thing. The replica of the lighthouse, the street names. Why had the powers that be sought to honor the infamous history of a small Massachusetts town? The Salem I had known as a kid was a theme park for witches and things that went bump in the night while Sugar Maple was New England's version of the American dream.

Or was it? In less than a week I had seen Fourth of July fireworks explode every time Chloe and I touched. I had seen a snifter of brandy hover over my lap like a Harrier jet. Hell, for a few moments yesterday I had almost believed I had levitated from one end of Carrier to the other. And not under my own power.

People left footprints in the snow when they walked and I hadn't left a single one. When I asked Chloe, she had looked at me like I was hallucinating. Disappearing black ice on a thoroughly dry street. Wonky electronic equipment. Snapping power lines. A lightning bolt with my name on it.

There was something going on there, and it had nothing to do with apple pies and white picket fences.

I had noticed an abandoned dirt road a

few hundred feet back. The forest was in the process of reclaiming it, but I was pretty sure my truck was up to the job. I had a full tank and a good sense of direction and the growing certainty that Sugar Maple wasn't what it seemed.

And maybe neither was Chloe.

CHLOE

Isadora was waiting for me when I burst through the front door of Sticks & Strings.

She wore a purple velvet cloak embroidered all over with silk thread in the colors of the rainbow. Her magick was so powerful that the room shook from it.

Tonight I saw her through eyes opened by my own blossoming powers and her beauty was astonishing. Ribbons of silky jet-black hair that cascaded to the floor, luminous turquoise eyes, skin the color of heavy cream tinged with the slightest touch of pink.

I could feel myself growing smaller as I stood there, diminished in every way possible by the faerie woman standing before me.

"So it's true," she said as she motioned me into my own shop. "Your powers have begun."

I dodged the issue. "What are you doing here?"

"We've come too far for pretense," she said with an amused chuckle. "The Book of Spells should be mine."

I had to hand it to her. I had been expecting the usual Fae game of thrust-and-parry, but she went straight to the heart of the matter.

"Only a Hobbs woman can own the Book," I reminded her.

I was flung across the room like a bag of roving. The edge of the worktable stopped me before I went headlong into the fireplace. My right hip took the worst of it and I was grateful for every quart of Ben & Jerry's calcium I'd ingested lately.

"You might want to have your meds adjusted," I muttered as I struggled to my feet.

Fortunately wise-ass humor was lost on most Fae.

"The facts are these," she said, imprisoning me in a silver net that clung like a damp spiderweb. "I will have the Book.

Your powers are not yet sufficient to fully claim it. You can defer to my greater powers and be rewarded, or you can fight me and lose everything you value."

"You forgot the third option," I said as I shrugged off the silver net with a surprisingly effective display of my own newfound magic. "I could fight you and win."

LUKE

The road came to an abrupt stop about a half mile from Snow Lake. I could either retrace my path and try to find another route or ditch the truck and go the rest of the way on foot.

I ditched the truck.

The woods were thick. Very little moonlight filtered through the dense cover of pine and spruce. I kept myself on track by focusing on the clearing that I assumed opened onto the lake itself. An owl hooted from somewhere close by, but there was little sound beyond that and the crunch of ice-encrusted snow beneath my feet.

I had the sense I was being watched. The woods were filled with creatures, most of which came alive at night. I figured as long as I didn't hear a banshee, I was ahead of the game.

I reached the clearing at the southwest edge of the lake. The place was deserted and I figured the entire village was over at the Playhouse, where Scrooge should be putting it all together right about now.

Most lakes of this size in northern Vermont had been deemed safe for skating by Thanksgiving this year. No warnings to the contrary had been posted at Snow Lake. The kids had played hockey and practiced for the upcoming festival without incident just two days before Suzanne's accident. By all reports the center ice had been unmarred by signs of wear or weakness.

The frozen surface gleamed smooth in the moonlight as if it had been Zambonied. It was as if yesterday's half foot of snow had never happened. I decided against walking the perimeter of the lake. Walking across it was faster and it would give me a chance to see the spot where the accident happened. I walked out toward center ice. I had grown up skating natural ice and I trusted my gut the same as Suzanne had that Snow Lake was solid.

I stopped a few feet away from where she went in. Where I had expected to see the usual angular breakage common to this type of accident, I saw the smooth edges of a perfect circle.

For the second time in my life my blood ran cold as my hand closed over the star pin in my pocket. I stood there staring at the opening where Suzanne had dropped into the icy lake and experienced an overwhelming sense of dread that I couldn't explain.

I backed away from the spot then turned and walked quickly toward the enormous sugar maple I had noticed on my first night. The tree was halfway between the lake and the street, the tallest of the maples in that stand. I ran a hand over the bark. The circle wasn't new. Dried sap had long since formed scar tissue over the initial injury but hadn't obliterated the smaller designs.

Burned into the once soft wood were the symbols I had noticed in the news clipping: a small crescent moon and a sun whose rays shot off in every direction. The same symbols as those on Chloe's parents' grave markers.

There was a third symbol, however, that

hadn't been in the news clipping. A star like the one in my pocket. When I leaned close, I caught the faint scent of burned wood and I felt the residual dampness of sap against my fingertips.

"Too bad about that one."

I turned to see one of the golden boys standing behind me. He wore a long black coat and a wide scarf that covered much of his face.

"What do you mean?"

"Your friend," he said, unwinding the scarf. "I don't remember her name."

His face was magazine-cover perfect. No bruises or scrapes. It was the cross-country skier but without the good-natured charm of the other night. This man made me wish I hadn't left my gun in the truck.

Something ugly was taking shape and I didn't know where it was heading.

"Her name was Suzanne," I said.

His smile was white and gleaming. "Suzanne," he repeated. "I've never been good with names."

"You were with her that night." It wasn't a question.

"I wondered how long it would take you."

His smile widened. "Not bad, Detective. I'm impressed."

"Where did you meet her?"

"Are you asking as her friend or as a cop?"

"Would it change your answer?"

"If you want to know if I fucked her, the answer's no."

I didn't say anything.

"C'mon," he taunted. "Take a shot at me. You know you want to."

I kept my cool.

"So what is it? She wouldn't give you the time of day."

I still didn't respond. I wasn't going to be goaded into doing something stupid.

"She'd been drinking," he said, "but she wasn't drunk. She saw the lake and she wanted to go skating."

It sounded like Suzanne. She wouldn't have thought twice about skating in some skimpy evening dress. Of the old crowd, she was the one who had always thumbed her nose at convention.

"She said she could teach me to skate a star into the ice."

Definitely Suzanne. She had taught

herself to skate figures as a kid just for the hell of it.

I knew where this was going. Dane had figured he would put up with her skating in the hope that it would lead to something else, and when it didn't, he lashed out in rage.

"Too linear," he said with a grin.

Shit. The guy could read minds.

"Figured that out too. Damn, you're good."

"You killed her."

"Now there you're wrong, Detective. I didn't kill her but I could have saved her. A small distinction but an important one." He studied me carefully for my reaction. "The human body doesn't do well in those temperatures. My mother counted on that."

"What the hell does your mother have to do with Suzanne's death?"

"Who do you think melted the ice beneath her feet?" The son of a bitch actually laughed. "You should've seen your friend's face when she realized what was happening. She kept grabbing for the edge of the ice and it kept melting beneath her fingers."

If I'd had my gun, I would have used it.

The fury I felt burned away rational thought. I swung at him with a right hook that should have flattened him but didn't. The guy didn't even blink.

"You get one free shot," he said. "Next time we play by my rules."

I swung at him again, but this time I was lifted off my feet and flung backward into a spruce tree. My head slammed against the trunk with a thud.

I tried to get up but couldn't. Every time I lifted my head, pain pushed me back into the ground.

"I didn't think you'd be much of a problem but I was wrong," Dane said, standing over me. "I'm going to have to do something about you."

His boot connected with my gut and I vomited blood into the snow.

"Poor bastard," he said. "Too bad there's nobody around to help you."

I heard the words but I was having trouble putting them together into a whole. The pain in my head was bad but the pain in my gut where he'd kicked me helped take my mind off it.

He was a psychopath but I didn't think

he was a cold-blooded murderer until he kicked me in the right kidney and things went black.

I don't know how long I was out, but when I opened my eyes again, there were two of them battling it out six feet above the lake, which was ablaze with what looked like some kind of flaming glitter.

I was either dead or brain damaged. Nothing else made sense.

Unless it was magic.

I pushed the idea as far away as it would go. As far as I was concerned, magic was a Vegas lounge act performed by a middle-aged guy with a bad rug and a twenty-year-old assistant looking to fast-track her way into show business.

One of the brothers crashed to the ground a few feet away from me. His bloodied face sported some older bruises so I knew it was Gunnar. He tried to say something to me, but an unseen blow threw him back against the big sugar maple tree.

Maybe it was time to rethink my position.

Three symbols. Three accidental deaths. And now the faint outlines of two new symbols were beginning to form in the bark while I watched.

I pulled myself upright. Near me Gunnar groaned. But where the hell was his brother?

I glanced around the lake. The mirrorlike surface of the ice was thick with steel blue glitter. There was no sign of either brother. People didn't just disappear like that, did they?

"Shit," I said out loud. In Sugar Maple they did. I thought of the woman I'd met at the cemetery and the way she'd seemed to vanish into thin air.

"That was our mother."

I followed the sound of the voice and saw Dane standing on the branch of a winter-bare oak tree looking down at me. "She does a pretty good Boston accent, doesn't she?"

Bad enough he had read my mind but now I heard Jack's voice as he had sounded on the cell phone that morning. *Hey, Mac. We're having a memorial for Suz on Sunday. The old crowd . . .*

The dead electronic equipment. The busted water pipe.

"Mine," he said.

"The black ice?" I asked out loud.

"Pretty good, huh? Then again I've had a lot of practice."

"Jesus," I breathed. "You killed Chloe's parents."

"Can't take credit there but I gave you a few good scares."

"Did you cause that school bus accident too?"

"Guilty as charged."

When a suspect started spilling his guts, it usually meant one of two things: he was either ready to give himself up, or you didn't have to worry about what to do on your summer vacation. My chances of making it through the night were shrinking fast.

"You're in over your head, MacKenzie. You're messing with shit you can't comprehend. You would've lived longer if you'd gone back to Boston and stayed there."

He vanished with the last word, but he left his calling card in the form of a thunderbolt that split the night sky with a thunderous crack. It gathered speed as it looped the lake, then entered a trajectory headed straight for me. I moved left. So did the thunderbolt. I moved right. It did too.

A thunderbolt with my name on it. Why not? It was as believable as anything else that had happened to me since I arrived in Sugar Maple.

There was something ironic about a cop buying it in a town without crime. Maybe one day, in some afterlife Zen kind of moment, I'd find the humor in it.

The thunderbolt was so close I could feel its heat when Gunnar threw himself in front of me.

I bellowed as a red-hot current zapped my right leg.

Gunnar was motionless but watchful. His scorched flesh smelled like a combination of toasted marshmallows and motor oil.

Our eyes met. He had taken a blow meant for me.

"Why?" I asked as I stared down at him. "You don't even know me."

"Chloe loves you," he managed. "Save her."

"From what?"

His eyes opened, closed, then opened again. ". . . Mother . . . knit shop . . ."

I slipped my arm under his shoulder and

helped him to his feet. "You're badly hurt," I said, stating the obvious. "We need to get you to the nearest hospital."

But there were no hospitals in Sugar Maple. Or doctors, for that matter. I hoped some of those brochures in the truck had the information I needed.

"You're . . . not . . . listening," Gunnar said, grimacing as he pulled away from me. I watched as he seemed to gather strength from some unseen source. "It's an ambush . . . we have to get to the knit shop now."

I started for the car but he grabbed my arm hard enough to stop me in my tracks, uttered a few syllables I didn't understand, and we were pulled backward into darkness.

23

LUKE

We exploded into the back of the knit shop in a blaze of smoke and light. Gunnar stumbled but stayed upright while I crashed to the ground like deadweight. As a cop I was used to facing the unexpected, but this was off the chart.

"Holy shit!" The words tore from my throat as my molecules reassembled themselves. I felt like a human jigsaw puzzle with a few pieces missing. And a hell of a lot of questions to ask when this was over.

The knit shop was alive with special effects not even Hollywood had dreamed of. A yarn tornado spun furiously in the center of the room while a human-sized web of knitting needles clanked and danced near the window like an empty bird cage. Magazines and papers swirled across the floor. Bookcases had been overturned, the books crushed beneath them. A dark-haired woman hovered two feet off the ground, directing the action like a crazed conductor.

I zeroed in on Chloe. That son-of-a-bitch Dane had her pinned up against the wall. His black coat was shredded. His face was splattered with blood. He looked wild, out of control, and triumphant as he wrenched her arm hard for emphasis. Pain was clearly evident in her face but she didn't utter a sound. My respect for her soared sky high. I had known cops who went out on permanent disability after a whole lot less.

Gunnar flung himself at his brother in a blaze of silver blue glitter and heat. Dane threw Chloe to the ground and met his brother's attack with the kind of ferocity I had only seen in stone-cold killers as I half walked, half crawled over to where she lay.

"Are you okay?" I asked. "What the hell's going on?"

"Get out," she said. "Get as far away from here as you can."

"Not without you."

I helped Chloe to her feet.

"This isn't your fight," she said.

"It's your fight. That's enough for—"

"So the knight in shining armor has come to save our heroine," the dark-haired woman said from across the room. She was focused solely on Chloe. "Give me the Book of Spells or he dies."

What the hell was a book of spells?

I stepped in front of Chloe as recognition dawned. "You're the woman from the cemetery."

"Luke." Chloe sounded a warning. "Isadora means what she says."

"Listen to her, Luke," the woman said. "She wouldn't lie to you."

Cops aren't real good with threats. I stepped forward and the next thing I knew I bounced off the wall on the far side of the room.

Isadora cocked her head to one side

and hovered in front of Chloe. "Do we understand each other?"

"Perfectly," Chloe said. "You're still not
getting the book."

Isadora glanced at me over her shoulder. I felt like I was thinking my way through
a headful of oatmeal.

"Detective, it looks like you should have
stayed in Boston." She spread her arms
wide and a giant anaconda suddenly appeared five feet in front of me, jaws open,
fangs glistening with yellow slime.

I'm not a fan of snakes. Especially not a
thirty-foot specimen with a body as wide as
a steel girder and a head bigger than your
average trash can. It lay coiled on the floor,
glistening black eyes watchful, forked tongue
lazily testing the air in search of prey. Suddenly I felt the atmosphere change. The
snake uncoiled slowly, deliberately, rising
higher and higher until its outsized head
brushed the ceiling. Its movements were
sinuous and dangerously compelling, a
rhythmic swaying movement that was a pre-
lude to disaster. I'd be lying if I said I didn't
want to grab Chloe and get the hell out of
Dodge.

Unfortunately two thousand pounds of snake were blocking the exit.

Isadora made a quick cutting motion with her left hand and the snake swooped forward, head swaying back and forth like something from a bad horror movie. Its mouth gaped open, jaw unhinging wider as a hissing sound surrounded me and the sour smell of wet ashes filled my nostrils. Chloe scrambled toward me and I yelled for her to stay away, but she didn't listen and the snake sent her flying with one flick of its tail.

CHLOE

I slammed into the floor hard. My left hip took most of the fall, but my head hit the edge of a chair and I guess I blacked out for a second because next thing I knew the monster snake was coiled around Luke's torso and legs. Luke struggled wildly against the increasing pressure, but he was no match for whatever fresh hell Isadora had set into motion. The sorceress side of my lineage might be kicking into high gear, but the human side was still vulnerable to pain.

The look in Isadora's eyes told me she would take this as far as she needed to.

I struggled to my feet. It was probably a good thing I didn't know where the Book of Spells was hidden because I would have handed it over to Isadora then and there. I dragged myself across the floor, crying out as Luke's face went from angry purple to deathly white to a waxy blue. The gargantuan snake slowly turned its head and settled its black-eyed gaze on me for what seemed like forever. I saw triumph in its eyes. Ropes of spittle dripped from its fangs as its hellish maw opened obscenely wide.

The snake reared back, exhaled an acrid plume of black smoke from its nostrils, and Luke's head disappeared from sight.

Before the scream could tear from my throat, Luke appeared on the ground next to me. I glanced quickly around the room and realized Gunnar had taken his place.

We both watched in horror as Gunnar was slowly pulled deep into the serpent. The hideous pulsing of powerful muscles marked the deadly progress. My brain shut down in self-defense against what was happening there in front of my eyes. Nothing in my life had prepared me for the sight of pure evil.

Then as quickly as the snake had appeared, it vanished in a swirl of pale yellow smoke. I waited for a triumphant Gunnar to reappear next to us ready to take on the next comer but the room fell into a profound silence. The silence stretched longer and deeper and the realization that the unthinkable happened finally hit me when Isadora's howl of rage blew out the doors and windows of my shop and sent the roof spinning up into the night.

Next to me Luke made a sound somewhere between a grunt and a groan. Blood poured from a gash over his right eye, and he seemed to be having trouble breathing. He also had the glazed expression of someone who was on sensory overload. He was a cop. He knew better than most that humans were capable of doing terrible things to each other, but I was certain he had never seen anything close to what he had witnessed tonight.

Our eyes met and held for an instant. We barely knew each other but somehow the bond between us was intense. I hoped it was strong enough for him to accept that this was my world, not his, and the rules he lived by didn't apply. He had to follow my lead or we were both lost.

Around us Isadora's towering display of grief sucked the oxygen from the room. Dane hung in midair, his torn black coat billowing behind him like a flag. Without his mother's direction, he seemed powerless.

Right now I was the only one on her radar.

"It's always you," she roared. "Is no sacrifice enough to satisfy your selfish needs? Sorcha. Your parents. Now my son. All dead because of you."

I felt Luke's questioning glance but I didn't dare acknowledge it.

"Sorcha stayed in this realm for you . . . she sacrificed for you . . ."

I tried to ignore the words, but her voice only grew louder.

"Gunnar loved you and how did you repay that love? He made the ultimate sacrifice so you could find happiness with a human . . ."

I refused to listen.

"And your parents." Her laugh sounded like metal against metal.

Next to me Luke tensed. I shot him a warning look.

"You're a liar," I said to Isadora. "The car skidded on a patch of black ice. It was an accident."

"And how do you think the black ice got there?" she countered.

"You killed my parents?"

Isadora had sent Dane to do the dirty work, but he was young and inexperienced in the dark arts and he hadn't figured on me being safely buckled up in the back-seat. "Unfortunately you survived but we did manage to eliminate Guinevere."

My mother's death was cause for cele-bration. My father's didn't even merit ac-knowledgment. I realized at that moment that I was capable of murder too.

"I was six years old. What could I have possibly done to make you hate me that much?"

"You have been a thorn in my side from the first. Our town came into being as a ref-uge from the cruelty and fears of humans. It isn't right that someone with human blood would have dominion over us."

I opened my mouth to speak but Luke stepped forward. "You killed Suzanne. You melted the ice beneath her feet and you both watched her die."

"It was the expedient thing to do. My sons both show a weakness for human females."

Luke was either crazy or the most courageous man I had ever met. He didn't back down an inch. "One of your sons is dead. Was that part of your master plan too?"

"Enough talk." Isadora pointed toward Luke. "Kill him."

"With pleasure," Dane said as loops of heavy gold chain the width of boat mooring sprang from his fingers and began wrapping themselves around Luke, tighter and tighter, attempting to finish the job the giant snake had started.

"Another fool sacrifices himself for a worthless specimen. Sugar Maple will thank me for this."

"Stop!" The word exploded from the depths of my soul. "Let him go!"

We all stared in amazement as my cry caused the chains to snap then disappear. Luke slumped to the ground, knocking over the almost empty basket of roving. He lay perfectly still, and for a second I thought he was unconscious. But there was a different quality to his stillness this time, a tension that made me believe we still might have a chance.

"This is growing tedious," Isadora said, visibly unsettled. "Perhaps I'll kill you both now."

"You won't kill me," I said. "You know as well as I do that if I die before you can claim the Book from me, it will be absorbed into the Universe."

"We don't need the Book any longer," Dane said. "Gunnar is dead and I inherited all of his powers. We can claim the town and make the transfer without it now."

Isadora's eyes burned with a zealot's fire. Whatever grief she had felt over Gunnar's death was swiftly fading as dark excitement took its place. *Hello, Mommy Dearest.*

Isadora, brandishing a flaming sword, swooped down like a bird of prey. The sword spiraled from her hands and headed straight for Luke, who rolled out of the way a moment before it plunged into the wall behind him.

Dane lunged for me, but somehow Luke was on his feet and he tackled him. They careened off the minitwister that was still spinning in the center of the room, then slammed into the cage of double point needles bouncing along the ceiling. Luke's blood splattered the walls.

With a mighty cry, Isadora launched a death bolt. Instinctively I flung out my hand and a glass shield spun outward into the path of the bolt, stopping it just inches before it reached Luke.

Isadora's bolt bounced off the shield, turned end over end over end, sparkling in the moonlight that flooded through the space where the roof used to be, then jack-knifed through Dane, slicing him cleanly in two. Like matching halves of a perfect diamond, the mirror images began to rotate slowly at first, then gathered speed until they vanished in an explosion of steel blue glitter.

Isadora's screams were the stuff of nightmares. They came from a hell I couldn't imagine. They peeled the skin off her hands and exposed the purple veins lying beneath.

She turned to face me, and I knew only

one of us would still be standing when this was over. Our eyes locked as a death bolt split the air just left of my ear.

This wasn't the Isadora I had known all my life. This was the woman I'd first seen at the Town Hall meeting: angry, vengeful, out of control. She began to spin like the twister, flinging lightning bolts and flaming swords wildly at Luke, but one after the other missed the mark. Enraged, she turned on me. I glanced toward the cage of double point needles clanking in the corner then back again at Isadora and jumped back in amazement as it surrounded her slender body, imprisoning her.

If this was what it was like to have magick, I think I liked it.

She burst from the cage and I was immediately slammed into the north wall, crushed against the bricks by an invisible panini press.

A pure Fae couldn't be harmed by the actions of a human, but I wasn't a simple human any longer. I had three centuries of magick coursing through my veins. Somewhere inside me was the power to stop her heart forever. All I had to do was use it and the battle would be won.

My fury matched hers. My need for revenge was equal to hers.

She deserved to die. To be erased from this world and any other she might inhabit. She deserved no more mercy than she had showed to my parents or to Suzanne or, in the end, to Luke.

But there was one important difference: I couldn't bring myself to take that final step.

"Fool," she spat. "I wouldn't hesitate."

Her huge turquoise eyes were focused directly on me with the kind of concentration only the Fae possessed. Luke, motionless on the ground, no longer mattered to her. I was all that mattered, and my time was running out.

I knew I would have only one chance and I had to get it right. Would a flaming sword appear in my hand when I needed one? Isadora's powers were at their peak while mine were just beginning to flow through my body. She knew exactly what to do and how to do it. Me? I was still flying blind.

But I had watched enough TV crime shows to know not to react when I saw Luke lift his head and take in the situation.

Relief that he was still alive threatened to undo my resolve. I couldn't let that happen no matter how much I wanted to run to him.

Luke started to crawl slowly toward the flaming sword embedded in the wall behind Isadora. I forced my expression to stay neutral, but there was nothing I could do about the fact that my heart was pounding so hard I had trouble breathing.

Isadora said something but I couldn't make sense of her words. I was too busy trying not to betray the fact that I was watching as Luke pulled himself up then grabbed the hilt of the flaming sword with both hands and yanked it from the wall.

I felt powerless as he slowly moved closer to Isadora, who was hovering a few feet above the ground. No second thoughts. No doubts. He would do what needed to be done even though he had seen things tonight that would send most mortals running.

Isadora stopped speaking and I could feel the heat of her gaze intensify. I literally stopped breathing as Luke moved behind her, raised the sword high overhead, then made to plunge it into her back.

I don't know if it was something I did or if Isadora's Fae senses alerted her, but she spun around so quickly that she vanished from sight for an instant then reappeared as a lightning bolt shot from her hand straight toward Luke.

The scream tore from my throat like jagged pieces of glass as the bolt slammed into the center of his chest and sent him through the shattered front window and into the night.

He was only mortal. He had withstood multiple onslaughts, but this time Isadora had achieved her goal. He was gone. I had never experienced pain like this before. It burrowed deep into my bones and worked its way outward, devouring everything within reach.

If my magick had been stronger, if *I* had been stronger, this never would have happened. But I hesitated and this was the result.

Luke deserved better. My parents and Gunnar and Suzanne deserved better.

I had no death bolts at my command, no flaming swords. All I had was the combined power of generations of Hobbs women.

I heard the voices of Aerynn and Maeve, Bronwyn and Guinevere, and all the others who had come before me. Their strength and wisdom were mine for the taking.

Banish her . . . banish her . . .

The voices grew stronger inside me.

Banish her!

I was a descendant of Aerynn and this was my time.

"Banish!" I cried out as I lunged for Isadora. "Banish!"

I scaled the air as if it were a flight of steps and grabbed her by the shoulders.

"Banish!"

I could feel the power surging through my body, the strength flowing into my muscles and bones. I lifted Isadora over my head and laughed out loud as the word *Banish* literally danced in the air before me, crisp and shiny black as patent leather. It widened and elongated and wrapped itself around a stunned Isadora, and then as the last letter fell into place, I summoned up all the magick at my command and hurled her through the missing roof, over the treetops, through the clouds, and into the void.

It was done.

I watched in silence as my shop reassembled itself around me. The roof slid back into place. Windows pieced themselves together. Bookcases righted themselves. The crazed twister began a counterclockwise rotation that sent brightly colored skeins of Noro and Elsebeth Lavold and Araucania flying back to their proper places. Penny was sleeping soundly in the overflowing basket of roving as if nothing had happened.

I stumbled out of the shop and stood on the sidewalk, gulping in the clean, cold air. I felt empty. The town had been saved but the cost had been high. My best friend had sacrificed himself so I could be with the man I loved, and in a terrible twist of fate, the man I loved gave his life so I could live.

Hobbs women loved only once. We were given one chance to be happy, one tiny moment in time when our hearts were open to the future.

And now mine was over.

I caught the scent of woodsmoke in the air, the faint tang of pine. The purple mist that had blanketed the town was gone. Sugar Maple was back to picture-postcard perfection, safe and snug beneath Aerynn's protective spell. In a few weeks it would be as if none of this had happened. The town would go on the way it always had, happily flying beneath the radar.

I would have given everything I had to be able to forget the past week. To see Gunnar one more time. To erase the memory of Luke from my mind and the pain of loss from my heart.

In a thousand lifetimes I wouldn't have enough magick to do that.

I was about to head for home when I heard my name. At first I thought it was my imagination, but the sound grew closer, the voice more insistent.

"Chloe."

It was Luke's voice. I closed my eyes and gulped in more fresh air to clear my head. My imagination was running wild.

"Turn around, Chloe."

I felt a hand on my arm, a warm human hand, and I spun around.

He looked like he had been to hell and back, but he was all in one piece. Tall. Strong. Alive.

Relief did to me what fear couldn't: I felt my knees go out from under me, and it was Luke's arms that kept me from falling.

"You're here," I whispered. "You're still here." If this was all I ever knew of happiness, it would be enough.

"I was afraid I'd lost you," he said. "When she—"

"I thought you were gone. That bolt went straight into your chest."

"I had a little help."

"You were wearing a vest?" I didn't mean to sound skeptical, but I doubted there were too many bulletproof vests out there that also protected against magick bolts of lightning.

He reached into his jacket and pulled out a small square book. "This saved my life."

"A schoolkid's marble notebook saved your life?"

"I know," he said. "Sounds nuts, but after the things I saw tonight, I'd say anything's possible."

A funny tingling sensation started working its way up my spine. "Do you always carry a kid's notebook around?"

"I found it in the cat's basket when I fell. All that talk about a book of spells, I figured it might be important."

He handed it to me and I gasped as the

cheap composition book suddenly mor-
phed into a huge dark green leather-bound
volume the size of an unabridged library
dictionary.

But not even the Book of Spells was as
important as the fact that after everything
that happened, we were there together. I
placed it on the ground at my feet and met
his eyes. "It saved your life. That makes it
extremely important."

"I have questions," he said, drawing me
into his arms.

I slid my hands inside his jacket. "I figured that."

"But they can wait."

I looked up at him and smiled. "I figured
that too."

Our eyes met, and for the first time in my
life I let down my guard. I let him see me
the way I really was, not the way I wished
I could be. Tall, blond, skinny, big feet, small
boobs, part human, part magick, and head
over heels in love.

And the amazing thing was he loved me
too.

It was the last thing he said before he
kissed me and the world disappeared.

But this time in a good way.

Did you ever wonder why things happen the way they do?

I finally had the answer.

It was so we could have moments like this.

EPILOGUE

CHLOE
SUGAR MAPLE—FIVE DAYS BEFORE CHRISTMAS

Gunnar's death cast a shadow of deep sadness across the town that neither Dane's death nor Isadora's banishment could match.

I spent a lot of time with the Book of Spells those first few days, reinforcing the protective charm and searching for a way to reverse Gunnar's fate even though I knew it was a lost cause.

If any volume contained such a secret, this would be the one. The Book was a living, breathing organism that put pop-ups to shame. The word *lavender* became a scent I could breathe in. Music from the pages sounded throughout my shop. I felt the ocean lapping against my ankles, the wind in my face, the velvety softness of a baby's cheek. But not even the Book could undo what was already written.

The best I could do was to hold Gunnar's memory in my heart and hope that somehow, somewhere, he knew how much I loved him.

Gunnar had made it possible for Luke and me to have the chance to build a future together, but unfortunately he forgot to tell us how.

I was putting the finishing touches on the better-late-than-never Sticks & Strings Christmas tree when Luke appeared in the doorway.

"Don't say it," I whispered. "If you don't say it, I don't have to believe it."

He said it anyway. "I don't want to leave, but I can't . . ."

He didn't have to finish the sentence. I knew exactly what he was going to say. I even understood. We were everything he wasn't. To him, our magick looked like un-

leashed chaos, our freedom and individu-
ality like a recipe for disaster.

He was a cop. He lived by the rule of
law. His world was imperfect but it made
sense. It had logic and form and predict-
ability.

So did Sugar Maple, but first you had to
be willing to push past the selkies and
trolls and shapeshifters to find it. Asking
him to turn his back on the warm comfort
of being human in order to throw in his lot
with us was too much to expect of anyone,
although for a moment I had almost convinced myself that he might.

And let's face it: I was a descendant of
Aerynn, and unhappily-ever-after endings
came with the magickal powers.

I tried to force a laugh. "Just don't say,
'It's not you, it's me.' Anything but that."

"Okay," he said, with a smile as phony
as my laughter. "I won't."

Our eyes locked over a small mountain
of kettle-dyed merino I'd been meaning to
wind. The thought that I would never see
him again made me want to grab the Book
of Spells and call up every trick used by
every sorcerer who had ever walked the
earth and make him mine forever.

But I couldn't do it. I loved him enough to let him go.

At least that was what I kept telling myself.

"You'd better get going," I said over a giant-sized lump in my throat. "There's a blizzard on its way down from Canada."

I wanted him to tell me that he didn't care about blizzards, that he didn't care about anything but staying with me forever, but he didn't and I had to remind myself that this was the real world of mortal men and women, who didn't have forever to get it right.

He nodded and I could see the emotions breaking through his steely resolve like small seismic events beneath the surface.

Let him go, I told myself. *If you love him, you'll let him go.*

I knew how it felt to be deeply lonely in a world that wasn't yours, and I wouldn't wish that on him.

"This doesn't have to be good-bye," he said. "I'll drive back to visit or maybe you can come down to Boston. We'll figure this out."

I didn't say anything. I was reasonably

sure my expression didn't change but he knew just the same. You know that flat, dead-eyed stare cops acquired with the badge? That was how he looked at me. "What aren't you telling me?"

"You know about the protective charm."

He nodded.

I took a deep breath. "The town wanted me to take it a step further."

"What does that mean?"

"They wanted me to cast a spell on you." I took another deep breath, but that one didn't help any more than the first. "To make you forget."

His eyes never left mine. "So I would forget what happened that night? I gave the town my word and I'll keep it. The town's secrets are safe."

"Not just that night," I said. "To make you forget everything."

For a second he looked like he was going to laugh at the absurdity of it, but then he caught himself. This was, after all, Sugar Maple. "Gunnar? Isadora? Midge and her vampire family?"

I shook my head. "Just be some nice eccentrics you bumped into along the way."

"What about you?" I don't know if it was my imagination, but for a second I thought his voice broke. "I'll remember you."

"Yes, you'll remember me," I said, my own voice breaking in response, "but I'll be the knit shop owner next door."

"Nothing more?"

I shook my head. "Nothing more."

"Nothing could make me forget how I feel about you."

"This would have," I said, "but I couldn't do it."

Whatever happened between us, I wanted it to be real.

Who knew Samantha and Darrin had gotten it right after all?

I couldn't help it. I started to cry. He tried to pull me into his arms, but I kept my distance. "This is hard enough," I said. "If you hold me, I'll never be able to say good-bye."

"You could come with me," he said one last time.

I shook my head. We both knew my life was here in Sugar Maple and always would be.

There was nothing left to do but say good-bye.

ONE HOUR LATER

"I'm fine," I told Lynette and Janice for what seemed like the hundredth time. "We said good-bye. He left. It's over."

"You don't look fine," Janice observed. "You look like crap."

"It's been a rough couple of weeks," I said dryly. "A girl gets tired battling the forces of evil."

I was only half kidding. The confrontation that night here in the knit shop had left me drained and shaken to my core. Banishing Isadora had taken all of the burgeoning powers at my command and I was still refilling my well of magick. According to the Book, I had executed the most rudimentary of banishing spells, and as soon as my powers were up to speed, I would need to supplement the original banishment with a few booster spells.

The irony wasn't lost on any of us. Gunnar was gone forever, but Isadora might return. Whoever said life was unfair had really nailed it.

"After all we did to piece Luke back together again, you'd think he would stay awhile," Lynette said. "It seems kind of rude if you ask me."

"I agree with Lynnie." Janice fiddled with a tiny manger ornament. "Would it have killed him to hang around for the holidays?"

"It's better this way," I said. "Like ripping off a Band-Aid."

They both nodded although neither one of them had ever used a Band-Aid in her life. Over the centuries our two very different worlds had come to share the same references.

Lynette glanced at the clock across the room. "He's probably nearing the state line right about now," she said quietly.

Janice pushed a platter of Chips Ahoy toward me.

Three hands grabbed for the remaining three cookies, which proved chocolate truly was universal. We all watched the clock and thought our own thoughts.

"He should cross it in the next ten minutes," Janice said.

"You're thinking highway time." Lynette broke off a piece of cookie and popped it into her mouth. "He has about thirty miles of country roads before he hits the high-way. I'd say give him forty minutes more before he gets there."

I polished off my own cookie and gath-ered up the crumbs on a fingertip. "It's more like thirty-three minutes."

"Not that you're counting."

"Nope," I said. "Not that I'm counting." I loved them like sisters, but I didn't tell them that I hadn't cast the spell over Luke.

"Okay," Janice said, fixing me with one of her I'm-the-boss looks. "So you're heart-broken. I've been there. But there's an up-side."

Lynette and I exchanged eye rolls.

"I saw that," Janice said. "You fell in love. You got your powers. Now it's time to take the next step."

"Jan!" Lynette sounded aghast. "It's only been an hour. Give her time."

"How about I call my cousin Haydon and tell him your powers came in big time. He'll be joining us for Christmas dinner. Maybe—"

"No," I said. "Absolutely positively not."

"I wouldn't give cousin Haydon a second chance either," Lynette said, "but Cyrus met a perfectly adorable werecat at a winter solstice festival last week who would be wonderful for you."

"A werecat?" Janice was dismissive. "She's not the werecat type. I see her more with another sorcerer or maybe a selkie."

"A selkie! You know how she feels about selkies."

"Where are you going?" Janice said as I pushed back my chair and stood up. "It's snowing out there."

"I heard the mail drop," I said. "I'll be right back."

They were my friends. They meant well. I knew what they were saying even though they were trying to be uncharacteristically polite. Just because I had my powers didn't mean Sugar Maple was in the clear. There was the small matter of pushing the Hobbs line forward another generation.

I didn't want to think about any of it. I wanted to go outside and throw myself into a snowdrift and wait until spring thaw. Luke had no idea how lucky he was. I wished the Book could help me cast a spell that would make me forget him. Anything would be better than the hollow aching emptiness where my heart used to be.

I stepped outside and shivered under the awning. We weren't at white-out conditions yet but we were getting there.

Holiday lights twinkled from every shop window. The gas lamps shimmered through the snow. A few hardy shoppers trudged by with heads down against the wind, but there didn't seem to be any knitters among them. The town was blanketed not just in snow but in silence. Except for the steadily increasing wind, there wasn't a sound to be heard.

I turned to go back into the shop when the crunch of tires through snow stopped me. It could have been anyone: UPS making a delivery, the power company, a day-tripper who wouldn't let a little thing like a blizzard slow her down.

But I knew it was Luke.

I stood there beneath the awning in my heavy Lopi sweater while the snow swirled all around me and I waited.

Don't go getting excited. There's a blizzard out here. The roads are probably impassable. He hasn't changed his mind. He just changed his plans . . . temporarily.

But that didn't stop a totally ridiculous,

implausible, doomed-to-disappointment sense of hope from leaping to life in that big empty spot inside my chest.

I know, I know. Crazy, wasn't it? Like a man would suddenly decide to abandon everything that was real and solid and dependable to throw in his lot with a sorceress-in-training, but I couldn't help myself. I used to believe in Santa Claus, the Easter Bunny, and Tom Cruise too.

His truck rolled to a stop in front of Sticks & Strings. He cut the engine and I stopped breathing.

This doesn't mean anything . . . he needs a place to crash for the night . . . this doesn't mean anything . . .

The driver door swung open and he climbed out.

I still wasn't breathing.

He walked around the rear of the truck and headed straight toward me. Who would have guessed that hope could hurt more than a double root canal?

"I couldn't do it," he said, stopping just inches away from me. "I tried but I couldn't."

"The snow," I said. "Better to wait until the roads are clear."

"Let's give it a shot."

I stared at him but no words came out.

"Did you hear me?" He looked excited, hopeful, uncertain, and a little scared. "I said I want to give it a shot."

"You mean stay here in Sugar Maple?"

"I mean stay here with you."

"But—"

He raised his hand in front of my lips. "You've already told me all the reasons why I shouldn't. Now let me tell you the only reason why I should: I love you."

I swallowed hard. "That might not be enough."

"Then we'll figure it out as we go along. I love you, Chloe. Let's give it a chance and see where this leads."

"I can't guarantee what the future will hold, Luke. I've never had magick before. Anything might happen."

"I'm willing to take my chances as long as I can be with you."

"Hobbs women don't have much luck when it comes to happily ever after."

"That gives us something to shoot for."

"I can't convince you to go."

He met my eyes. "Tell me you don't love me and I'm out of here. No questions asked."

"I love you, Luke MacKenzie," I said as I threw my arms around him. "That's the one thing that will never change."

His mouth found mine, and we both jumped as silvery-white sparks shot into the air around us, sizzling against the falling snow.

"A good sign?" he murmured against my lips.

"The best," I said as fireworks exploded overhead.

I almost thought I heard the voices of three hundred years of Hobbs women cheering me on.

If this wasn't the happy ending I'd been dreaming about, it would do until the real thing came along.

BARBARA BRETTON'S TEN THINGS YOU NEED TO KNOW ABOUT KNITTING

1. A dropped stitch isn't the end of the world.

2. Frogging isn't a mortal sin . . . or a sign of knitting inadequacy.

3. One knitter's great project is another's week in hell.

4. If you don't love the yarn, you probably won't love the process.

5. Knit for people you love who also love the fact that you're knitting for them.

6. Knit a swatch! Knit a swatch! Knit a swatch!

7. Stitch markers aren't a crutch for a lazy knitter. Neither are row markers or counters.

8. Take photos of your projects. One day you'll be glad you did.

9. Spit-splicing really works.

10. It's all just knit and purl.

Barbara maintains the blog *Romancing the Yarn* with authors Fran Baker, Elizabeth Delisi, Jamie Denton, Nancy Herkness, Cindi Myers, Laura Phillips, Dallas Schulze, and Janet Spaeth. You can find them at http://romancingtheyarn.blogspot.com.

WENDY D. JOHNSON'S TEN THINGS YOU SHOULD KNOW ABOUT KNITTING LACE

1. The good news is that the needles can be large. The bad news is that the yarn can be as fine as sewing thread.

2. If you drop a stitch, you are almost always screwed.

3. If you tell people you are knitting lace, 50 percent of those people will call you Granny.

4. If you tell people you are knitting lace, 50 percent of those people will ask you to knit them something lacy.

5. Delicate gossamer lace makes a great summer knitting project: it is almost lighter than air.

6. Stitch markers are your friends.

7. Really pointy needles are also your friends.

8. Cats/dogs and lace knitting do not mix.

9. Gripping television drama and lace knitting do not mix.

10. Any angst and trauma you experience during the knitting of your lace project is more than made up for when you block it and see it in its completed glory.

WENDY D. JOHNSON'S TEN THINGS YOU SHOULD KNOW ABOUT KNITTING SOCKS

1. Sock yarn is an addictive substance.

2. If you knit socks for other people, 50 percent of those people will save them for "best" and never wear them.

3. If you knit socks for other people, 50 percent of those people will wear them out and beg for more.

4. Knitting a sock in public will always attract strangers.

5. No matter how large your sock in progress is, 99.9 percent of these strangers will ask you if you are knitting a baby bootie.

6. You can impress the hell out of people by turning the heel of a sock.

7. You can astound and amaze people by telling them that the yarn for a single pair of socks can cost $20 to $30.

8. You can effectively keep people from bothering you by threatening to stab then with your sock needles.

9. A sock project in your bag is the perfect antidote to a traffic jam.

10. Once you slip a pair of hand-knit socks on your feet, you will never look back.

Wendy D. Johnson is a lifelong knitter who since April 2002 has maintained a popular knitting blog: WendyKnits.net. Her designs and articles have appeared on the knitting website *Knitty*, and she has been quoted or featured in major knitting magazines. She is currently working on a book of sock designs to be published in spring 2009.

DAWN BROCCO'S NINE TIPS FOR KNITTERS

1. Fixing a miscrossed cable

Arrange the stitches (sts) on your needles (ndls), so that the miscrossed cable is next on your left hand (LH) ndl. Slip the cable group off the LH ndl. Pull out each row of yarn from just those cable sts, until you get to the cross. Pull out the miscrossed sts, rearrange them so they are crossed correctly, then place them onto a double point needle (dpn) of the same size as your working ndls.

With a second dpn, knit across these sts using the bottommost free yarn strand. Slide sts to other end of dpn, then knit across them using the next free yarn strand. Repeat until all dropped yarn strands have been knit up, then replace the sts onto the LH working ndl and continue on.

There always seems to be a greater length of yarn hanging free, which causes gaps on either side of the reworked cable sts. To more evenly distribute the yarn, I knit up each st, then pull up a smidge more yarn. You can also pull the extra looseness into the adjoining sts.

2. Crossing cables without a cable needle
Slip the to-be cabled sts (in this case, 4 sts) to the right hand (RH) ndl, pinch the last 2 off the RH ndl and either hold in front or back, as per the direction of the cable, slip the remaining 2 sts from the RH ndl back to the LH ndl, then replace the 2 pinched sts to the LH ndl and knit all 4 in their newly crossed position.

3. Measuring gauge across ribbing
Don't even try to measure from a purl stitch! I always measure ribbing from the center of a knit sts to the center of another knit sts, being sure to count the first and last 1/2 sts.

4. Keeping shoulders from flaring when binding off in cable pattern
Decrease within the cable's sts, as you bind off (BO), to keep the edge from flaring. The ratio? Approx. 1 st for a 4-st cable, 2

sts for a 6-st cable, aiming for a Stockinette BO gauge.

5. Weaving in ends as you go

I always weave in yarn tails as I knit. But to alleviate the bulky ridge that forms as well as alleviate any distortion on the face of the fabric, don't weave in both yarn tails at once.

I alternate them, as follows: *The old tail goes over the working yarn, knit 1 st, the new tail goes over the working yarn, knit 1 st, the old tail comes up from under the working yarn, knit 1 st, the new tail comes up from under the working yarn, knit 1 st; repeat from * until all tails are woven in. If the fabric seems tight, just give it a stretching sideways to loosen the woven tails a bit.

6. Stranding 2 colors on dpns

It can be difficult to keep a loose-enough stranded tension when working on dpns, especially when working socks at tighter-than-sweater gauges. Be diligent about moving the sts over on the RH ndl and always weave in the unused color at the end and beginning of every ndl junction. This will keep the stranding from puckering at the ndl junctions.

7. Heel flap depth

Regardless of the height of the heel flap given in a pattern, work your heel flap to your personal dimension. Measure from your ankle bone to the floor, to get your flap depth measurement. Adjust the number of sts to be picked up and knit at the gussets.

8. Amount of negative ease in socks

Socks bag out in wear, so negative ease is used to give a better fit. Most sock knitters use between 10 and 15 percent negative ease. If you are working a colorwork stranded or Fair Isle design, however, only decrease approximately 5 percent for negative ease, as stranding reduces the stretch of the fabric.

9. Dawn's 6-Point Star Toe Shaping (a change from a 4-point toe and grafting)

Knit around, decreasing sts to give a number divisible by 6, *if* your stitch count isn't already divisible by 6. Knit 2 rounds (rnds). If I only have to get rid of 1 or 2 sts,

I don't knit 2 plain rnds, I go right into the toe's decreasing.

So, for example, on a sock with a stitch count of 48 (8 groups of 6):

(K6, k2tog) 6×=42 sts remain. Knit 2 rnds.

(K5, k2tog) 6×=36 sts remain. Knit 2 rnds.

(K4, k2tog) 6×=30 sts remain. Knit 2 rnds.

(K3, k2tog) 6×=24 sts remain. Knit 2 rnds.

(K2, k2tog) 6×=18 sts remain.

(K1, k2tog) 6×=12 sts rem.

(K2tog) 6×=6 sts rem. End off.

EXTRA TOE TIPS

- For an even rounder toe, I'll skip the 2 plain rnds after decreasing to 24 sts.

- The number of plain rnds needed can vary with gauge and/or the desired depth of your toe box.

- This toe can be used as a peasant heel. Adjust the number of plain rnds to give the desired heel depth.

Dawn Brocco is a well-known knitwear designer whose patterns can be purchased online, through various catalogs, and in local yarn shops across the country. You can visit Dawn at her website: DawnBrocco.com.